BOOKS BY KB FISHER

Promoted with Tenure
Admit Two

PROMOTED
WITH
TENURE

KB FISHER

This book is a work of fiction. All names, characters, places, and events are products of the author's imagination or are used fictitiously. Any resemblance to actual events, locales, or persons, living or dead, is coincidental.

Copyright © 2024 by KB Fisher.

All rights reserved. This book or any portion thereof may not be reproduced or used in any manner without written consent of the author. If you would like permission to use material from the book (other than for review purposes), contact the author at authorKBFisher@gmail.com.

First Edition: February 2024

Paperback ISBN: 979-8-9880200-2-8
eBook ISBN: 979-8-9880200-3-5
Library of Congress Control Number: 2023923718

For BENTON—

my son

Acknowledgments

I thank my wife, Carissa, for providing feedback while writing the original draft. Our talks are valuable beyond words.

I also thank my incredible editor, Dylan Garity. Your guidance is second to none.

The deepest sin against the human mind
is to believe things without evidence.
—Thomas Huxley

part one

FLY NO FLY

I

BLADES WERE THE TOOL, and tools were made to be used. It didn't matter much in what fashion—only that steel broke flesh on the right occasion.

Darkness was approaching, and time was of the essence.

Steve nocked an arrow, pulling the shaft against the string. Then he lifted his bow into frame, inch by heavy inch.

Treelike shapes, devoid of light, stretched their hands across an open food plot of crimson clover and wheat, as off-white tines of bone rose and fell at a leisurely pace. Each step of the hoof, every taste of land, was silent as a glimpse of tan pelage marched its way broadside.

A single red pin came into view and floated behind the front shoulder of the target as his finger brushed the release.

The broadhead opened as the arrow passed through the figure and skipped into the wood line, leaving behind nothing more than an ephemeral trail of green light from a glowing nock and a faint stream of scarlet, pumping from the now-startled deer.

Steve plodded through dense foliage, trailing each drop as blackness draped the swamp. One trace of red led to another as the beam of his headlamp swept across fans of palmettos and over the stench of mud.

The crack of a branch, followed by another hollow snap of wood, sounded not far from the carcass and echoed from one cypress to another, pushing a barred owl into flight.

"Hello?" he called into the black, his torch jerking with each twitch of the eyes. "*Hello?*"

The only response was that of the night—fireflies and mosquitoes and the like, swarming in blankets above the warm yet cooling harvest. The Louisiana wetlands had provided, but they also could steal away.

Upon returning to camp, he switched on an overhead spotlight and lowered the hoist before dragging the body onto the wooden deck. After hanging the deer from the gambrel, Steve began to cape his trophy. A sense of pride, a feeling of accomplishment, washed over him as eight points hung hardly out of reach of the blood-washed floor. He smirked as his knife made its way through the hide—as smooth as silk.

Before he could work the coat any farther, the yellow light was smothered. His only remaining sight was a poor result of the night's quarter moon.

The blade slipped from his control and jabbed his palm, and he dropped the tool in pain. "Goddammit." He winced.

The dull sound of boots treading on wood echoed from beneath the skinning shed.

"Hello?" Steve's voice rattled as he clenched his hand, the warm, tacky fluid dripping from between his chilled fingers.

He caught the flash of a grin below heavy shadows as blue latex gripped sharpened steel.

The scalpel melted into the hunter's throat, the blade sliding with ease from ear to ear, a tacky mist enveloping the night air. He failed to glimpse the responsible party as he clenched at his throat, drenched in helplessness. The last image he saw was those gloved hands as he collapsed beneath the darkened shed.

• • •

"Mommy, how much longer?" Angela asked from the back seat.

"Not much farther, sweetie. We're almost there."

The night was young, and Meaux was the only driver on the desolate road. Bleached headlights turned corner after winding corner, the thin highway pressed against a line of hardwoods on either side.

"Are you excited to see Daddy?"

"Yeah, I miss him," she said, her speech delicate.

"I'm sure he misses you too, love."

Meaux glanced in the rearview mirror. Her daughter was watching the pitted ball float, motionless, behind a passing, broken forest. Hunting season was always rough on the mother-daughter duo. One weekend after another, Meaux revisited the pain in her child's eyes.

The small gray car crept along the gravel road of the family camp, the cabin notably dark beneath a pinpricked sky.

"Looks like he might be asleep already, Angie."

A minute later, Meaux walked through the front door, feeling along the walls for the elusive switch. Little Angela all but hung from her mother's leg, ducking the night. The woodsy sweetness of pine filled the room and floated through a kitchen window, cracked above the sink. Meaux drew a deep breath and closed her eyes, although the room, naturally, could not have been darker.

"Hello? Daddy?" Angela called.

"Steve, we're here," Meaux echoed.

As she opened the back door, a flicker of porch lights illuminated a scene from which she could not turn away.

"Mommy?" Angela pointed to the shed, her beige teddy bear falling face-first to the floor.

Two bodies hung side by side—predator and prey.

2

"WE'RE HERE TO ACKNOWLEDGE and celebrate the work of Doctor Mitch Olivier for his contributions to the field of behavioral ecology and white-tailed deer research," said Bryan Guidry, Dean of the College of Sciences. "Your work on host-parasite evolution has greatly impacted the field and the department. As a result, your promotion to associate professor with tenure has been approved. Cheers."

Beers were raised. Bottles clacked. Ass-kissing abounded.

At least, on the surface.

The dreary, white conference hall was filled with the University of New Orleans's most revered biologists, including Mitch himself. "Thank y'all for showing up," said Mitch. "I know most of you probably have better things to do on a Saturday evening, so I really appreciate it."

"Of course," said Bryan. "Although, I thought you were gonna miss your own party there for a second. I suppose I knew better, though. Someone as big-time as yourself can't miss such an occasion. Not when it's all about you," he said with flared nostrils, slapping Mitch on the shoulder.

"Yeah, sorry about that. Time never seems to be on my side." He grinned, flashing his teeth beneath the blanched fluorescent lighting.

Mitch was now one of them, a *tenured* professor. He had managed to do what was considered impossible in the academic world—remain at one's graduate institution as both a postdoc and a professor after receiving his PhD. To the outside world, he was merely another biologist working for the greater good of the establishment. On the inside, he was God.

"Trust me," said Aura, Mitch's wife. "Mitch is great at many things, but being on time has never been one of them. Lucky for him"—she turned to face him—"most of us are already here, working on the weekends." She batted a seductive eye.

Aura Theriot was a full professor who'd served on Mitch's PhD committee as his advisor in the department nearly seven years prior. Eight journal articles and half a million dollars in funding later, they were hitched. Not the greatest look according to human resources, nor the dean. But Mitch loathed the fact that his marriage needed to be monitored by his profession. As if he couldn't be trusted after all he had sacrificed for the cause.

"Well, at least I have better timing than your boy Steve," Mitch said to Bryan while popping the top off his second beer on the table's edge, the cap bouncing to the floor with a high-pitched clank. "He can sit in the middle of the woods chasin' tail every weekend from October to February but can't show up for someone he just promoted in his own department. I thought chairs were supposed to support their faculty. Sounds like he has his priorities backwards, no?"

The corner of Bryan's mouth turned up, hinting at the you're-an-asshole smile peeking from beneath a faux façade. He carried himself as if his superior title somehow made up for the fact that he was beyond vertically challenged.

Mitch rarely observed the dean looking up to the professors below him.

Aura shoved her elbow into her husband's ribs. "I think we

can all agree that we're busy. No need to point fingers. I'm sure he's just running late."

"Besides, aren't you just as obsessed with killing innocent animals?" Bryan asked. "I'm willing to bet you, too, have been out in the middle-of-nowhere swamp over the last few weekends, sitting for hours at a time with some cypress knee stuck up your ass, helping the mosquitos catch a buzz."

"I'll be over here." Aura gestured to another group of faculty before downing the remainder of her beer. "Sounds like y'all need to iron this out on your own."

Mitch moved in closer to Bryan. "Innocent animals . . . Guilty animals . . . It doesn't matter. All of my work is approved by the Institution's Animal Care and Use Committee," Mitch said sardonically.

"Oh, come on. You and I both know IACUC only cares about the deer—the ones with a backbone. Those blood-sucking flies and ticks you collect are drowned with a higher-percent alcohol than what's in your hand. And for what? So you can count them under a microscope? At least *some* of the scientists in the room are doing the real legwork. I'd take a good look at yourself, Mitch, before you begin trash-talking your boss. After all, he had to approve this shit show before it landed on my desk."

Mitch nodded and glanced around the room, making sure his words wouldn't carry. "So, what you're saying is that the university will never care about animals like yourself." He spoke gently. "And I suggest you swap out that cerveza for a water. The department isn't so blind to your problem as you might think," he said from the corner of his mouth, waving to Aura with a come-back smile. Her mosaic eyes of smoky, burnt honey drew him in without fail, time and time again. Regardless of where her attention was aimed, they pulled at him day and night—a moon against the seas.

Bryan turned his back to the crowd and walked Mitch backward into the wall. "Listen, you ungrateful prick—we all have our disagreements, but Steve has done more for this department than you can imagine. If you think for one second you're going places just because you're screwing someone who puts you on their papers in exchange for some ass, you're sadly mistaken. You can either step up your game and play nice, or you'll be teaching Freshman Bio as associate *bitch* for the rest of your career."

"You did this," Mitch said, shooting a bro nod to the room. "You're the one who approved the paperwork at the end of the day. Don't threaten me if you can't follow through."

"Yeah, I did. And I can just as easily undo it. The only reason the department approved your packet is because of that little dollop of cream you follow around like a lost puppy. You know, not all universities support spousal hires," Bryan muttered, raising a satirical toast. "Don't forget it."

"You boys playing nice?" Aura interrupted. "How's the vibes?" she asked, balancing on her imaginary surfboard.

"Peaches," Mitch said with a tense leer.

3

THE MEAT WAS STILL fresh. Both bodies, in fact.

Red and blue lights beamed in circles across the surrounding forest. The strobes flooded Hunter's wide eyes as she observed the two slayings—one legal, one not. It was her first murder, second week on the job. They were the first on scene, only minutes after the responding officer.

The one thing more gut-wrenching than seeing a dead father hanging from a shed's rafter was listening to his daughter's cries while examining the body. A family's sorrow, distant as it might be, made the job nearly impossible.

"No one said forensic pathology was gonna be an easy career," said Parker.

"That's not it," Hunter mumbled, shaking her head in little Angela's direction. Hunter's gaze was stuck on the dining room window of the cabin, the girl's whimpers framed in a dim, golden light as she sat with her mother at the dining room table.

Meaux appeared to be fighting to catch her breath as mascara-stained tears sprinted down her flushed cheeks. Angela was gripping a stuffed bear that was apparently named Mr. Snugglesworth, his cotton leaking at the seams. The daughter held the one-eyed beast as if it had never felt so soft.

"Number one: rigor mortis is absent," said Parker as he

knelt next to the body, pulling the thermometer from the professor's abdomen. "Liver temperature is ninety-two degrees."

The decedent's wife had provided an ID. He was Steve Daigle—professor and chair of the biology department at UNO. Husband, father of one.

"Hunter, time of death."

"What?"

"Time. Of. Death," Parker repeated.

"Oh . . ." Hunter looked down at her watch. It was 10:15 p.m. "Six to six thirty," she said casually. No afterthought required. "He probably isn't far."

A body cooled at roughly one and a half degrees Fahrenheit per hour after death. But the estimate was complicated once other factors were considered, such as ambient temperature, body mass, whether the decedent was clothed, and so on. Hunter knew Parker didn't care for certainty in the reporting of such estimates. An approximation was what he was after.

"Shouldn't it be you down here? I'm not the one in training, after all."

Hunter turned to the bodies, her head tilted, vision tapered. The buck hung from a metal gambrel, inserted between the bone and tendon of its hind legs. Typical processing. Steve's corpse, however, dangled from the roof by two ropes, each fed through one of his legs in a similar fashion to the venison. Not an easy feat.

"You hunt, Parker?"

"Me? Hell no."

She turned up her flashlight to where frayed ropes met weathered ceiling joists, then back down to the bodies as they swayed in a delicate breeze. "Someone has a real hankering for it."

"What about you?"

"Only as a teenager. Duck hunting with my father, mostly."

She crouched between the carcasses, dragging her light from the deer's snout up to its neck and back to Steve's body.

"You know he had a license, right?" Parker said with a grit in his voice. "This is a *single* homicide, in case you haven't noticed."

"There's a reason for it."

"Come again."

"There's a reason. His body wasn't strung up like this on a whim. It's too particular. Too calculated."

Parker looked to the scene then back to Hunter, his attention wandering.

"Detailed, perhaps. But they couldn't be any more different. The decedent had his throat slit, and the deer was shot. They're hung in different ways."

Hunter reached into a black leather case and removed a thin pet comb. It was the same metal comb she used on her retriever at home. Not the exact one, of course.

"We should wait for Homicide to get here with the coroner, remember?" Parker said. "We've been over this."

"And when do they plan on getting here?"

"Soon, why? They usually show up around the same time."

"There's no telling how long that'll be," Hunter said in a no-bullshit tone, glaring at the deer's pelt hanging from its midsection. "You said it yourself—their timing is unreliable. My goal is to do what I gotta do and be on my way out before the party starts. You opposed to that, boss?"

"You should know the answer to that. It's something else we've been over—get done what you gotta get done and get out. Clean but efficient. Besides, this is an outdoor scene, so we're working against the clock."

Hunter began combing the pelt along the deer's neck. "He clearly didn't finish field dressing it before he was killed. Lucky for us, that means the coat is at least partially intact."

"Which brings me to number two: you're the entomologist. What are ticks doing on the body?"

She pulled a pair of forceps from the case and held out her light. "Hold this, will you." Then she leaned her head in close to Steve's face, a familiar stench pouring from the gaping wound below his chin. Pests crawled from his nostrils and into the unforgiving cut.

The circle of life.

Hunter unscrewed the cap on a glass vial that was filled with ethyl alcohol before pushing the tweezers into Steve's sinus cavity. She slowly, meticulously, removed one of the insects and dropped it into the tube.

"Well look at you," said Parker. "Goin' all Mr. Miyagi on their asses."

Hunter capped the vial and lifted it overhead, white light hitting the bottom of the glass and scattering across her hand.

"If he was killed around six fifteen like you said, what are crawling insects doing here so quickly when he's off the ground?" Parker asked.

"Two mistakes," she said while rolling the vial in her hand, peering at the specimen. "One—ticks aren't insects. They're arachnids."

Parker snapped his head as if she had insulted his mother.

"Two—this is a flying insect. At least, it was. Don't feel bad, though. Most hunters can't even tell the difference."

"Okay, now you're just confusing people."

"Bonus question," said the student to the teacher. "Is a fly with *no wings* still a fly?"

• • •

"Sup, buttercup?" said David, looking away and pulling in a nervous breath the moment he spoke.

Hunter glanced over her shoulder as she clenched the glass vial.

As if the night wasn't stiff enough.

"It's about time y'all showed up," Parker said with an extended hand, robbing Hunter of the chance to respond first. "It's been over an hour. Thought we were gonna be going at this one alone."

David looked at Hunter while he shook Parker's hand. Hunter held her eyes to the floor, doing her best to avoid the inevitable.

One-night stands tended to mix with a new career as well as oil mixed with water. Cold water.

By day, David was a seasoned technician on Homicide's forensics team. By night, he was Hunter's acquaintance—a friend, if the imagination stretched far enough. Some friendships walked a fine line between acquaintance and guilty pleasure. A line as sharp as unbroken glass under the pressure of one's palm.

"David, this is Parker," Hunter said with a tilt of the head. "He's showing me the ropes for a while."

"I believe we've met. Y'all are already acquainted, though?" Parker said.

David held his grip. "You could say that."

"Well, we're almost done here, but I'll let y'all catch up while I go inside to see if there's anything else they got from the mother and daughter. Bring him up to speed, will you?"

Hunter nodded with evading eyes. "I should get you caught up then," she said emphatically. "If you wanna step over here, we can take a look at how the—"

"You know, you never did explain this to me," David said,

nudging the simplistic red "A" tattooed on her wrist—a small reminder.

She looked around to the rest of the forensics team scattering like ants, their cameras outflashing the lightning bugs.

Then she pulled down her black hat; eye contact was the killer of comfort.

"Like I was saying, we can take a look at how the body is similar to, and different from, the deer. I think it's obvious that this was premeditated."

"Looks pretty messy to me."

"Messy and planned aren't mutually exclusive."

David offered an upside-down smile. He twisted the edge of his pointed, salt-and-pepper mustache and let out a curious, "Huh."

"The work is too detailed. Too intentional," she continued. "Plus, there's this." She tossed him the vial.

He lifted the glass to just above eye level. "The bug expert is handing me a bug? Can't say I'm surprised."

"Bugs aren't shocking. The type and location, however, are the intriguing parts."

David fidgeted with the tube. "I don't follow." He tossed back the sample and moved his flashlight to the bodies.

"It's a parasitic fly," she said.

"A blow fly? We see those all the time on bodies."

"Different family altogether. Blow flies belong to *Calliphoridae*. This is a hippoboscid. A deer ked. That's not the most interesting part, though."

"Well, I see a deer. There's a *deer* ked at the scene. I'm blanking on the interesting aspect."

Hunter ran her light from the deer's neck down to its head. "I combed the deer's body. At least, what hadn't been skinned. There's no deer keds. Only winter ticks and a handful of blacklegged deer ticks. No keds."

"Okay, so they flew off the deer and landed on the ground. I don't see what you're getting at."

"I found the fly on him," Hunter said, running the white beam of light to Steve's corpse.

"I think you're reading too much into this. Flies are found on deer, there's a dead deer at the scene, and parasitic flies move from host to host. What am I missing?"

She tossed the vial back to David. "Look again."

"Are you sure this is a fly?"

"*Lipoptena mazamae* drop their wings when they find a suitable host, and they remain associated with that individual for the remainder of their lifespan. The chances that they all flew to a human corpse and not the deer within the short timeframe since the murder is highly unlikely. Besides, if they were on the deer first, it's also improbable that they still had wings to switch hosts."

"A fly with no wings, huh." He tilted the sample between two fingers, the fluid swashing from side to side. "So if the entomologist is confused, what hope is there for the rest of us?"

"Who said anything about being confused?"

4

Hunter could hear Drake barking as she parked her old, black Honda Civic on the oyster-shell driveway. Regardless of the hour, day or night, he was waiting at the front door.

Their tiny home lay on Michoud Boulevard—a short, secluded stretch of road off I-10 near the southeast side of Lake Pontchartrain. The street sat near the west side of Bayou Sauvage National Wildlife Refuge and wasn't far from the park's boardwalk, a trail visited frequently by Hunter and Drake on days off.

As she opened the storm door to her home, she was met with a ten-hour buildup of slobbery kisses and anxious paws. Lowly handshakes and a wet nose.

That was what best friends were for.

A floorboard creaked from the bathroom, inciting Drake's whimper as he ran in broken circles, his tail banging into the nearby cabinets.

"What is it, bud?"

The door inched open as black clogs shuffled across wood floors. Hunter's hand instinctively reached to her hip, but her gun wasn't there. She hadn't carried to work that day.

She looked over to the small safe peeking out from above the fridge. Could she grab it in time?

Hunter sprang to her feet as a woman stepped out from the bathroom in cut-off, denim shorts and a white crop top.

"*Seriously*, girl? You ever heard of a text message?" she asked Deborah.

Deborah took a sip of red wine from the tumbler in her hand. Then she swirled the glass before shrugging off Hunter's concern.

"You ever heard of a lock? I just walked right in. Hey, boy," she said, stooping down to pet the wagging tail attached to four legs of excited brown fluff. "You know, if you had some other type of dog, like a rottweiler instead of a lab, you wouldn't need to worry so much."

"Oh, is that how it works? Bigger dog, smaller lock?"

Hunter's experience had taught her that big dogs and even larger locks were key. Calm pups and an absent mind were her current problem.

Deborah stood up and grabbed her by the waist, pulling Hunter in for a kiss.

"I'm glad you're here, though," Hunter said. "It's been a long one."

"Too long."

Deborah's lips tasted of peppermint—a sweetness outshone only by their softness.

"So I guess that if you're getting in this late, you finally popped your cherry, huh," Deborah said. "I know it's only been a couple of weeks, but you never leave the office this late at night." She opened a cabinet above the stove and grabbed a family-size box of Cheerios.

"Is this the journalist asking or the girlfriend? And you know that's Drake's cereal, Deb. I just got him that." Hunter snatched the box from her hand and placed Drake's bowl onto the floor. The clangor of cereal hitting the aluminum dish drowned out Deborah's crunching as she shuffled a fistful of Os into her mouth.

"I'm off the clock, but does it really matter?" Deborah asked.

It does if this is an interview.

"We had a pretty rough homicide called in late this evening—a hunter who was out bow hunting ended up getting the shaft, strung up next to the damn deer he killed. Of course, things were made even more difficult once David and the rest of Homicide decided to show up late."

Deborah stopped chewing, her cheeks blown up worse than a chipmunk with a newly minted stash.

"David?"

"Yeah. Me and the supervisor were on the scene for a good hour before they decided to show."

"Jesus Christ."

"Yeah . . ."

"So David, huh?"

Hunter looked at her with a grimace and a roll of the eyes. "We're not doing this, Deb. Not now."

"Doing what?" she said with an obnoxious gulp.

"It was before things were official. You know that."

Deborah crouched next to Drake, snatching one last O from his bowl. "That's what you keep telling me. I'll let you rest, though," Deborah said as she walked over and pushed Hunter's long and burnished chestnut hair from her face. She leaned in and gave Hunter a gentle peck on the nose. "We can talk whenever you're ready. Just wanted to stop by to see how your day was."

"Thanks. I'm glad I have you waiting around after days like today."

Deborah turned to the door as Hunter struggled to let go,

holding on to her with a single finger before the tenuous grasp was broken and her hand fell to her side.

"Hey, Deb," she said as Deborah opened the screen door, Drake wagging at her feet. "Supplemental material, yeah?"

"Of course. I was never here," Deborah said, pulling an invisible zipper across cherry-stained lips. Drake pawed the door as Deborah looked back with reluctant eyes from the bottom of the stairs.

"What?" Hunter said to him once the door closed. "Don't look at me like that. I had to. She was gonna eat all your food again."

Hunter sat on the floor with her back against the wall, the dog sprawled across her lap. "It's okay, bud. I'm not going anywhere," she said, scratching his head. Her phone vibrated in her pocket as an itch crawled up her thigh. She entered her four-digit code, only to see David's name across the screen.

5

TEACHING WAS PURELY AN obligation. Research was what had driven Mitch to the top, peering down at his flock.

It was Monday morning, and the small classroom with stadium seating and blue plastic chairs was packed to the gills with juniors and seniors. The crossover course shared by the two classes was the most desired lecture in the department.

Sit down and shut the hell up.

"Alright, everyone, let's get started shall we?" Mitch said to the class, speaking from behind the podium. "Last week, we left off with our discussion on evolutionary mechanisms. Who can remind me what they are?"

A junior in the front row threw up her hand faster than a cougar on blow. But this was no middle-aged night stalker; her pigtails and cartoony smile said she was twenty-two at most. Mitch did his best to avoid the overeager ones up front. The ones who seemed all too excited to be sitting in outdated desks, packed into an ice-cold classroom that hadn't seen a fresh coat of paint in thirty years. But the teaching came with the territory. Unfortunately.

"What ya got?" Mitch droned.

"Mutation, genetic drift, gene flow, and selection," the youngin squealed. "If you want, I can define it too."

"Define what?"

"Evolution."

Mitch scanned the room, his eyes narrow, questioning whether anyone else had heard the nails dragging down the board. Surely, he wasn't the only one being subjected to such torturous ignorance.

"Is this Bio 4524—Evolutionary Mechanisms?" Mitch asked.

"Yes . . ."

"Did we define evolution in our first lecture?"

"Um . . . yeah."

"Do you think that you should already know what evolution is as an upperclassman taking an evolutionary mechanisms course?"

"Yes?"

"Thank you." Mitch smirked. "That was perfect."

She scrunched her nose. "For what?"

Damn, it's gotta feel good being so clueless. So comfortably numb.

"Don't worry. I'm sure someone will explain it to you. Moving on to material we *haven't* covered." He turned to the whiteboard. "If we think back to the fundamental theorem of natural selection, we can say that the rate of change in fitness of an organism is the product of its genetic variance in fitness at a given time. The problem with this is that biologists don't entirely agree on what fitness is, exactly. It's measured many different ways in practice, but we can say, generally speaking, that it's the product of survival and reproductive success. Now, who was responsible for developing the fundamental theorem of natural selection?"

Mitch turned back to the girl in the front row and raised a speculative eye. "No? Nothing coming to mind?" he asked derisively. "Anyone?" He looked around.

"Darwin!" someone shouted from the middle of the class.

"Oh, come on," Mitch said. "That's just lazy."

The room broke out into uncontrollable laughter as he walked back to the board. "I'll give you one hint: he developed the ANOVA."

The majority of the room bowed their heads in what was clearly shame. Mitch knew that they had heard the term before in countless courses and were forced to use it incessantly, but it appeared as if they hadn't the foggiest of clues.

"Fisher," a girl said with conviction from the back corner of the room.

"Very good, Miss . . ."

"Wallace," she answered. "And no, the irony is not lost on me."

The corner of Mitch's mouth crept upward by a fraction of an inch.

A soft knock interrupted the flow of lecture, Aura's head peeking from behind the thick oak door. "Dr. Olivier, can I have a word?"

"Go ahead and review the notes on defining fitness," Mitch said as he left the room.

He walked into the hall and eased the door shut behind him. "What's up? I thought you had a meeting with Bryan this morning?" he asked Aura.

"I did."

He sensed that something was sour. She was avoiding eye contact worse than a crushing teen walking out of the movie theater after sucking face for two hours.

"Mitch, Steve passed away."

His head moved back as his eyes doubled in size.

"He was killed."

"What do you mean 'killed'?"

"He was murdered, Mitch. Saturday evening. That's why he

couldn't make the party. His wife and daughter found him at their camp. They're saying it happened at some point that day."

"What did Bryan say?"

"That's about the extent of it. He was pretty shook up, obviously."

"I can only imagine how bad that was for his little girl. How bad it is for his wife *and* girl. What about the cops? They have any leads?" Mitch asked hurriedly, popping the marker cap in his hand.

"No idea."

Mitch folded his arms with his back against the wall, his focus darting. "Really? That was it? Bryan didn't say anything else? I mean, he's gotta have a plan for what to do next. Someone's gotta take the reins."

Aura hesitated. "That's what you're concerned about right now? Who's gonna step up as chair? I'm sure he has some sort of plan, Mitch, but you really think your wife is the person he's gonna share that with? Y'all aren't exactly copy and paste."

"Sure. I'm just wondering who's gonna pick up the slack. These kids aren't gonna fail themselves."

6

ON MORE OCCASIONS THAN not, Hunter had arrived at work before the sun had dealt its hand. And she put in ungodly hours late into the night, with an obese lunch block in the middle for the purpose of avoiding colleagues. The chatty ones, at least. She was pleased that her job didn't call for much interaction with coworkers—only persistence and a sense of self-efficacy.

Swiping her access card at the door, she walked through the lobby of glass windows, whose crystal-clear panes stretched their borders from floor to ceiling. Her steps resounded off the marble walls as she walked down the abandoned hallway and unlocked her office door, motion lights jumping to life like falling dominos from above.

She reveled in the quiet of a day's first light.

The New Orleans Forensic Pathology Center was located in a simple two-story structure connected to the medical examiner's building on Earhart Boulevard, also home to the coroner's office. The larger forensics team was attached at the hip with the Homicide unit on South Broad Street. Each of the departments communicated with one another at various levels, depending on the nature of a crime and what each branch demanded of the others.

Within the Pathology Center, the primary laboratory rested

between her and Parker's offices. Hunter's workspace was festooned with a private yet overwhelming collection of preserved insects and other specimens, organized to a T in tall wooden cabinets and glass showcases, housing everything from blow flies to louse flies, bat flies, butterflies, dragonflies—the Bubba Gump headquarters of forensic entomology. Her master's diploma, displayed next to her medical degree above her desk, reflected the obsession.

Pulling her long ponytail from the opening in the back, she removed her hat and tossed it onto her desk. The day's work called for the organization and inventory of specimens and various evidence collected from what Homicide was calling the "revenge murder."

Simply put: the hunter got hunted. Apparently, the boys over at Homicide thought they had a sense of humor.

Before getting covered up with paperwork, she wanted to examine the flies more closely to confirm the taxonomic classification she had made in the field and sketch some illustrations for later reference; photos were useful but difficult to annotate. Hunter removed the glass vials from their carrying case and placed them in an obsessively neat row next to the light microscope at the center of the lab. An overhead light shone down onto the bench, outlining an island in an endless sea of laboratory equipment. Waves of high-end centrifuges and precision pipettes. A beacon of beakers.

Pencil drawings of endless varieties, taped to the shelf in a perfect line behind the scope, decorated the microscopy station. Each rendering was shaded to perfection.

The deer keds she had collected from the scene were otherworldly creatures, not familiar to most of the hunting community—flat, auburn-brown bodies; large, red compound eyes; wingless flies unable to do what their name intended. The microscopic was another world entirely. A product of design, some had said.

As Hunter began the sketch on a clean sheet of paper, the bug-eyed insect once again springing to life, she heard the quiet click of the lab's lock finding its mate. She glanced at the skylight, which was not yet accepting the morning's rays.

"You know, there's other lights in here," said Parker, breaking her concentration.

"Yeah, I'm less distracted if all I can see is my work. The darkness is my blinders, I guess. You're here a bit early."

He pulled out a stool across the aisle from her workbench, the chair's metal feet dragging across the smooth cement floor. "You're still at it with those flies, huh? You find anything new, or you still hung up on the fact that they weren't on the deer?" Parker asked as he sat down.

The best theories were ones that withstood the most scrutiny. After all, that was what made a theory a theory and not a hypothesis. Hunter welcomed the doubt.

"I know you don't agree, but I think there's more to it than mere coincidence."

"Oh I agree that it might not be a coincidence, but couldn't they have all just fallen off the deer before the same happened to the decedent? I mean, the deer was killed first, so it would have cooled down first. These guys need blood to feed on, which they wouldn't have once a host bleeds out and starts to cool."

"True, but as is the case for any idea, the data don't lie. At least, not without the help of an analyst. Research shows that they remain on harvested deer for hours far beyond death. There's no reason why they would have abandoned the deer that quickly. He wasn't even done caping it yet, much less field dressing it."

Parker glanced at the bare bones of a sketch next to the

scope. Hunter could see the uncertainty painted in his eyes. "Well, keep at it, and let me know if you come across anything else. We need to focus on the whole picture, too. Not just the entomology. Hopefully we'll hear from the coroner's office sometime soon."

"Of course."

"Aside from the recent case, I wanted to talk to you about something else before you got too busy. You have a minute?" Parker asked.

"Sure, what's up?" She placed her pencil down on the desk and turned toward him, hands folded in her lap.

"My church group is having a retreat next weekend, and I was wondering if you wanna go. It's only Friday through Sunday, so we wouldn't miss much work. You can even bring Drake."

"Why are you inviting me, of all people, if you don't mind me asking? I'm sure there's some rule against fraternizing with trainees, no?"

Hunter was in no way curious as to why he was inviting her. Her question was nothing more than a mechanism to create a brief window of time for her to drum up some reason, any reason, to side-step the invitation.

"Well, it's a good group of honest, god-fearing people, and I could use a break from this place. And if I'm gone, you can be too. At least, for the weekend."

A grin climbed its way to the surface from beneath her otherwise vacant gaze. But she kicked it back down, stepping on its grip from above as it held tight to her ego. *We're at work*, she reminded herself. "God-fearing, huh. Dare I ask which one?"

And there it was.

"Which one?"

"Yeah, which god? Which one were you born into? I'm curious. I'm more of a nature gal, myself."

"I wouldn't really say I was born into anything, but it's a Christian church if that's what you're asking."

She paused. It was the precise response she had expected. "And your parents? I suppose they attend the same church?"

"Of course they do."

"Well, I appreciate the sentiment, but I'll have to pass. The idea of God has never been my thing—any of them, really. Not enough evidence for me on the logic front."

Religion—the one topic for which Hunter had zero filter. And no regrets.

It took Parker a moment to respond. "Okay. If you change your mind, you know where to find me."

She could sense he didn't care to drag the conversation any further. It was suffocated just as quickly as it had been ignited.

Parker stood up and pushed the stool back under the bench. Hunter was all too familiar with the uneasy silence. They all responded the same way. Family, friends, coworkers, acquaintances. She had found that, at least through her own experience, the South in general repelled "the A word" like water from a duck's back. Without the shield of social media, no one wanted to have the discussion. As a scientist, it saddened her from the inside out.

He began to shuffle away but turned back before reaching his office door, his hand suspended midstride, frozen at the doorknob. "Forgive me for asking," he said, looking back over his shoulder, eye contact elusive, "but what would be 'enough evidence'?"

Hunter didn't dare look away from the microscope, just inched her head back, her focus drifting over the drawing before her.

Then she spoke with a flat tone of assurance. "Simply . . . any."

• • •

Hunter's classification was dead-on—the flies were hippoboscids of the species *Lipoptena mazamae*. Her knowledge of the *Hippoboscidae* family only reached so far, though. The more common blow flies that typically infested the deceased were studied ad nauseam by the forensic community. After a quick search of Google Scholar, the predominant database of published research, she realized the majority of literature on deer keds came from academic labs—wildlife biologists, in particular, were obsessed.

As she scrolled through the laundry list of manuscripts, three names repeatedly floated to the surface: Steve Daigle and Mitch Olivier from the University of New Orleans, and Robert Hebert from Louisiana State University. The remainder of the studies were largely authored by professors from Mississippi State and a handful of researchers dotted across Texas and Georgia.

The parasitic, ostensibly, was of interest to the Southernly.

Royal light radiated from the monitor and scrolled across Hunter's face, one line after another flowing over the bridge of her nose and cutting across her razor-sharp chin. She shook her head. The papers were a rabbit hole. One author had cited a colleague, who cited themself, whose paper regurgitated their own work even more so. It was one raging clusterfuck of citation-hungry egos. And at the top of the list was Doctor Steve Daigle.

"Is the darkness supposed to be a reflection of your soul?" David spoke dryly from the door.

Hunter nearly fell from her chair. "Goddammit, are you serious?" she snapped in response, her words wobbling, hand on her chest. "Between you and Deb, one of y'all's gonna put me in the hospital."

"The door was open."

"And just like her, you're allergic to knocking."

He flipped the light switch at the door, flooding the room with cool flickers that led to a striking brightness.

"They were off for a reason."

David didn't entertain it. "I came by to see if there's any more information you have on the samples you collected."

"No, there isn't anything else other than what I told you at the scene. The samples found on the decedent are deer keds, but there weren't any on the deer. Other than that, I'm still digging."

"You gonna let me know when you have more?"

Hunter snatched a pack of gum from beneath the computer screen and began jamming one piece after another into her mouth. She took her time and filled a bubble at her lips until it could no longer handle the pressure. Then she began smacking as loudly as possible, fluttering disdainful lashes.

"Alrighty, then. Glad I made the drive down."

"Look, if you're wanting something to bring back to the unit, just give me a little longer. I'm looking at some things that might be of interest. Alright? Besides, I still need the coroner's report, so I'm working with what I have. We've already estimated time of death and provided the most likely cause of death. Based on the samples I collected from the scene, I'm focusing on what I think is most relevant for the time being. And that's the entomology."

He walked around the desk and peered with tunneling vision at the computer screen. She pounded the escape key and slammed the laptop closed, the larger secondary monitor flashing black.

"Well, okay then," he said.

"Like I told you already—give me a few."

"Fine. Just be careful running around with your girl from

Crescent Crimes. Homicide already has a bad impression of the writers over there. I'm sure you don't want them pointing fingers at you too with your new, personal ambitions and all."

"I think a magazine is the least of your worries. Don't you have tech work to do that doesn't involve obsessing over past flings."

"Flings, huh?"

Before she was able to pull the punch, she could see it was a low blow. The damage done.

"I guess I'll let you get back to it, then," he said over his shoulder as he turned toward the door. "Just remember—the department goes through pathologists like they're going out of style. They don't keep y'all around for long if you don't perform. For your own sake, I'd try to get the ball rolling on this sooner rather than later."

"And what makes you so concerned all of a sudden?"

"I have my own job to do, which unfortunately relies on you to some extent."

She stood up and followed him to the door before he turned back and rested against the doorframe.

"Are you sure there isn't anything else you wanna share?" he asked. "Maybe we can talk about the case over dinner."

"Give the unit my best."

Hunter flipped the light switch, killing the glare, and shut the door, leaving David on the other side.

7

THE BIOLOGY OFFICE WAS hidden on the second floor of the Computer Center, where it was impossible to find without an up-to-date GPS—a quirk of UNO's superb sense of modernity. A cement staircase, tucked away and shadowed within a brick, soot-filled tower, led to double doors at the building's foyer. As Bryan strolled into the office, Jessica was sorting through mounds of paperwork in the filing cabinets behind her desk.

His wife ran the department with greater precision than most professors did their labs. And much like academia itself, keeping a department well-oiled was sink or swim.

"Well there's my short stack," Jessica said. "What brings you to this neck of the swamp?"

"There's something I wanna get your opinion on."

To the unfamiliar acquaintance, they were a peculiar couple. She was a good foot taller than Bryan and sported shoulder-length blond hair, tapered to the front. He, on the other hand, was the epitome of Rogaine failure. Bryan was the professional, she the untamed edition. The woman behind his fury.

The sun was rendered unconscious by tinted windows, and a Southern dampness swept through the office each time the door of the building was thrust open.

"Sure, what's goin' on?" she asked.

Bryan swiveled the office door shut and flipped the handwritten "gone for lunch" sign at the glass. They sat at a modest corner desk flanking the immense drawers of department paperwork. The office—the building, in fact— sported a mothball-like aroma and a lackluster motif carried straight over from the flowering '60s—block walls painted a light aquamarine from the waist down and crème to the drop-tile ceilings. Dusty carpet floors harbored decades' worth of who-knew-what beneath their mud-stained edges.

"Well, I need to figure out some way to cover Steve's course load after what happened. It might seem a bit soon to start thinking about, but someone's gotta teach the class, not to mention run the department."

"Who do you have in mind?"

"Remember that postdoc from a while back, Kole LeBlanc? He's over at LSU with Robert Hebert."

"I think so. He was here for his PhD, right? You had said something about him changing up his research?"

"That's the one. I was thinking it might be quicker and more affordable to see if he'd be interested in an adjunct position for the time being, until we can hire someone tenure-track. Likewise, I need to find someone in-house who can serve as the interim chair. We basically lost a two-for-one."

"Do you think he would be interested? I mean, most postdocs don't wanna be bothered with an adjunct position when they're already on a short timeline to complete their work. Don't most of them have about two years on their contract?"

Bryan looked toward the door. The sign was carrying out its due diligence.

"I'm not really worried about whether he's a postdoc," he said softly. "Mitch has been feelin' all hot-shit since his promotion. I'm not sure if you remember, but they were actually here together, working on their doctorates at the same time, competing to see who was the better grad student. I think Mitch needs a reality check."

"And how is that gonna be a reality check? Bringing in someone who used to be his academic rival is only gonna piss him off. Don't you think?"

"Maybe." Bryan squeezed the knotted muscle at the back of his neck, his jaw tensed in pain beneath his bloodshot eyes. Sitting behind a computer 24/7 not only caused him physical pain, it also made him bitter. And he was fully aware of the fact. "It'll show him that even someone like Kole, someone who didn't slide straight into an assistant professorship after half a postdoc, can still teach in the same department as him. As you already know, I was on Mitch's graduate committee. His research was, and still is, top-tier. But his teaching skills could use some work if he's gonna stick around. If anything, it'll show him some humility."

"Mitch's evolution class is one of the most sought-after courses in the department. And what about pay? Adjuncts make pennies compared to postdocs. I'm not sure that plan is gonna get you very far, hun."

Bryan raised his shoulders, only to let them fall. "Just because you have a bunch of happy students getting As doesn't mean they're being taught properly. And postdocs are poor, you know that. Kole can't be making any more than $40 or $45K over at LSU. He'll still be doing research over there, but teaching here would be a good way to supplement his income, put some more teaching experience on his CV."

"That is, if he cares about teaching."

Bryan had the dual reasoning all worked out in his head. On one hand, the department really did need a good instructor to pick up Steve's Ecology course. On the other hand, Mitch needed to be around more professors in the department who didn't worship the ground he walked on. Kole was perfect. It was a roundabout way for Bryan to both save money and push Mitch in the right direction. The idea was a stab in the dark, but he was willing to give it a shot.

"I sure hope he does—if he's looking to stay in academia at least. Besides, he won the GTA fellowship while he was here. I can call Rob and ask, but I don't think Kole's teaching at all right now. The only problem is whether he's willing to commute a little. We'd need to advertise the job, emphasize that we highly encourage everyone who *isn't* a white male to apply, and interview an applicant pool that includes as many different types of people as possible."

She huffed from her nose. "Dare I ask who you have in mind for interim chair?"

His mouth inched open to an absence of words—a tentative gape.

• • •

"Hey, Rob. How's it hangin', man?" Bryan spoke with enthusiasm as he pressed the phone between his ear and shoulder, his head slanted at an awkward angle. He bounced down the steps and exited the brick stairwell, the day's sunlight reflecting off a newly poured but dry concrete pathway. Then he pulled his sunglasses from the inside of his coat and covered his eyes. "You got a minute?"

"Sure, what's up?" said Robert.

"Kole LeBlanc is still in your lab, right?"

"Yeah. He's got about a year left on his current postdoc. We've been struggling to scrape up the funding for him to stay here for as long as he has, though. It's about time for baby bird to be pushed out of the nest. He's done with his field work out in Bama, so he's mostly just writing and doing some data analysis here and there. Why?"

Bryan walked through the UNO Quad, in front of the library, where students were battling it out at swampball—the annual mud volleyball tournament played in an excavated dirt pit lined with water at the center of campus. The brown sludge stood out amid the pristine grass heavier than a mole on ginger skin. Each year, the hole was backfilled and covered with fresh grass, as if it had never existed. Vanished into thick air.

"Well, first of all, I'm sorry about Steve. I know y'all were close." He strode up the library steps and onto the walkway beneath the building's towering overhang. "But I'm wondering if you think Kole would be interested in an adjunct position over here at UNO, teaching Steve's Ecology course for the rest of the semester. We might even be able to work something out if he wants to stick around once the semester is done."

"Isn't that a bit of a commute?"

"It's a little over an hour. I drove farther than that for five years during my PhD. Besides, he was doing field work two states away for the better part of a year, and the drive here would only be a couple days a week."

All Bryan could hear was ambient splashing from a number of crystal-blue fountains lining the walkway as he abandoned the library's shadow and ambled toward the amphitheater. He stopped at a tiny metal bench at a fountain's edge, a copper shimmer shifting beneath the onslaught of droplets disturbing otherwise tranquil water. A greenhead plunged itself beneath the ripples, then shook the liquid from its plumage as it opened its wings, just enough to roll the wetness from the tips of its black-and-gray feathers.

"Why don't y'all just temporarily hire someone who's already there? Wouldn't it be easier for one of the postdocs or professors in the department to cover it?"

"We'd like to, but we don't really have anyone who has the time. And those who do have the time aren't qualified." He rested on the bench and leaned forward, his elbows teetering on the edge of his knees, head down. He could practically feel his half-bald crown shimmering as sweat mystically appeared from nowhere beneath the day's damp temperatures.

"I guess I can ask him. Let us get some revisions submitted, and then I'll bring it up sometime soon," Robert said. "What kind of timeline are we looking at?"

Bryan leaned back, looking skyward to brown and golden pinecones, lost and blurry in a jet-blue sky.

"As soon as possible, really. The students are currently paying for a course with no instructor. We need to complete an official job search through HR, though, and follow through on the interview process with an applicant pool."

"And don't forget the diversity statements. You need diversity statements, Bryan."

8

BAYOU SAUVAGE WAS AN entomologist's wet dream. Languid canals and brackish marshes meandered in broken webs between Lake Pontchartrain and Lake Borgne. In the midst of the Lord's six-legged creatures, flying and crawling over the brush, sat Hunter's home for two.

Boardwalk hikes through the refuge served as a way of ridding her mind of the day's urgency. And the company of woman's best friend made the walks all the less lonely.

She set the hook on her pup's leash and pushed open the screen door, leading him down the porch steps one heel at a time. As they left the driveway and befriended the road, Hunter heard the familiar crunch of shells in the driveway from behind. She turned back as Deborah's car skated to a stop before the reporter slid from the driver's seat. Deborah shuffled at a half jog to meet them on the street, her keys jangling in hand.

"Hey, wait up," she said in a slur of heavy breaths.

Drake lunged forward, then bowed with his front legs sprawled out to receive his anticipated head rubs, yanking his owner at the far end of the lead. Hunter's shoulder pulled at the rest of her body as she threw her free hand into the air.

Deborah spoke in an overdone baby voice: "Dare. Him. Is." She dropped to her knees and accepted her slobbery greeting.

"Mommy didn't wanna wait for me, did she?"

"If only your timing with us was as good as your writing," Hunter said.

As she rubbed his ears, Deborah looked up to her with thin eyes. "Oh. Now my writing is good?"

"Well, I did say good, not great. Don't tell anyone, though. I'm with the fuzz, remember? I'm obliged to loathe every word."

Deborah pulled her lips taut as she moved the unseen zipper across her mouth. "Supplemental material."

Then she stood, and they began walking side by side along the dusty road. A five-minute amble from the house led to the entrance of a trail, harboring a narrow timber bridge—weathered, smothered in character, and flanked by lofty, greenish-brown grass. Drake pulled ahead as Hunter struggled to keep a hold of his leash. Deborah lagged behind at the center of the road, alone.

"You coming or not?" Hunter asked.

The red ball was beginning to dip its face behind swaying weeds, and a solid shadow inched its way down the path. Gnats swarmed in an ever-changing mass above the tattered bridge. Deborah stepped forward and met Hunter on the crossing. "I was hoping we could talk about the case a little."

They stepped off the edge of the decaying, wooden passage and into the brush. The tall reeds shaded the wind and brought with them a dense humidity.

"The case? What case?"

"Your case."

Drake pulled at the rope, expressing his want, his need, to be farther down the trail. Hunter's arm wrenched forward as if it had forgotten it was connected to the rest of her body.

"*My* case? You mean . . . the one I just told you about the other night?"

Deborah responded without a word, only hopeful eyes.

"I told you about that in confidence."

"And I didn't say a word to anyone, I swear," she said with a raised hand. A scout's honor. "As a writer, I just can't help but be interested in what you're working on."

"As a *crime* writer, you're interested in cases you can write about. Not because you're 'just interested,' no?"

"I don't have to write about everything we discuss. Or anything for that matter. And no one has to know what we talk about."

Hunter glanced ahead, down the trail, as it shed its light one shadow at a time. The lab whimpered at her feet.

"I don't think that's a good idea. It's a conflict of interest. It doesn't only look bad—I'll lose my job if someone finds out that I'm discussing a case with a journalist after only a few weeks on the job. I just can't, Deb."

The sun held a fragile grip as it rolled over the edge of the horizon. A single streetlamp blinked as a needle's prick a distant two blocks away. The day's clarity was sparse.

"Come on, you know me. I can leave work out of it. This isn't my first rodeo being with someone in the industry. Unfortunately."

"No, you can't. And I'm not putting myself in that position. I think it's a good idea to keep work off the table."

Hunter was surprised she had brought it up. Deborah didn't have the greatest track record with dating someone who worked all too closely with the reporting industry. Her last relationship had ended after a solid two-year run. He was the director of media and photography for the Baton Rouge crime scene unit. Unfortunately for Deborah, his ex-wife was an analyst in the same department. One thing led to another, and one day, Deborah had caught them in the copy room when she was surprising him with lunch. Needless to say, the copy machine was out of order.

But Hunter didn't want to push it. Deborah was bringing up the past, and Hunter could see how her work with David was sitting in the background, simmering on high heat. Her words treaded carefully over swampy grounds.

"Okay. Can you at least tell me how work is going? Generally speaking," Deborah said, putting her hands up in front of her in what appeared to be a defensive gesture.

They paused, standing at the center of the overgrown trail. Hunter was being tugged in opposite directions. She had worked tirelessly toward her newfound career for years. One semester after another of graduate school, menial jobs in academic labs, rejected applications. She wasn't about to throw it all away over some story. Over a relationship.

"I don't mind telling you about work generally, but, you know . . . I would think that you wouldn't wanna discuss work at all, after what happened with your last relationship. Don't you wanna keep work separate? Focus on us?"

"You mean—keep work separate so you can keep David separate?"

9

THE FOLLOWING DAY, HUNTER strode into the lab at dawn's first blush. Just enough morning had crawled over the horizon to paint the top floor of the building blood-red.

Upon entering the lab, she assumed Parker was still relishing a comforter's comfort, as the lights in his office were yet to be awakened. After all, not everyone put on a smile at working the hours of a baker.

The assistant pathologist took a seat behind her desk. A small table lamp, shaded with fern-green glass and a gold pull chain, furnished the room's trivial amount of light. Dim—as she liked it.

Today, it was more than pathology that was wreaking havoc in the back of her mind.

Going into the relationship, Hunter had known that Deborah had a past. Not a shady one, but a history, nonetheless. Just as everyone did. She was well aware of her partner's last relationship, and how it had ended on a sour note, but that didn't matter to Hunter. Deborah was the one who'd gotten screwed over. Besides, Hunter was new to the whole "woman" thing, and she needed to test the waters at some point. With only her toes at the shore, it was a bit nippy thus far.

As far as her own relationships were concerned, David was

a borderline case of casual dating. She realized how college-y it sounded in her head, but at the time they were involved, she was only aspiring to slide into a pathology position at some point in the distant future. Once she had realized it would soon become a reality, she hesitated at the thought of getting wrapped up in something with a colleague whom she would be working with directly. And so she had pulled it up by the roots before it truly had a chance to flourish.

As bad as it sounded, Deborah was the safer option, given Hunter's new career. But, personally, perhaps safe was . . . difficult? Just as Hunter knew of Deborah's recent breakup, Deborah had voiced her opinions on Hunter's most recent relationship. Although, Hunter thought that the woman's use of the term "relationship" was a bit strong. "Acquaintances with benefits" was perhaps more suitable.

As she sat at her computer, caught up in the glare of a blank screen, Hunter heard the office doorknob struggling and failing to turn. She couldn't see it clearly through the vague light of the room. She hadn't noticed whether the lab's lights had been turned on, either—the small gap beneath the office door was black as black could be.

Parker?

Her office entrance to the lab was locked; only the second door, the front door, which led to the hall, was open.

The doorway shook against its frame, the knob coming to life yet again.

"Hello?"

She stood up and advanced toward the lab entry. Heels met the ground first. Toes followed. One slow foot at a time.

"Parker?" she said lightly.

The knob's movement ceased.

Just rip it off, she thought. *Get it over with.*

Hunter drew a breath. Then she twisted the lock and yanked open the door, an indoor wind shoving her hair backward. Parker stood at the center of the lab. He halted midstride, turning toward her.

"Hey, was that you?" she asked.

His voice hung vacant, just long enough for her hair to steady itself as it fell across her shoulders. "No."

She looked out across the lab, then back to her colleague. "You see anyone?"

"Yeah, I think someone was looking for you. I saw somebody from my office, but they walked off when I came into the lab. You expecting anyone?"

Hunter shook her head with a frown fit for the bewildered. "No. I was waiting for you to get in. You got a minute?"

"Sure," he said.

Hunter stepped to the side and opened the door while glancing out to the lab entrance.

"What's up?" he asked, walking into the room. He took a seat, massaging the unshaven edges of his chin between his thumb and index finger. Even seated, his tall, thin frame towered over her. "Everything goin' alright with the case? Good job on that preliminary report, by the way. I know the coroner's office is a fan of the quick work."

"Thanks. I appreciate it. I was actually wondering if I could pick your brain about something for a minute."

He smiled. "That depends."

"You know Deborah Doucet from a while back, huh? I think y'all were both working in Baton Rouge at one point?"

"Yeah, I see Deborah around every now and then, doing her reporter thing. She wrote up a few of my cases while I was working under the coroner's office out in Baton Rouge. I didn't know y'all were friends. How is she?"

"Well, I guess we're friends, too," Hunter said. "Dating, actually. She's good. Still working over at *Crescent Crimes*."

"I think that's who she was with then, too. She got transferred out here not long ago, mostly working stories in NOLA and Chalmette, I think. Dating, huh? It's a small world, I guess. Although, I don't see her but once in a blue moon."

"Definitely. Anyways, I wanted to let you know that we've only recently got involved with one another, but I also wanted to see what your thoughts are on the whole dating-a-journalist thing. Especially when they work so closely with our office from time to time."

"Huh . . ." For a moment, he looked unsure as to whether he would provide any advice at all. But Hunter felt that if she could get an objective opinion from anyone, it was Parker. "Yeah, I mean . . . I don't really have any expertise in that area. My wife and I got together long before I got wrapped up in this crazy mess of a career. I'd say as long as y'all keep work at an arm's length, everything should be alright. Thanks for letting me know, though. We can have you fill out a conflict of interest, but it isn't anything the front office can't handle."

It was the response she was hoping for, really. At least now it was out in the open.

"That's what I was thinking," she said. "Maybe a few ground rules would do us some good."

"I don't see why not."

Perhaps it could work. For a moment, she no longer felt so guilty about drawing a line in the mud when Deborah had asked about the case. Either way, she needed to smooth things over with her before the tension began to fray. She couldn't let the benefits of past acquaintances get in the way. Of her relationship or her career.

10

EVERY BUSINESS DEALT IN one form of currency or another, and academia was no different.

The trick was learning how to game the system but doing so in a seemingly legitimate fashion. At the end of the day, success bred success. That was the hard truth behind thriving as a well-to-do professor. To catch the attention of the gods, you needed to pull off a miracle or two. Working the system was also necessary for surviving in the trenches as a postdoc worth mentioning. One who—withstanding adequate therapy—might be lucky enough to garner a phone interview following six or more years of voluntary purgatory. As a "doctor," of course.

In dealings of the academy, however, there were no bills or coins, at least not in the traditional sense. Scanty salaries prevailed. Instead, scholars dealt in grants, papers, and citations—often from the bottom of the deck. Outside of the pyramid scheme itself, nonscientists often believed that grants somehow benefited professors personally, although this was rarely the case. If anything, external funding picked up the summer salaries for nine-month, tenure-track appointments. To a department, grants were a status symbol and a means to an end more than they were a road to wealth. They kept a lab afloat, albeit on a yacht chartered by the university.

Rafts were for the flock.

Robert not only knew the system inside and out, he played it like a fiddle. He orchestrated successful award applications that were funded with ease, published in top-tier journals that were more business than scientific enterprise, and (by questionable means) racked up more citations than what was considered humanly possible. Religiously, he taught his postdocs each and every note.

His lab was pure and simple but well-ordered. A single square table lay at its center, surrounded by black workbenches against the walls, where light microscopes and computer monitors were dotted among the graduate students and postdocs. For the time being, one postdoc occupied the space.

Windows, stained and fragile, funneled little light through their soiled panes. Unfortunately for professors, sports programs and campus image were the university's top financial priorities, as research was of little concern to prospective freshmen.

As Robert entered the room, Kole was laboring over the R code on his computer, positioned at his corner desk. R was both a blessing and a curse. The program was the number-one data analysis tool in biology but also a primary source of emotional breaks and prolonged dissertations for the analytically challenged—and the impatient. More often than not, Kole could be found glued to his monitor, modeling data with an energy drink or coffee in hand.

"You fix that figure for the meta-analysis yet?" Robert asked, removing his wiry glasses.

Without breaking his view of the orange code, pasted against a black screen, Kole pushed a piece of paper down the table and toward his boss. Robert picked it up and nodded with approval.

"This should work," he said as he dropped the printout over his employee's desk, the document floating from side to side before jamming itself beneath the edge of Kole's laptop. "Make sure you get it submitted before the weekend. We can't afford to drag it out any longer. It's been under review for six months as it is."

The professor slid his blue-and-gray plaid sports coat from his arms and draped it over the chair behind his desk, which sat catty-cornered to the postdoc. He dragged his palm down over his unruly goatee to tame the stray, rusty hairs. Then he pulled out his chair and jolted the mouse, his computer emerging from its sleep.

"Reviewer 2 better be satisfied after all of this. Three pages of comments is ridiculous, aye," Kole said from across the lab. His fashion was lost somewhere between poor graduate student and aspiring academic—ragged, skinny blue jeans, a plain black T-shirt, and black-and-white Adidas. His coat hung over the back of his chair but rarely moved.

"Reviewers only care about two things," Robert said. "As long as they remain anonymous and convince the authors to cite a few of their papers, they're satisfied. Unless, of course, the paper goes against their own ideas that they've peddled their entire career. Then it's a free-for-all. At that point, it becomes a tug of war between two egos. Something along the lines of who has the bigger h-index."

"So much for objective science, then. I was under the impression that journals want to publish good research, regardless of who the authors are."

Robert snorted an exhale in decibels only he could perceive. "Objective science, huh. There's a reason peer review is single- and not double-blind—at least in biology. In today's day and age of p-values and journal impact factors, you're more likely to find a pink unicorn fucking a one-legged Chihuahua than you are to run across true, objective science."

"Well that's cynical, no?"

"Not at all. That's the realization you'll eventually come to after being on the inside for far too long. That's reality."

Kole shoved his foot against the wooden leg of his desk, spinning his chair around full circle as he looked up to the ceiling, squinting. "Well, Reviewer 2 clearly doesn't share our affinity for synthetic reviews. So, hopefully the editor makes the right call." He scooted back to the desk and spoke over his shoulder. "By the way, I emailed you the latest draft for you to look over before I send it back in. If you can take a quick look at the highlights, we need to fill in a few of the citations. Of course, Reviewer 1 is asking us to cite three papers that are all Smith et al. I only wonder who the reviewer is," he said in a mocking tone of voice.

"Alright. Give me a sec."

After looking over the draft, Robert shook his head, his lips pursed to one side. "That's a negative, Ghost Rider. You can add Hebert (2019), Hebert et al. (2020), and Hebert et al. (2022)."

Kole appeared hesitant, providing Robert a window of opportunity to offer up an explanation. But nothing came through.

"Excuse me for asking," the postdoc started in, "but isn't that a bit subjective? Perhaps a little self-serving?"

"Like I said—reality."

For Robert, it was only another day at the top.

II

DEBORAH RESIDED IN A reserved tan-brick home not far from Hunter but a few clicks deeper into New Orleans East, off Hayne Boulevard. She stood on the front porch under a bubbling, soapy sky, where the ambience of passing cars mingled with a lakefront breeze. She lifted her chin to the sunlight, the warmth feeling like a new pair of heels. The busy roadway put her at ease on luminous days when the house windows could be trusted unshut.

Silence provoked an uneasiness within her.

She walked inside and set the tumbler down on the kitchen counter before grabbing a fresh bottle of cabernet. After twisting the cork free with her teeth, she topped off the glass, then returned the bottle to its home at the back of the stovetop, the wine's predominately maroon counterparts organized in an orderly lineup.

The writer's work had flowed more freely with the red ghostwriter by her side. How much of the creativity was her own, however, she was unsure.

Deborah was grateful to have reeled in an employer that allowed her to work from home more days than not. Her workspace wasn't really an office, per se, but a small reading nook that was tucked between the kitchen and living room—an all-white space with four bookshelves stacked above her desk, stretching to the ceiling. It was the "writer's corner" as she liked to call it. Deborah was a homebody, and she loved it. Working from home gave her peace of mind and allowed her to write sporadically as the thoughts rolled in—ideas made visible by her liquid coauthor. She was never one to work a nine-to-five, and the freedom of her position at *Crescent Crimes* afforded her the chance to move about the day unhindered.

A knock at the door indicated lunch had arrived.

"Hey, you," Deborah said as she opened the door, where Hunter greeted her with a kiss on the cheek.

Hunter handed her a steamy paper bag, which sheltered a ball of newspaper. The verdict on its contents was irrefutable, the aroma unmistakable.

"Oh my god, I can smell 'em already," Deborah said.

"It never gets old, does it?"

"Crawfish? Never. Let's sit out back. It's beautiful outside." She gestured to the back door with her head.

The porch was furnished with a set of wooden benches and a rustic pallet-wood table, shaded beneath a black-and-gold umbrella awning. Deborah could feel the salty breeze brush the side of her face, dampening the warmth of the day's sun. She had hoped that eating outside—surrounded by the blueness— would soften the impact of the inevitable conversation she was about to drop on Hunter. She had no intention of blindsiding her partner, but Deborah was uncertain how to avoid it. So she eased into the moment.

"How's work?" Deborah asked. "*Generally speaking*, of course." She threw out the emphasis as half-genuine, half-good-hearted jab.

Hunter appeared to brush it off with a delayed response. "It's good," she said with a lack of taste. "I think I'm finally starting to get the hang of things. Although, I'd be lying if I said my first case was a simple one."

"Well, I won't pry, then. I'm glad to hear things are going well."

Deborah lifted the newspaper ball from the bag and placed it onto the table. She peeled back the layers like one of the onions inside and let the contents fall into place.

The journalist in her wanted to pry about Hunter's newfound career. But the girlfriend had bigger fish to fry.

"What about you?" Hunter asked. "You normally aren't big on getting together for lunch. It's usually dinner."

"Well, that's the thing. We need to—"

"Oh, before I forget!" Hunter continued. "I got you something." She pulled a folded envelope from her back pocket and placed it across the table. "I know our anniversary isn't for a few more days, but I couldn't wait."

"Hunter, we should—"

"Come on. Open it. I've had it for over a week as it is. Don't make me wait even longer. Come on." Hunter sat wide-eyed with her arms flat on the table. Watching. Glaring.

Deborah pulled the envelope toward her and unfolded the crumpled paper, which looked as if it had earned its character beneath Hunter's backside over the past several hours. Perhaps more. She reached inside and removed two tickets, turning them face up at a curious pace.

"I scheduled it a ways out so we have time to plan. Two weeks. Me and you. Just us and the open ocean." Hunter was beaming widely. "*Alaska.* Whattaya think? Yeah? I got it all planned out. We leave on Friday, come back on a Sunday. It's perfect. We can—"

"Hunter."

"And it's paid for. All inclusive. You don't have to put up a dime. Just show up and—"

"*Hunter!*" Deborah said, in command of the table. She had finally garnered Hunter's attention. It was time to pull the pin. Toss it overhead and as far as possible. "Like I said, we should talk."

Hunter's expression faded from a lakefront sheen to black, skipping gray altogether.

"Okay . . . What's up?"

Hunter grabbed a fistful of crawfish and a head of garlic, then dropped them onto her tray. She wasted no time digging in. She popped the first one in two and put the head to her lips, pulling the juice from the flame-red shell with a slurping inhale. Deborah sat with her hands in her lap.

"Well, I've been thinking about this for a while. And I'm not really sure how to go about saying it. Or, explaining it, I should say."

Hunter's posture, once poised at the table's edge, downshifted from evident excitement to a low-end slouch.

"You remember what I told you happened with my last relationship, right? Me and Jake were together for years, working in the same department. Everything was great, until—until it wasn't."

Hunter's eyes sank beneath the weight of Deborah's words. Her shoulders rolled back in a subdued frustration.

"Yeah. I remember. You've told me several times."

Deborah looked off to the side, recalling the complete story from years past. "I was on cloud nine. Blissfully in love. *Blindly* in love. He had told me about his ex who worked in the department and that I had nothing to worry about. That their relationship was in the past. And I was naïve enough to think nothing would happen. I just went along with it."

Hunter dropped the head of garlic she was just getting into, her seasoned hands dangling in front of her. "Deb, what are you getting at?"

"Well, I know there isn't anything you can do about having to work with David from time to time, but—"

"Oh come on, Deb. No. I really don't wanna do this right now. This is what you're gonna bring up? Again?"

"Can you at least hear me out instead of getting all defensive about it?"

"I'm not getting defensive," Hunter lashed back, "I'm just tired of hearing about something that isn't an issue. Something you're *making* an issue."

"If I tell you it's an issue for me, then it's an issue for me. Plain and simple."

Hunter shook her head and refused to make eye contact. "If you say so." She grabbed a roll of paper towels and began to wipe the juice from her hands.

"I know that you've told me that I have nothing to worry about when it comes to David. And yes, we've had this conversation in the past. I was fine with it before. It was a brief history, and the two of you broke it off. I get it. But things are different now. You've been at this new job for all of a few weeks, and you're with him on a regular basis. How would you feel?"

"How would I feel? If you were working with someone you had a fling with over the course of a few weeks? I don't think I'd get too worked up over it, Deb. Not to mention, Jake didn't cheat on you with a past fling. It was his ex-wife."

"I just can't, Hunter. I can't do that to myself again."

Deborah held the tickets in her hand, rubbing the cardstock between her fingers. She placed them back into the envelope and held it out, suspended, over the table. "I'm sorry."

"You're kidding me," Hunter said, the water welling to the surface of her grayish-greens.

Deborah's hand hung over the piping-hot pile of crawfish, the condensation dampening the paper between her fingers.

"Please," she said. "Take it."

Hunter looked at the folded paper, then back up at Deborah. She snatched the tickets from her hand and placed them back into her jeans. Then she wiped a lone tear as it raced across her freckles, down to the corner of her lips.

"This isn't something I wanna do," Deborah said. "I don't want to end this. End *us*. I just . . . I feel like I have no choice. I feel like I'm setting myself up for the same thing to happen again. Please don't be mad at me."

Hunter pushed out a short breath, the corners of her mouth beginning to quiver as another drop sprinted down the side of her nose.

"Please don't," Deborah begged. "This isn't any easier for me than it is for you." She repositioned herself on the bench. Anything was more comfortable than sitting motionless, watching Hunter drop one tear after another.

"So, that's it?" Hunter asked. "You're leaving me because I have to work with someone when I don't have a choice? Really?" She sniffled and wiped a droplet from the tip of her nose.

"No, I just feel like I need to protect myself before I get hurt again. I thought everything was fine last time. And it wasn't. Can we please just finish our lunch and talk for a little while? Please?"

Hunter smeared the wetness from the corner of her mouth with her sleeve and stood from the table.

"Hunter, please. What are you doing? Please don't."

She pulled back her hair and secured it with the scrunchie from her wrist. "You know what the worst thing is about all of this?"

"Please sit down."

Hunter snatched the black Ray-Bans from the V of her shirt, shading her eyes against the once-attractive day. "I'll continue working with David. And it has nothing to do with you."

12

THE BIG MAN UPSTAIRS had been granted tenure. Eternal life.

That is, until he would be up for full professor another five years down the road. As it turned out, the pearly gates granted you access to . . . another set of pearly gates. And so the pyramid was built.

Mitch hadn't spoken to Bryan since the party, but he needed approval from higher up before he could recruit new students to his lab at the upcoming graduate student recruitment day; his flock was thinning. The event was hosted by the College of Sciences each spring to indoctrinate new master's and doctoral students for the coming fall. And now that Steve was, well, no longer in the picture, the dean was the department's go-to. For the time being.

"Good morning, Dr. Olivier," the secretary said from behind her desk as she paused her organized assault of the keyboard. "Let me see if he's ready for you."

Mitch waited in the corner of the room with his arms interlocked, gawking at a picture of Bryan with the president of the university. A picture that was all too obnoxious for the cramped reception area.

"You can go in now," she said with a broad, psychedelic grin from the doorway, overly excited to be escorting faculty through holes in the wall.

As he entered the office, Mitch recalled how absurd it all was—the dean's spectacle. The display was more obscene than a peacock's strut, but at least the bird's show served a purpose. The room, on the other hand, was comparable to a small library, decorated with endless dust-peppered books that looked as if they had not been and never would be touched, plaques and other awards reminiscent of a childhood bedroom, and more photos of Bryan with the who's who of university administration. Three desks for one man was surely overkill.

"Have a seat," Bryan said from his kingly leather chair.

"Please. Don't get up," Mitch responded in a thirsty manner, arid as summer blacktop. "I know how *incredibly* busy you are."

An empty rocks glass, filled with ice at the corner of Bryan's desk, caught Mitch's eye. And Mitch noticed that Bryan noticed his noticing.

"Thirsty much?" Mitch asked.

Bryan leaned forward and eased his computer closed, then sat back and crossed his legs. His black-and-blue-checkered socks filled the gap between pantlegs and black dress shoes. "Let's get this over with," he said, glancing at his watch. "I have brunch in twenty. What is it you need this time?"

"This time? I don't recall there being a last time."

"Is that so? You're welcome—for the pay raise, that is."

Mitch smirked from his pearly yellows. "Look, recruitment day is coming up, and I need to bring some more students into my lab. The problem is that I'm still waiting to hear back on my NSF grant, so I can't bring anyone on as an RA just yet. There any TA spots available?"

"How many?"

"At least two—one master's, one PhD."

The dean raked his fingertips across the side of his face as he peered through the window and out across the greenish St. Augustine campus.

"Fine. I think Biodiversity Lab needs some help. But I do have a stipulation."

Mitch stuck out his neck, turning his ear toward the administrator. "I'm sorry. A *what?*"

Bryan reinforced his ask. "A requirement."

"Of course you do."

Mitch instantly regretted the meeting. He had always preached that it was better to ask for forgiveness than permission. Too bad he had failed to follow his own advice.

"Your lab's been doing great on the DEI side of things. All of the grad students and undergrads you've brought in over the last few years were recruited based on your desire to diversify your lab and bring in underrepresented groups. That's great. But I need you to focus on the qualifications of these next two you bring in. Make sure the PhD hire actually has teaching experience, preferably someone with a master's. And both of them need to have some sort of prior research involvement."

"I'm guessing you haven't made a decision on interim chair, then?"

"What does that have to do with you bringing in grad students?" Bryan asked.

"Well, deans are never involved in deciding which grad students are accepted to departmental labs. That's usually between the PI, the department chair, and the GPO. You're creating conflict where it doesn't exist."

"I don't see the conflict. As far as you're concerned, I am the department chair. At least, until I decide otherwise."

Mitch flipped his grin and nodded to an empty corner of the room. Of course Bryan didn't see the conflict. He wasn't on the receiving end of such a demand.

"Usually, chairs are the ones who approve graduate recruits," Mitch said. "We've always used the ranking system that Steve put in place, then the chair and graduate program officer approve or reject it. Isn't it up to me how I rank my recruits? Besides, why does it have to be a this-or-that type of thing? Why can't I bring in a diverse group of students who are also well-qualified?"

"Absolutely. As long as you put their qualifications first. Based on the performance of your recent graduates, I'm concerned that your students aren't teaching enough, nor leading enough projects. Your PhDs should complete a minimum of four chapters. Preferably five. And most of their work should be submitted and under review by the time they defend."

"With all due respect, don't we have enough people like . . . us? In the department?"

"Okay. Then you should have no problem handing in your resignation and giving your position to someone less privileged. Someone who isn't a white male benefiting from the patriarchy." Bryan's nostrils flared—his signature "gotcha."

"That isn't the point, and you know it."

"Oh, I think it's quite pointed."

Perhaps self-sacrifice for a greater cause wasn't as easy as Mitch had led on. Were his seemingly good intentions backfiring?

Impossible. How dare anyone, much less Bryan of all people, question his place in the academy.

"It's easy to check some boxes so you look good for your colleagues," Bryan continued. "It's easy to follow the herd. To blend in. But it's something else to walk alone in the opposite direction, toward the slaughter."

Mitch felt the pressure crackle and pop along his jaw as he bit his teeth with chipping force, his scowl smoldering.

• • •

Wives, too, bathed in the academy's clout. Bubbles and all.

Aura's office, the entrance included, was far from modest. She was one of the more senior professors in the department, and she had no problem making it known. Mitch loved her outspokenness, her pride, when it came to her career.

Just outside the door, in the hallway, was what seemed like an endless bulletin board, lined with row after row of peer-reviewed publications from his wife's lab, papers he had never seen touched by passersby. Only one CNS article—that is, an article from either *Cell*, *Nature*, or *Science*, the top-dog journals— was pinned at the center of the board and framed by what the academy would call "lesser publications." Aggrandizing CNS papers wasn't admitted outright, but it festered like an infection through underground whispers. A puss-filled ooze that was not only welcomed but celebrated by its host. Lucky for Mitch, he was co-first author. It appeared that marrying into your department had its perks after all.

Of course, Mitch's name was listed second on the paper, which meant his fame and fortune would forever live under the shadow of "Theriot et al." It was a loss he hoped to one day avenge.

Mitch rolled his knuckles across the door before entering her office. Aura was seated behind her desk, glaring at the computer with her hands in wedlock behind her head, leaning back and swiveling from left to right. Her lips were poised in what appeared to be a thoughtful duckface.

"Don't think too hard. You'll blow a fuse," Mitch said.

"You're not gonna believe the email I just got. Come here." She pushed herself aside in her rolling chair and made room for

Mitch behind the desk, resting her head on her hand at the table's edge. "Read this." She lifted her chin to the monitor.

It didn't take long for Mitch's brow to form a single, mile-high summit. The email had been delivered only seconds after Mitch had left Bryan's office, mere moments prior.

Dear Dr. Theriot,

As you know, the department is grieving the loss of our chair, Dr. Daigle. Such a loss leaves us not only saddened but in a bind. We have both an undergraduate course that needs to be covered and an interim chair position to be filled. I am contacting you because I believe you are the best candidate for the latter.

We plan to begin a formal search soon for someone to fill the position permanently, but for the time being, I need an existing faculty member to step up and run the department. If it helps, you would have myself to consult regarding any uncertainty during the assignment, and you will still be able to fulfill your obligations as professor and mentor, teaching your existing courses and overseeing your lab group. As such, your obligations as chair would be minimal until we can hire someone long-term.

Let me know if this sounds like something you are interested in. We can meet soon, perhaps over lunch, to discuss the details if so.

Sincerely,

Bryan Guidry
Dean
College of Sciences
University of New Orleans

A rampant chuckle bled from Mitch's voice. "That little prick wasn't even man enough to mention it when I was in his office just now."

"In his office?" Aura questioned. "What were you doing in his office? I'm surprised you walked away in one piece."

"Yes, it was a mistake. I had asked him to meet so I could get a feel for how many TA spots are available in the department before recruitment day gets here."

"And?"

"And it turns out, for my lab, two. That is, if I—and I quote—'focus on their qualifications.'"

She didn't bother to respond. She simply waited for it.

"Exactly. That's the look." He pointed to the Grand Canyon of a gape where her lips had once met. "That's the expression I assume was on my face."

"He actually said that? Focus on their *qualifications*? What the hell else are you gonna do? Hire them for their looks?"

"I know, right. Apparently, I'm doing great with DEI but need to make sure the PhD student has teaching experience and both of them have some sort of research under their belt. Like those aren't things I would consider."

"That's bullshit. Between our labs, we're responsible for, what, 70 percent of the department's outreach? If anything, he should be grateful."

"Well according to head honcho, I'm just another white guy benefiting from the patriarchy."

"That seems like a strange thing for Bryan to say. Even considering his push for the college to focus more on scientific advancement than—"

"Maybe I'm stretching it a bit, but that's how it came off." A sea of politics ebbed and flowed through Mitch's mind, churned by whitecaps of power. Tides of lies. "This, on the other hand." He pointed to the computer screen. "This is some sneaky shit."

"Why sneaky? You don't think it's a good idea for me to step up as chair?" Her voice had grown defensive.

"Maybe sneaky is the wrong word. It's just . . ."

"Divisive?"

He turned to his wife with a bleak look. "Precisely. Divisive. He's giving me ridiculous rules and restrictions while proposing that my wife run the department. And keeping it from me, at that. You're his saving grace, and I'm his—"

"Fly in the ointment?"

13

As Hunter drove back to the scene, back to Steve's family camp, one of Louisiana's fleeting afternoon rains had begun to wither over the Deep South's wetlands. A grayish haze wormed at the pace of an hour hand across the rural country streets, which gradually devolved into the swamp's sinking roads as the Honda smoked its way farther into the middle of nothingness.

She felt the blood drain from her hands, from a pumping warmth to a numbing chill, as she turned down the secluded, residential driveway. It lay a crowded distance from the neighboring property.

Hunter parked her car to the side of the residence and walked around the house, out back to where the professor's body had once been displayed. As she turned the corner, the corroded metal gambrel that had once held the cervid caught her eye. It was left hanging from the decaying rafter at the center of the shed, swinging in a gentle breeze and knocking with a rhythmic thud against the rotting wood of the small shack. If it had been up to her, the gambrel would have been collected as evidence. But it wasn't her call. Her focus was expected to be on the decedent and not the deer, which was briefly examined and then discarded by Homicide. In her mind, this was a grave mistake. The rope, on the other hand, was gone, gathered with the professor's body—now *that*, she had had some control over.

What keeps this thing from collapsing is a mystery in and of itself, she thought.

As she gazed at the scene, a deep voice floated toward her from the adjacent property. Hunter looked toward a line of shrubbery at the camp's edge—a blend of palmettos, ferns, and mature cypresses. A skinny path led down to a rusted barbed wire fence, which was hidden among the flora there.

The modest double-wide trailer next door was hardly visible. And the plants between the properties were overgrown, twisting and winding between the barbed wire. Too thick for a clear line of sight. She needed to get closer, so she treaded lightly down the muddied path.

Hunter swatted the flies from her eyes, their wings hissing the air, drawn to her heavy exhale. The twisted wire of the fence brushed against her pantleg as she thrust the plants aside, straining her vision to glimpse the adjoining home.

No one had mentioned a nearby neighbor. If she could only work her way between the spiked cables, she could get a better look.

Hunter pushed down the middle of the three cords and bent over, sliding one leg through to the other side. Balancing.

"Fences usually keep people out," a man said gently.

Hunter slipped and fell bottom-first on the slick path, her calf catching one of the razor-sharp prongs. "Shit," she murmured.

The man's boney face peered down at her from the other side of the property line. "Can I help you?" he continued, arms straight at his side, eyes empty.

It took a second. One that felt like an eternity. But she eventually recognized the narrow, scruffy face and paw-paw ears, held up by a pair of toothpicks in brown loafers. It was one of the professors from UNO—she recalled his picture from her online search.

Hunter adjusted her hat and brushed the fallen hair from her freckled cheeks. She couldn't find the words. "Hey," she said. She took a moment to collect herself before standing, attempting to wipe the mud from her legs. The stains seemed to have other plans. "I was just, uh . . . I'm just taking a look around." She gulped, her throat dry. "We had an incident here the other night with Steve . . . I mean, Mr. Daigle. You know him?"

"Sure," he said as he glanced over her shoulder to the skinning shed. To the gambrel. Hanging. "He was my boss." Swinging.

She had strong feelings about eye contact, but they held no weight in his presence.

"Do you think, uh . . . you think maybe I can—"

"Hunter?" She heard someone from behind, the back door of the camp slamming shut. She turned to see David walking toward her.

"Hey! I didn't know you were stopping by. I'll be right up," she called. She turned back to the fence—back to a line of green fans below a drapery of Spanish moss. The professor had vanished as quickly as the airborne pests had arrived, and she still couldn't recall his name.

"What are you doing down there?" David shouted from the trailhead.

Hunter looked at him, then back to the fence line, her gaze roaming like an abandoned puppy in unfamiliar streets.

"Be right up," she said with her back to the trail.

Reluctantly, she turned around and walked back up the path, grabbing the weeds for balance along the way. David was standing in front of the skinning shed, pulling at the ends of his mustache as usual. "I wasn't expecting to see you here. What a pleasant surprise."

"I could say the same."

"Yeah, the boss needed me to stop by for some more photographs. He wants duplicates in the daylight." He unzipped the case hanging from his shoulder and removed the camera. "What about you?"

"Same. Parker says I need to focus on more than just the entomology, so I thought I'd swing by and take another look. I'm just hoping there's something else that might point us in the right direction before we hear back from the coroner." She scanned David's face while doing her best to avoid any expression of her own.

Hunter wasn't entirely sure how he would feel about her interest in the investigation, beyond the Pathology department's usual involvement. Profiling was largely left to Homicide. She had gotten a halfway-decent grasp of the type of person David was outside of work, particularly after their involvement with one another a few months prior. Her understanding of the politics between the departments was more tenuous, though. She wasn't willing to risk overstepping her bounds so early on in her new position, even with someone as understanding as David.

There was no reason her idea about the professor at the fence shouldn't remain quiet for the time being. At least, that was what she told herself.

She heard a car door slam in the direction of the driveway.

The two of them looked back to the drive, only to see Meaux waving at them from beyond the yellow tape that enclosed the backyard. "Hey, is it okay if I come down?" Meaux shouted from the perimeter of the backyard.

"Sure, just be careful," Hunter said. "Follow the path."

It was Meaux's property, but given the murder of her

husband, the yard was a crime scene first and foremost, and off limits to anyone and everyone until further notice. Including the owner.

Meaux ducked beneath the yellow ribbon as the tape dragged across the top of her back, her dirty-blond hair dangling to the ground. Then she walked with a deliberate care down the dirt path connecting the driveway to the backyard. Her deep, tanned skin glistened in the day's sunlight.

"I didn't know anyone was gonna be here today," Meaux said.

"Just gathering some more info," said David. "We can head inside to talk if you'd like."

Hunter looked to David. She could see the concern on his face. She, too, was uncomfortable standing with a victim's wife so close to where her husband had been violently murdered.

"No, I'm okay," Meaux responded. "I'm only stopping by to organize some of my husband's belongings, if that's okay. One of his long-time hunting partners has some of his things here, mixed in with his. So I'm trying to sort through what I can and take my mind off of everything for a little while. If that's even possible."

"Of course," David said. He nodded to the skinning shed. "Out here is really the only scene that we're working with. Feel free to do what you need to inside."

She spoke in a soft, windy tone. "Thanks. I wasn't sure if that'd be a problem."

David shook his head with an approving frown.

Meaux's undying focus was on the gambrel. It didn't seem to matter that her husband's body was gone, the rope collected. Hunter watched the wife's eyes as they walked up to the rafters, then back down to the metal hanger. And Hunter could feel it too, what she suspected Meaux was sensing—the once-innocent shed now radiating a permanent glow, steeped in death.

"You okay?" Hunter asked.

Meaux didn't blink. Didn't respond.

"Mrs. Daigle?" David said.

Hunter placed her hand on the back of Meaux's arm. The woman jumped, startled by the touch.

"I'm so sorry," Meaux said.

"No worries at all," said Hunter. "Your husband's hunting partner—he have a name?"

David looked at Hunter as if she was being a touch too inquisitive. Insensitive, perhaps. Hunter stared at him with an I-got-this look.

"Yeah, sure," Meaux said. "His name is, uh . . . Robert. Hebert. He's a professor over at LSU."

"How long did he know your husband?" David asked, looking to Hunter with a pair of *we*-got-this eyes.

"Um . . . quite a while. Probably about twenty years or so. They used to work together from time to time. Not so much lately, though. They've just been hunting together more than anything."

"Well, if you remember anything that you think might be important, give me a call," David said, handing Meaux his business card. "I know you're already in touch with our Homicide unit, but I work closely with them as well, as part of the forensics team."

"Yeah, will do," Meaux said, taking the card and holding it up to her eyes. Her face went white. "Thanks, but I . . . I gotta go." She pointed to the porch, then turned away.

14

BRYAN SAT IN THE corner of the student-infested dining hall on the first floor of the University Center, waiting impatiently for Aura to join him for lunch. The ball of his foot hurriedly patted the blue-speckled, white tile. Lunch meetings were the worst, especially with the building's air set to "freeze your ass off." He folded his arms in tight. If he was going to convince her to accept the interim chair position, he needed to meet with her in a way that would require her to stick around for a reasonable amount of time. Free lunch had seemed like the surest bet.

What academic didn't pounce on a free meal?

He wasn't afraid to consider his ulterior motives. He was hoping that Robert would talk to Kole about the adjunct position sometime soon. The course couldn't be in limbo indefinitely. Bringing in Kole would not only be great for the students, given Kole's excellent track record with teaching, but it would hopefully also give Mitch the kick in the ass that he both needed and deserved. Getting Aura to take the chair position was just a bonus. The interim chair would technically be responsible for interviewing and hiring Kole.

What could possibly go wrong?

The dean spotted her walking across the way, her washed-out umber hair held up in a haphazard bun. Aura had apparently ditched the usual full-length skirt for a pair of denim overalls and what looked like tan work boots. Bryan thought it was an odd choice, even for her.

"Hey, you order yet?" she asked as she approached the table, her hands folded inside the front of the baggy overalls.

Bryan stood and began walking alongside her. "Nope. What you in the mood for? Looks like our only options might be Subway or sushi."

"Sushi?" Aura spoke with a suggestive tone, slightly higher than her usual pitch.

He held out his hand, face up, toward the sushi counter. "After you."

"So, interim chair, huh," Aura said. "Your email didn't say much about your choice, other than you thought I was the best candidate."

"Well, you're tenured and you don't mind being involved with departmental responsibilities outside of your lab. You're one of the most productive professors we have who can juggle things outside of teaching and research."

They approached the register to order. "You first," Bryan said.

Aura looked up at the menu. Bryan'd had no idea she was a regular there—her order was in before they had reached the counter.

"Hey, Doc," the lady spoke from behind the register. "You having the usual?"

"Sounds like a plan," Aura responded.

"The usual?" Bryan said. "What's the usual?"

"Spicy tuna roll and a side of edamame."

Bryan wavered for only a second. "Make it two." He handed the lady his credit card.

"You don't need to do that," Aura said.

"I know I don't *need* to, but I did invite you out to lunch, after all. And I am trying to butter you up so you accept this position." His nose widened.

Maybe he shouldn't have been so straightforward. But the satisfied look overtaking Aura's face told him he was on the right track.

The lady handed Bryan a tall metal card holder with a number. "It'll be right out."

They walked to a small window-side table at the back of the diner. He placed the holder down on the table and adjusted the number so it could be seen by the waiter.

"So," Aura started in, "I'm tenured and can do things other than research and teaching."

Bryan shrugged a single shoulder. "I just don't see anyone else doing well with the position right now. Everyone's either getting ready to submit their tenure packets, has just gotten tenure, or has previous research obligations that would keep them from doing the job the way it needs to be done. I'm assuming you're on board, or at the very least interested, if you took the meeting."

She completed a string of quick, shallow nods. "I am. I just wanna make sure that I'll be able to keep up with everything else I have going on right now. I might not be as tied up as everyone else, but I do still have a lab to run and a class to teach. Not to mention, I'm in charge of the Scientific Outreach Institute next semester, which still has a ways to go before it's up and running."

"Of course," Bryan said. "Like I said in the email, you'll have me to consult with about any uncertainty in the position. There's really only one thing right off the bat that I'll need your help with. It's short notice, and HR has my hands tied."

Aura scrunched her eyebrows, which narrowed her nose only a touch. "Okay."

"We have you to fill the chair position—if you accept—but we still need someone to teach Steve's Ecology 6093 course. Like . . . yesterday. I'm bringing in a postdoc from LSU who did his PhD here. Kole LeBlanc."

Aura sat back in her chair and folded her arms. Bryan didn't need to ask her opinion. Her eyes spoke volumes.

"Here we go," the waiter said, setting down their food. "Is there anything else I can get you?"

Aura kept silent.

"No," said Bryan, "I think we're good."

"And you couldn't find someone in the department to cover it? Wouldn't that be the easier way to go?" She spoke with a jolting sharpness.

"No one fits the bill. Everyone's either too tied up or not qualified."

He had planted the seed, just as he had hoped. Bryan had seen it time and time again: academic spouses were the nucleus of departmental gossip. And Mitch would know of Kole's possible return soon enough.

"Okay, so what do you need from me?"

"An interview. Well, I need you to be in the room, at least. Since this is happening on such a short timeline, you and I will be the hiring committee. We'll need to have a graduate student representative there as well."

"As long as I can keep up with my outreach and DEI work, I'm all for it. I'll take the position. If I need to, I can pull a couple grad students off one of our research projects and have them be responsible for organizing the Outreach Institute. I can just oversee everything." Aura looked outside as she shuffled a cut of the tuna into her mouth, holding her hand over her lips as she worked on it. "Speaking of grad students . . ." she muttered.

Here it came. A testament to just how spot-on Bryan's

Theory of Spousal Gossip really was.

"I heard through the grapevine"—Aura continued while chewing—"that you're unhappy with the graduates in Mitch's lab."

Bryan chuckled to himself as he tried not to let any sound rush past the rice-wrapped fish melting in his mouth. A few seconds had passed before he was able to safely swallow. "Unhappy is an interesting word choice. Perhaps I'm a bit . . . confused. Mitch's lab is one of the most productive research groups in the department, but his students' work doesn't seem to reflect that very well."

"I don't get it."

"His PhDs are barely completing three projects of their own while they're here. And hardly any of them teach. I simply told him that if he's gonna recruit more, they need to have some research experience under their belt. And if possible, the PhD needs to have taught when they were a master's student. The focus needs to be more on the science. On the biology."

Aura's cheek hinted at a busy tongue working inside. Bryan could sense that she wanted to respond. Defend her husband, perhaps.

"And you don't think that's what he's doing?" she said.

He placed another roll into his mouth, then stabbed the wooden poles into the last piece of sushi on his plate. The dean folded his hands beneath his jaw, his elbows resting firmly on the table. "What I think is that you are now the chair of biology. Not the social sciences department."

15

BOOKS WERE HUNTER'S KRYPTONITE. Her to-be-read pile was sprouting faster than her disdain for how easy it was to enter a bookstore and leave several hours later with no money and a wilting dopamine rush. But she avoided the mainstream outlets.

Her go-to shop was a sheltered hole-in-the-wall owned by Mr. Pillet on Front Street in Slidell—a brief skip to the Northshore of Lake Pontchartrain. The once-small feel of the town had exploded since Katrina and pushed the quieter crowd either westward toward the Covington area or briefly south, across the lake to where Hunter had moved; she technically lived in New Orleans, but away from the hurry-up-and-slow-down of the city. Books were her excuse to run back to Slidell at least once a week. In some ways, she missed the former modesty of the town.

After parking in a ten-car lot that really only had room for seven Pinto-sized vehicles, she walked around to the front entrance, which was hidden down a claustrophobic alley, tucked away between a brick wall and the storefront windows of a bait and tackle shop. Each time Hunter entered the bookstore, she felt as if she had access to the city's buried treasure. Rarely did she see other customers there, but somehow, someway, old Pillet managed to keep the doors open.

The first time she'd visited the store, she was a bit turned off by its disarray, its overwhelming level of entropy. But over time, the uniqueness had drawn her in. A single long, tall bookshelf occupied the space, running down the center of the shop from front to back; if not careful, you'd run straight into it within three steps of walking through the front door. The rest of the store was nothing more than stacks of books, one on top of the other, that ran from the floor to head height or taller. It looked like the storage shed of a book hoarder who had been evicted from their apartment on two days' notice. But after enough chats with the owner, Hunter had realized that Pillet knew where each and every book was located. He was a walking database of literary inventory—title, author, format, and location, memorized to perfection.

"Hey, Reg." He called her Reg. It was short for "regular" since she visited the shop at least once every few days. "Let me know if you need anything."

"Thanks, P."

As she moseyed down the seemingly infinite maze of predominately paperback towers, the aroma of freshly cut conifers put her mind somewhere between nature and a cup of coffee. Beyond her addiction to reading itself, the bookstore allowed her mind to wander, unperturbed. More times than not, the biology section pulled at her heartstrings the hardest. But today, she found herself standing in the two-stack religion section, her eyes scanning the teetering piles from top to bottom. Dennett . . . Harris . . . Hitchens . . . Only one of the horsemen was missing. She set out to find something on Christianity or, perhaps, how to make religious friends. Religion in the workplace. Religion for atheists. Anything, really.

Perhaps I'll be better off over in philosophy, she thought.

She continued probing, then looked up to the folded,

handwritten sign made of college rule paper above the piles of books, verifying that she was, in fact, in the religion section.

Maybe "section" was a bit overkill.

After completing a thorough scan of the two pillars, she had found no titles for the nonreligious but endless texts to the contrary: how the religious could "communicate" with atheists. As if she were some sort of alternate life form. What she needed was a resource to help bridge the gap with Parker. Maybe she could simply reverse the message?

She picked up a few of the texts as Pillet spoke from the back of the shop. "I put on a fresh pot if you're interested. On the house as usual."

Hunter walked the full eight steps to the reading nook in the back corner of the store. The area was made full by a six-cup coffee pot, a toaster oven, and three chairs, which appeared as though they'd been rescued from roadside pick-up: a lawn chair, a dusty brown chaise lounge, and a black leather recliner that looked like it had been attacked by an impressive set of canines.

"Interesting selection," Pillet said as Hunter set the books down onto the rickety table between the chairs. The chaise lounge resembled less of a deathtrap, so she sat there. "If you're looking for a good perspective on atheism, we have some of Dawkins over in biology—*The God Delusion*, perhaps?"

"Ha. I've read that one. Not half-bad. I was actually looking for something in the opposite direction, like the ins and outs of understanding religion, maybe."

"Trying to get acquainted with both sides of the coin, huh?"

"Something like that," Hunter said.

"Hmmm. I don't think we have anything that broad. But I can take a look at my supplier. See if there's something I can order up?"

"Yeah, that'd be great."

Pillet walked behind the computer, next to the register, and began typing. "So, uh . . . what sparked this sudden interest in religion, if you don't mind me asking?" He lifted his chin and looked through the magnified squares at the bottom of his clouded glasses.

"Work, although my job has more to do with facts than belief. At least I like to think so. It's someone *at* work, actually."

"Ah. So that's the real interest, then. Communicating with coworkers," Pillet said, typing at the computer.

"You caught me."

The owner winked. "Remembering where I hid the mystery books in my own store isn't my only superpower."

"Really?" Hunter asked.

He nodded to the room. "You see a sign for the mystery section?"

She looked over her shoulder to the paper signs, dotted above the labyrinth of books. "Touché."

Pillet continued typing away at the crème-colored desktop computer.

"Hey," Hunter said, walking over to the counter. "Can I ask you something? A bit of a random question?"

"Of course. Although, it's 100 percent at your own risk. Just know you've been warned." He smiled over the computer screen.

"Fair enough." Hunter raised a hand, acknowledging the hazard. "If there's someone you spend a lot of time around, and they have strong opinions or beliefs that are completely different from your own, do you think that you're obligated to understand their point of view? Or just respect it?"

"I had a feeling it wouldn't be so random." Pillet stopped his typing and stepped to the side of the computer, removing his glasses and placing the frames gently onto the counter. "So would this happen to have anything to do with this coworker of yours who you need help communicating with?" He leaned forward with his hands folded on the counter.

"Maybe."

"Well," he continued, "I'll start off by saying that—in my personal opinion, full disclosure—you aren't obligated to respect any idea. But it's important to keep in mind that people are different from ideas."

Hunter's stare wandered as she ran the words through her mind. "So, what you're saying is that I don't need to understand their point of view?"

"No. I'm not saying that at all. I'm simply saying that, perhaps, people of differing viewpoints should be respected, until they give others a reason not to respect them. Their ideas, on the other hand, might need to be justified."

She bobbed her head in slow motion. "Follow-up question?"

"If you dare."

Hunter paused, making sure to phrase the inquiry appropriately and not be wasteful of the opportunity. "If you're saying that we should respect someone until they give us a reason not to, do people not need to earn your respect then?"

"Just like we can distinguish between people and ideas, we can distinguish between respect and trust. I think respect is something that should exist by default and takes effort to be maintained. Trust, on the other hand, needs to be earned. But perhaps we're getting away from your initial question. Isn't this really about ideas?" His eyes moved across her wrist.

"Yeah."

"Okay, then." Pillet stepped out from behind the counter and walked toward the biology section. "Follow me."

They moved an arduous seven steps before Pillet stopped

and knelt down to the bottom of the one and only bookshelf. Hunter stood beside him. "Based on your repeated visit to this section every week, I'm guessing your job has something to do with science?" He pushed aside a few books on the dust-riddled shelf, shuffling past a number of larger texts and what appeared to be century-old titles. "Here we go."

The owner braced himself against his leg and stood up. He handed Hunter a thin, small green book with all-black writing on the cover—*Huxley: His Life and Work* by Gerald Leighton, MD. "I think this will do you some good."

"Huxley. I recognize the name."

"Yeah, if you're into biology, I would expect that you do. He was an English evolutionary biologist who came up with the term 'agnosticism.'"

"Oh, wow." Hunter's words were genuine—she was appreciative of what she was holding.

"'Darwin's Bulldog,' they called him."

She opened the text and flipped through the front matter. On the first page was a perfectly preserved library stamp dated Jan 10, 1917.

"I know it's not really a religion text, but I suspect you'll find what you need inside. At the very least, it'll point you in the right direction."

She continued fingering through the pages, shaking her head. "I can't thank you enough. This is such a unique book, just sitting at the back of a shelf like that." She turned it over and ran her thumb across the bottom right corner where the barcode would usually rest. "I can only imagine what something like this goes for."

Pillet folded his arms and widened his stance. "Well, you plan on coming back across the pond to bother me with some more questions?" His brow waited in suspense.

"Of course. You don't think I drive out here just for the books, do you?"

"Then good." He threw up his hand before turning back to the counter. "We'll call it even."

Hunter held the book to her chest as the corners of her mouth drifted apart.

The man pointed to the door with his pencil. "Now get out of here before I end up blabbing about where the mystery section is."

16

COLOR BIOLOGY WAS GREAT and all. But behavioral ecology was Robert's bird in the hand.

He didn't mind helping Kole with his color work, but his expertise in the area was limited. The professor's bread and butter was parasitism and statistical modeling. In particular, meta-analysis. It was the one and only course he was required to teach once a year in the spring. The method was a synthetic review of sorts, extracting already-published data to run new analyses and answer questions based on existing literature. It was an acquired taste that divided the scientific community.

Was it legitimate? Or statistical wizardry?

Robert had finished lecturing for the day and had promised Kole he would take a look at some micrographs before leaving campus. Upon entering the lab, he was taken aback to see that Kole wasn't glued to the computer per his usual fixation. He was glaring at the colossal, seventy-inch flat screen TV, mounted on the wall at the head of the lab's King-Arthur-sized conference table.

Kole wasn't the first postdoc who had come through Robert's lab and tossed behavioral ecology by the wayside. Getting other scientists to follow in his footsteps wasn't the professor's aim. His goal was to collaborate with hardworking, productive biologists. And for good reason: more pubs led to more citations. Publications were endgame.

And rarely did Kole disappoint.

"What's up?" Robert asked, walking up from behind the postdoc. "A seventeen-inch monitor isn't good enough anymore? Gave in on the upcharge?" He placed his coat onto the table before folding it neatly in half, brushing a strand of fuzz from the lapel. Then he adjusted his black, silk knit tie.

"Nah. I'm just going through these images from the copepod study. I'm wondering if my eyes are starting to play tricks on me or if I'm really seeing what I think I'm seeing."

"And what's that?"

"This."

Kole bent down to his laptop and zoomed in on the microscopy image, projected on the TV.

"What the hell is that?" Robert asked.

"Uh-huh."

Robert was in no way as familiar with the color world as Kole, but he mentored the postdoc as a favor to a colleague. An old friend, at that. *I scratch your back, you put me on a few papers.*

What made it work was that Kole had a unique familiarity with parasitism work. An interest that had hung around after he graduated with his doctorate from UNO. Robert had no problem tapping in on his mentee resource from time to time.

All it had taken for him to take Kole under his wing was a phone call from a hunting buddy. And Steve had been addicted to the chase.

Robert inched closer to the black-and-white image that filled the TV screen, enamored by what an electron microscope was capable of. His eyes moved across the picture like a toddler, drooling and lost in his first toy store.

"When did you take these images?" Robert asked.

"A few days ago. Why?"

"No reason. Just wish I would've been there. They're a textbook type of clean." He placed his hands above his eyes, shading his view from the sunlight pushing its way through the lab windows.

A single cell nearly filled the seventy-inch monitor. The micrograph showed the edge of a copepod—the model organism Kole studied to better understand how colors were produced in nature. Red coloration, in this instance. But something was off. Robert recognized the image. It was clear as day—only, it was different.

Scientists lived on different.

"I see the exoskeleton," Robert said. "But what are these?" He pointed to a row of white spheres in the animal's protective layer.

"Well, I have an idea. But I don't think you're going to buy it. Hell, I'm not even sure if I buy it."

The postdoc handed him a clipboard with some calculations written in pencil. Robert ran his finger down the writing, then looked over at Kole.

"Seriously?" Robert said. He looked back up to the TV screen. His eyes relayed the signal, but his mind doubted the message. "Structural color? Really? You model this yet?"

"Not yet. But the numbers work. It checks out."

"Well, I'm curious to see what R says. Run it through, and then we'll talk. You should also look into refractive index matching. I don't know the details on how to do it, but I wouldn't be surprised if reviewers end up asking for it anyway. I can hear 'em now. 'What *I* would've done . . .'"

"Already on it. I ordered the ethyl cinnamate this morning."

Robert handed the clipboard back to his postdoc. "Nice. I

think it'll be a great addition to your CV. If it all checks out, maybe we can shoot for something high up. Maybe *Nature* or *Nature Communications.*"

The boss could see Kole's eyes beginning to salivate. Just the word "nature" itself, in a publishing context, made any academic twitchy. In a good way, of course. But then again, Robert thought every one of his papers should be in *Nature*.

"I'm not going to argue with you on that one," Kole said.

Robert sat back onto the conference table and folded his arms. "Speaking of CVs, it might be time to give yours a once-over. I got a call from the dean himself over at UNO. They're looking for someone to cover Steve Daigle's Ecology course."

Kole's voice shot up an octave. "That's something I'm still trying to wrap my head around."

"I figured as much. But if you need to talk about it—"

"Yeah, it's something that I just need time to process. You know?" Kole pushed his fingers back through his boyish vampire hair. Then he went to work on his thumbnail in what appeared to be a nervous habit.

"Well, I think you should consider it. It would be a great opportunity to get back into teaching and get another line on your CV. You should be applying for positions at this point anyway."

"That's a lot of driving, aye?"

"True. Just think about it, though. It's adjunct, so you wouldn't be there more than maybe two days a week. Plus, Guidry said something about you being able to stay past this semester if you need to. So if you can't find a tenure-track position, you'll have something to fall back on. And even if you do get an interview, the position won't be until fall of next year."

"I'll think about it."

"Good. Just don't think too long. They need someone now.

I told Bryan that I'd let him know soon enough."

Kole looked down to his half-eaten nub.

"Besides," Robert continued, "don't you think it would be nice to return the favor?"

"Favor?"

"Well Steve got you this position. He might not be around anymore, but wouldn't it be nice to do something for his department? Head back to where it all started?"

17

CRESCENT CRIMES WAS AN everyone-for-themselves feeding frenzy, an ocean of chummed waters. And Deborah's cubical was a cage with an open door.

The journalist thrived in the action, though. It was an adrenaline rush. One day she was covering an accidental overdose and the next she was writing on the heels of a prolific serial rapist. She always craved more, like the addict in her latest coverage—a newly engaged parent: "Mother of Three, No Longer Soon-To-Be."

Devising a title was her favorite part of the writing process.

Lately, her mind couldn't keep quiet for more than two seconds, and she was tired of treading water. A new case sat quietly, untouched, at the corner of her desk. Waiting to be written up. Brought to life. But she couldn't get past the flashing cursor.

Writer's block isn't a thing, Deb, she told herself. *It's just . . . writing. And writing is hard.*

Or maybe it wasn't the writing. Maybe it was the recent break-up that sat in the back of her mind, showing its face again and again without warning. Much like the one dream that was guaranteed to revisit her in her sleep, unannounced.

She was searching the halls for her class on the first day of high school, completely and utterly lost. Embarrassingly so. Then the bell rang. Students disappeared into the rooms. And there she stood—alone in the empty hallway. She looked down at her class schedule but couldn't read the writing. The sweat from her hands had soaked the page. She ran laps around the infinite campus but failed to locate the room. She was late. On the first day.

Waking up in a jolt of cold dampness was guaranteed. Time and time again.

It was either "late to class" or "rotting teeth," as she had named the dreams. The latter was apparently common, but that fact had never helped her come nightfall.

Deborah had abandoned her usual in-home workspace and taken up temporary residence in her official office, in hope that a change of scenery would get the creativity flowing. The idea had fallen short so far, and she needed a fix before her current writing assignment went untouched any longer.

She grabbed her lip balm from the desk drawer, along with a compact mirror. Then she scooped a small amount of the paste from the jar and patted her perfectly defined, bouncy lips. The peppermint drifted up to her nose, her shoulders dropping in response to the perceived comfort. It was silly—getting all fixed up for a phone call. But she didn't care. She pulled her hair from the white tie and let the tawny waves splash across her shoulders.

Picking up the crème phone on her desk, she dialed Hunter. She placed it to her ear and lifted herself up, squatting, just enough to see over the top of her cage. The boss wasn't visible yet.

Ring after ring, she waited. Just before she hung up, her ex answered.

"Hello?"

Sure, Deborah was the one who had made the call, but she

hadn't really expected Hunter to pick up. She was calling as a formality, not to actually talk. Just to satisfy the itch, more than anything. Convince herself she was well-intentioned.

Shit.

"Hey, Hunter."

"Deb . . ." Her voice was a hollow aftertaste.

"I was just, uh, calling to see how things are going."

At first it was awkward, as expected. A string of silence, right off the bat.

"Hunter? You there?"

"Yeah. It's going."

"You at work?"

"Uh-huh."

"Okay, then. Just checking in on you. Do you maybe wanna get together sometime? Talk about things?"

Then another brief vacancy. Was Hunter preoccupied, or reluctant to speak at all?

"Talk about what, Deb? I don't think there's much to say."

"Look, I'm sorry. Okay? As hard as it might be for you to understand, I'm not trying to hurt you. At all. I Just keep getting caught up in what's happened in the past. It has nothing to do with you. Really. It isn't your—"

"No. You're not gonna go there. It does. It has everything to do with me."

"Alright."

Pause number two. Awkwardness progressed to tension.

"You know," Hunter started in, "it has everything to do with me. And everything to do with what's completely out of my control, Deb."

"That's not entirely true, Hunter."

"Look, do we really have to get into this over the phone? At work?"

"Like I said, if you wanna get together—"

"No. I can't decide who I work with, and I have no control over what's happened to you in the past. What you're doing isn't fair. You're putting this all on me."

Now it was Deborah's turn to go silent.

"Look, I gotta go. I think it's best if you stop by sometime soon to pick up your things."

"Wow. That escalated quickly."

"What? You made it very clear that you need to protect yourself. We can't be involved. If that's really how you feel, then we need to break it off clean and clear. I don't wanna risk hurting you any more than I already have."

"Hunter, that's not what this is about."

"Let me know when you'll be by."

She heard the phone find its receiver at the other end of the line.

If anything, the call had only solidified the discomfort. And the untouched story, the one she had yet to write, still ogled from the edge of her desk.

• • •

Hours had passed, and all Deborah had managed to do was type her byline and stress eat a bag of stale Zapp's Spicy Cajun Crawtators. Maybe Hunter was right. Maybe it had nothing to do with her. She couldn't expect the woman to quit her job. Her dream job.

Was Deborah being unreasonable?

It was the same story, though. A shiny new someone comes along with a rusty old "It's over, I swear." As if "I swear" meant something.

She grabbed the untouched folder and opened it—another story on someone unable to control themself on Bourbon, then attempting to cross the Hwy 11 bridge at 3 a.m. But the story might not have been so dull after all. Slidell PD had found the guy half-ejected from the driver's window with his fly unzipped, pants around his ankles. The body of his female friend was leaning over into the driver's seat, lodged between him and the steering wheel.

This one's gonna be a mouthful, she thought. She giggled to herself as she touched her finger to the tip of her tongue, then turned the page.

Her cellphone rang. Distracted, she picked up her desk phone.

"Hello," Deborah said. She flipped to the next page of the report, which was a point-blank photo of the male decedent's head meeting the concrete rail of the bridge. Needless to say, it had lost its shape. The head, that is.

"Hello?" she repeated. Another ring told her she had picked up the wrong phone. So she answered her cell.

"Hello," she said once more, turning over the picture. The next one was a close-up of the woman, her head on the floorboard. Her neck was clearly broken, bent backward from hitting the door panel on impact.

"Hi, may I speak to Deborah Doucet, please?"

"May I ask who's calling?"

"Yes, this is Cadence Prudence, editor in chief of *MurderoUS Weekly.*"

Holy shit.

"Um . . . yes. Hello, Miss Prudence. It's good to hear from you."

"How are you?"

"I'm doing well," Deborah said in a positive tone. "Staying busy. And yourself?"

"Same. I'm calling to let you know that I spoke with our local representative, Cassidy, out there in New Orleans. She said that she offered you an opportunity, contingent on you being able to provide us with some information for a story. Is that right?"

"Yes, ma'am, she did. I'm working on it right now. I should be able to send something over to her soon."

"Good. I just wanted you to hear it from me—it's a legitimate offer if you can deliver. I've seen a few of your pieces, and I'm sure you won't disappoint."

"Well, thank you for the opportunity. If there's one thing about my work that you can be sure of, it's that I deliver on my assignments. And I do so on time."

"I look forward to seeing what you come up with," Cadence said.

"Yes, ma'am. I look forward to it as well."

Deborah tightened her grip on the phone and closed her eyes.

"Oh, one more thing," said the editor.

"Sure."

"This case . . . it needs to be something big. Something worth our while. I know all of you over there at *Crescent Crimes* are used to covering anything that comes across your desk. But we're focused on headlines over here."

"Yes, ma'am."

"I just want to make sure we're on the same page. It needs to be significant, Deborah."

She closed the file on the drunk driver, pushing the folder back to the edge of her desk. Suddenly, road head was no longer of interest.

"Oh, and I'm sure Cassidy already told you, but this is an exclusive offer. I expect this to stay between us, yeah?"

"Absolutely."

"Good. I hope to hear from you soon. I'm looking forward

to seeing whatever you dig up."

"Yes, ma'am. I'll be in touch."

18

AS SHE WALKED THROUGH the lab and into her office, Hunter was still crushing over the book Pillet had gifted her, holding on to the text with a death grip. She pulled the chain on her desktop lamp and set down the book as if it were made of glass. As much as she loved to read, needed to read, she was slow at it. Luckily, this one was paper-thin and could be devoured before lunch.

She removed her hat and tossed it onto the desk, where it landed on a thick manila envelope.

"Huh," she muttered.

Hunter pushed the hat aside and picked up the packet. It had a decent, important weight to it. *Steve Daigle, case file – COPY,* was handwritten in clean black print. The opening of the package was sealed with red tape.

Just below the metal prongs of the envelope, she saw a note attached.

Hunter,
Got this late in the evening.
Please review so we can discuss.
– Parker

She turned to the book. "Don't worry. I'll get to you soon

enough." She ran her fingers across the cover. "I promise."

Then she walked into the lab, hitting the light switch at the door. Usually, the lab lights weren't a thing for at least an hour after her arrival, and she had a gut feeling there would be some tell-all photos in what she was about to see. But she was too jittery with anticipation to sit in her office and open the packet. She needed the wide-open space of the lab to prevent her nerves from imploding.

Hunter sat down in front of the light microscope. She pulled the red tape from the envelope and turned the packet upside down, a slew of papers and cardstock falling to the desk.

"Well, this is gonna be fun."

At first glance, the packet contained a copy of the official coroner's report, which included notes on the cause of death. Also included was the autopsy report, with photographs of the post-mortem exam, handwritten diagrams of the findings, and a detailed list of anything and everything to do with the decedent at the time of death.

She spread out the documents and organized them into three relevant piles: coroner's report, autopsy, photographs. Being the neat freak that she was, she decided to create a report of her own for Parker's convenience, although it wasn't required. Show some initiative.

Sticky notes were Hunter's thing. Her reader's obsession, so to speak. She pulled a yellow stack from the table's drawer, along with one of her fine-tip, archival pens.

Neatness was key. Necessary, even.

The majority of the report was comprised of terminology she was never privy to as a trainee. Findings she never would have considered. Although she may have been a newbie assistant, one note stood out to Hunter, a somewhat random fact she was familiar with.

Oblique incision to anterior of neck. Cut begins below right ear and continues to left side of the neck at downward angle, ending at vertical midpoint. Incision slightly deeper on right side with tail abrasion on the left. Right carotid artery severed. Superficial cuts present surrounding primary incision. Indicates head was not immobilized or restrained from behind. Injury consistent with right-handed attack from front . . . Incision made with fine-edge knife or surgical blade . . . Cause of death: blood loss and aspiration of blood due to throat laceration.

Hunter didn't only favor the philosophy and biology sections of the bookstore—she was also a sucker for true crime. And something that had stuck with her was the fact that homicides from throat cuts were almost always carried out from behind. It was easier. More efficient. The killer could hold the head steady and pull with enough force so that a single, deep cut was enough. Cuts from the front were rare. More personal. Sloppy. Whoever it was, they had no quarrel with confrontation.

• • •

After several hours of the morning had passed, Hunter had made no more than a dent in the lengthy report. But she was making progress. She was surprised at how detailed a coroner's report and autopsy could be.

"Morning," Parker said as he walked into the lab. "You get my note?"

"Yeah, I'm looking through everything right now."

His hair was still wet from what she guessed was his morning shower. It appeared as though the gusty walk from the car had sent his style into disarray. He pulled a comb from his front pocket and gave his blackened do a few short swipes, shifting the obviously dyed, dampened hair back into its rightful place. A drop of black water raced down the side of his face.

She couldn't possibly bring herself to point it out.

"Good," he continued. "You have any questions? Anything noteworthy so far?"

Hunter rifled through the papers and pulled one to the surface. "Actually, there's this. Maybe it doesn't have much to do with our pathology work, but I think it's something that we can pass on to Homicide. Either way, I think it's relevant."

"Okay. What ya got?"

She handed him the paper. "More likely than not, the decedent was attacked from the front."

"And why is that important?" His gaze remained down but his eyes darted up, cutting above the document. "Sorry, I'm not saying anything either way. Just trying to gauge your logic is all."

"Yeah, of course. I remember reading somewhere—true crime I think it was"—Parker smirked, and she continued anyway—"that knife attacks from the front are pretty rare. It's easier for someone to hold the victim's head from behind and get leverage for a single deep cut. Cuts from the front require more effort and tend to be a bit sloppier."

"Okay. It's interesting, I suppose. I'll give it a once-over. Let me know if you come across anything else." He began turning away.

"I think it might tell us—tell Homicide—something about the killer's demeanor."

The boss stopped and turned back, but only halfway. "And . . ."

"And I think they might be looking for someone who either knew the victim or has a confrontational disposition. Someone who didn't mind seeing the victim's face beforehand. Like I said, this isn't so much pathology as something that just stuck out to me as important. Maybe."

He paused, then finally acknowledged the dye that had run

down the side of his face, casually wiping the water with a single finger. "Good work. I'll pass it along."

"Thanks."

"Just make sure you read the report with pathology in mind, yeah? But I like these little side notes. These are the kind of things that we need to communicate. Let me know when you're done. I wanna sit down and go over everything with you."

"Will do."

He began walking away yet again before turning back one last time. "Oh, and Romero . . ."

"Yeah?"

"This is your first case. Don't kill yourself over it." He pointed to the papers on the lab bench. "It's good work, though."

19

"SO, WHAT'D YOU TELL Bryan? Did you accept the position?" Mitch asked Aura as they sat in her office, eating sushi. Again. Mitch always gave in to her lunchtime demands. They were phrased as suggestions, but he knew better. "What'd you tell him?"

I'm gonna turn into a fucking tuna, he thought, shoveling another piece of the roll down his gullet. An acidic burn bubbled to the surface.

"What do you think I did?" she said.

"Well I'm hoping you told his midget ass to go to hell."

She closed her eyes and chewed with an oceanic gleam. "That was a rhetorical question," she slurred. Aura opened her eyes and looked toward the window, covering her mouth before she spoke. "On a side note, he did bring up something interesting." Her eyes flicked toward Mitch for only a second before changing their mind.

"Oh yeah? And what's that?"

Mitch wondered what it was about sushi that made his wife eat like a toddler with a smash cake. She pushed another roll into her mouth, which was already flashing "no vacancy" in neon-red lettering.

"Well," she managed to say, "he needs me to serve on a

hiring committee. He's bringing in an adjunct to cover Steve's Ecology course."

"Why wouldn't he just get someone in the department to teach it? We're already far enough into the semester. Besides, didn't you just accept the chair position? Why doesn't he leave the hiring responsibilities to you?"

"He said that everyone in the department is either busy or isn't qualified."

Mitch shrugged and dropped his chopsticks onto the sushi tray in front of him. "I couldn't care less about what he's up to. Other than the fact that you said yes to the chair position."

"It gives us a foot in the door, Mitch. An inside angle. I flat-out told him that my DEI work was a priority, and he still offered me the position. At least now I have some pull in the department."

"No. Now you have even more on your plate with a lab to run and a class to teach. Not to mention undergrads to babysit."

She finally waved the white flag. Threw in the napkin. Leaning back, she placed her hand on her stomach. "I'll figure it out. Like I told Bryan, I can pull some students off their research assignments and have them prioritize outreach. That way, I have time for departmental stuff. Although, he did push back a little when I mentioned it."

"Of course he did. Publishing research is apparently the most important part of our jobs. He's fuckin' lost it." Mitch wiped his mouth with the edge of his hand. "I wish I could be a fly on the wall during those interviews, though. I sure hope you plan on using your newfound prowess to bring in someone who can help us with this Outreach Institute."

Aura pleaded the fifth.

"What? Is that a shit idea?" Mitch asked.

She took a swig of sparkling water. "No. Not at all. It's just that my hands are tied. He already knows who he wants to hire. That's the other messed-up part—the whole hiring thing is basically a formality."

"And who is that?" Mitch asked, taking a drink of his own.

"Kole LeBlanc."

The water flew from his nose and across the table, a sparkling tinge dripping from his sinuses down the back of his throat.

"I'm sorry?" He let out one of his adolescent chuckles, mixed with a choking cough. "For a moment there, I thought you said Kole LeBlanc."

All she did was nod.

Mitch placed his forearms flat on the table and rocked his head, attempting to no-handedly work out the crick that had suddenly materialized at the back of his neck.

"Excuse me." He kicked his chair out from beneath him as he stood up. Then he wiped his mouth one last time, dropping a crumpled paper towel to the table. "I have an impromptu meeting."

• • •

"Dr. Olivier, hello. How are you—"

"I need to speak with Bryan. He in his office?" Mitch said to the receptionist. Short and to the point. Abrupt. "He in there?" He pointed to the door.

"Um, yes he is. He's here today, but I don't know if—"

He pushed open the office door to find Bryan sitting behind his desk, talking on the phone, his feet up in typical kingly fashion.

Mitch stood at the foot of the desk, huffing from his power walk across the parking lot. Staring. Whatever fatigue had come about from the stride over was vanquished by the heat of adrenaline coursing through his veins.

"Hey, I'll have to call you back. Something . . . annoying just came up," Bryan said into the phone. "Hello. Is there something I can help you with, Doctor?"

"LeBlanc? Really?"

"I don't get it. Is there a question in there?"

"Cut the shit, Bryan. You can very easily hire someone in the department, temporarily, to teach the class. Bringing someone in from the outside is just gonna cost the department time and money." Mitch threw up his hands. "What are you doing?"

The dean stood up from behind his desk and walked around, meeting Mitch face-to-face.

"We both know this has nothing to do with time or money, and everything to do with your ego. Grad school was a long time ago, Mitch. You really holding grudges over petty awards and friendly competitions?"

Bryan inched closer, the smell of ninety proof flowing from his breath. "And besides," he continued, "Kole isn't from the outside. He'd merely be coming back. He won the GTA award while he was here. He's gonna need something soon once his fellowship ends, and he's right next door at LSU. You really suggesting I don't hire one of our own because the two of you had some beef over who did it better?"

"That has nothing to do with it. If we hire someone in-house who can work on the Outreach Institute, it would really help us out right about now."

"Sounds like maybe you should reach out to your department chair."

20

HUNTER STOOD AT THE kitchen counter of her petite home. The adjacent wall was lined with planters holding rows of herbs. Basil, cilantro, oregano. They elevated her culinary chops—her lonesome nights hunched over a single-burner stove—and added an outdoor touch to the limited space. An arboreous innateness that brought the outside in.

"What do ya think, boy?" She looked down at Drake. "Yeah? Boudin and dirty rice? You read my mind." She rubbed her friend's head, his ears slapping from side to side. Then she grabbed a pair of stainless steel scissors from the kitchen drawer before walking out to the back deck. Drake followed.

Bending over the waist-high plants, she snipped a few of the green and red bells. The pup rubbed the side of his face against the leaves' edges. Hunter smiled. "I like a good scratch, too."

As much as she tried to shake it, to distract herself and take her mind off the negative, Hunter couldn't dodge what Meaux had said during their run-in at the camp. Surely, Homicide had made the connection by now. Or maybe it was only an irrelevant inkling on her part. Albeit, one with a respectable grip.

She placed the fruit down onto the cutting board and pushed it aside, replacing it with her laptop. "Let's see," she said as she opened the computer.

Robert Hebert LSU, she typed in the search bar.

The ponderous wheel spun on the screen, chasing its own tail, bringing Hunter's impatience to the surface. She looked back at Drake. "Hey, it's better than sitting through a dial tone. You weren't here for the days of AOL, my friend."

Then the screen loaded, choppy, from the top down like an electric waterfall. She pointed to the computer while studying Drake with hopeful eyes, wishing he too would share in the excitement. "Hey, we're in business."

Hunter scrolled down through the list of returned links. *Biological Reviews . . . Journal of Ethology Ecology and Evolution . . . ResearchGate . . .* "Ah. Here we go." *LSU Behavioral Ecology Lab* was listed at the bottom of the first page.

She clicked the link, which led her to the Contact page of the professor's lab website. She quickly realized that that was too risky, though. Too forward. Not quite her role as a pathologist. She backpedaled and selected "Lab Members."

Not that she minded getting a bit squirrelly, drifting and pushing boundaries, but she wanted to do it right. Both her curiosity and tendency to take initiative were something she always yielded to—work included. And if that meant spinning the tires, drifting a little, then so be it.

The lab group was relatively small: two grad students and a postdoc. Both of the graduates were master's students, recent additions to the lab. The postdoc, however, had joined the group several years ago.

Hunter clicked the name—*Kole LeBlanc.*

The link transported her to another website entirely. Drake whimpered at her side. "Yeah? You think so?" she said, looking to the pup.

She grabbed her phone from the counter and thumbed her

code on the screen, then navigated to the keypad. A part of her knew that this wasn't her place.

But the little guy hanging out, whispering in her ear—a pestering little shit—reminded her that she could.

At least, she was capable.

• • •

As far as Hunter was concerned, capable was enough; self-provocation was a familiar friend.

The Audubon Insectarium and Butterfly Garden was neutral ground. The perfect place to meet. A shared interest, even.

Hunter entered the indoor exhibit and was immediately eased by the calmative space. The echo of running water and somehow a simultaneous quiet satisfied the air. A brief wooden bridge enclosed by black rails spanned a luscious pond, framed by greenery and flowers, whose beauty even the most inventive parts of her imagination would not have been capable of conjuring.

And of course, the small bodies carried by patterned wings, floating among the vegetation. Exploring in their own little world.

She had never visited the Butterfly Garden. But she now saw a place, an escape, to keep tucked away in her back pocket. A hideaway for the less-than-happy days.

As Hunter crossed the bridge, the walkway let out a slight creak below her feet. Then his hair caught her eye. His lionesque mane. Forget the jeans and tattered shoes—it was the free-flowing tufts that announced their presence from afar.

She stepped down from the bridge as he raised his chin toward her, an invisible "hi" between them. Then the real one a second later.

"Hi. Doctor LeBlanc?" she asked.

"Please. Kole." He reached out his hand, keeping the other in his pocket. "Hunter?"

"Good to meet you," she said, not yet able to meet his orangey-brown eyes. "Up for a walk?" She pointed to the room.

"After you."

He definitely looked the part. Intellectual. Witty. Run down from nothing but work. Aspiring-professor-like.

"So, you said over the phone that you're in . . . pathology? Is that right?"

She nodded. "Yeah, I work for the city in their criminal Pathology department. Working cases to understand homicides, mostly."

"Nice. I bet that keeps you on your toes, aye."

"You could say that."

Kole held out his hand, his index finger extended and bent, toward one of the small fountains at the edge of the walkway.

"You think that'll work?" she said, a hint of skepticism lingering in her voice.

He remained still, waiting. "If you're patient enough, you can get just about anything."

Hunter saw it from a distance. A golden pattern on dark brown wings, dodging the air, fluttering toward them. Just when it looked like it would fly away, it committed, landing on the tip of Kole's finger.

"Looks like you know what you're doing," she said.

"Well, I don't have a membership here just to throw my money away." He moved his arm toward her.

"*Opoptera*." They spoke at the same time.

"You know your butterflies, then," he said.

"I studied in the entomology department at Southeastern for a while." She felt the pink flood her cheeks.

"Yeah, we mingle with that crowd from time to time," Kole

said. "It's part and parcel with Rob's parasitism work. He collaborates with a few of the researchers over there."

The creature floated upward to the ceiling, meeting its conspecifics along the way.

"Like I said before, I was hoping we could talk about your PI, Robert Hebert. He was pretty close with Steve Daigle, no?"

They walked the path to a small feeding station—a carroty-colored plate holding a variety of fruit for the grazing inhabitants.

"Yeah," Kole said. "They went way back. They collaborated on and off for much of their careers. Ended up spending a lot of time together outside of work, too. Hunting, I think. What I don't get is why you aren't just talking to him yourself."

Hunter looked down at the ground, careful with her speech. "Well, I already knew before talking to you that they hunted and worked together. The reason I wanted to get your perspective is because of that very fact. Sometimes, if you really wanna know something about someone—"

"They're the last person you should ask," he said.

"And for that very reason, I'm hoping this can stay between us."

"Look, I'm willing to do whatever I can to help. I just don't think there's much I can tell you beyond what you already know. I've worked with Rob for several years, but work is about all it's been. I don't really know much about him outside of our research together. I'd never even met him before Steve got me the gig."

"Steve?" Hunter's voice was divided between surprise and uncertainty.

"Yeah. I was at UNO once as well. But I have a feeling you already knew that, aye."

In fact, she had not.

21

THE GRADUATE STUDENT REPRESENTATIVE sat in the corner. Legs crossed. Silent. Fidgeting like a field mouse in the rain, as if he was unsure what the hell he was even doing in the room.

Aura sat a touch too close to Bryan on one side of the conference table. Kole would be arriving at any moment.

"What about this one?" She pushed a piece of paper in front of the dean—the CV of the second applicant they had interviewed the day prior. Candidate two of three.

Bryan glanced over and could see her notes, the "DEI Training and Certification" section of the CV circled and highlighted. Bryan shook his head with a give-me-a-break rhythm. Aura pulled the paper back in front of her. "Yes, *sir,*" she whispered with a thin sardonicism.

The student looked up from the book in his lap, his eyes barren. Then Bryan began writing on a piece of scratch paper, the student at the edge of his vision. *This is a formality. Hence, the kid,* the note read.

He slid the paper in front of Aura, the grad student looking up yet again. Bryan smiled in his direction, nostrils broad.

Kid ain't even reading a biology book, he thought. *What a waste.*

He caught sight of Kole through the glass door. He stood before the postdoc had a chance to enter the room, then rushed around the table with an extended hand and met Kole at the door. "Doctor LeBlanc. It's good to see you. We're glad you could make it."

Kole's handshake was a vise.

Aura remained glued to her seat, continuing to annotate the other applicants' CVs. Kole's application lay in a folder, closed, off to the side.

"Please, have a seat," said Bryan. He pointed to a chair at the opposite end of the table.

Kole put out his hand to Aura. "Good to see you again, Dr. Theriot."

"Yep," she said, and left it at that.

Bryan looked at her. He failed to speak but tried his best to get the message across. *Get it together*, his glare said.

They sat with synchronized timing.

"Thanks for coming out on such short notice," Bryan told Kole. "It's good to see you again. I take it Rob was able to tell you a little bit about the position?"

"Yeah, a little. He said you were looking for someone to cover Doctor Daigle's Ecology course for the rest of the semester." He leaned his head to the side for emphasis. "And that I should take the job."

Bryan flipped through Kole's CV, wading through the pages before him. Or rather, he pretended to. It was the academic song and dance—appearing official, formally dressed, the vague questions, when in fact nothing was official in the least. Bryan would ensure the job was his.

But . . . HR.

"That's about the extent of it," said Bryan. "If I'm not mistaken, you took the course while you were here as a PhD student, so you should already be familiar with it. It would only be for the rest of the semester, but like I told Rob, maybe we can work something out if you need to stick around a bit longer. We're always up for easing the load on our current staff."

"Sounds right up my alley."

"Besides," Bryan continued, "you did great as a TA while you were here, winning the fellowship and all. I think you'd do really well teaching the course."

"Well, I appreciate it. More than anything, I'm looking forward to—"

"So, I'm looking at your CV, here," Aura interrupted, holding the papers up to her eyes, "and I don't see much outreach experience. Is that something you've been involved with since you've been over at LSU?"

Bryan looked at the applicant. *Ignore it*, he thought. *I mean, answer it. Of course answer it. Just, ignore it.*

"We were hoping to bring on someone who could help with our Outreach Institute next semester," Aura said.

The air shifted from a laid-back informality to more of a calm rebellion on Aura's part.

"DEI efforts have become one of the department's priorities," she continued.

"Well, it's *part* of the department," Bryan said. He couldn't look at her. His gaze remained forward. It was already taking everything he could muster to keep his cool. To act like her questions were in some way valid. Sure, she was the new chair. Interim chair. But he had an angle to work, and he was still number one in charge, whether Aura recognized it or not.

"No," Kole said. "It hasn't been a priority of mine. I find that, as an academic, research is my number-one priority. I suppose that if I had the extra time, I could manage to work it in. But as busy as I've been with my lab work and looking for a tenure-track position, I don't see that happening in the near future."

Aura huffed at the CV, cinching her lips. "Well . . . people tend to make time for the things they *want* to make time for."

Kole looked to Bryan, who flashed a wink, the eye hidden from his cocounsel by the bridge of his nose.

22

LAB MEETINGS WERE PITCHED as a necessity. An evaporative watering hole on the open savannah for an academic pride. In reality, they were a mirage engrained into the academic persona.

To Mitch, the weekly get-togethers were nothing more than a rally of the less accomplished. His following, looking up to the pulpit, desperate to learn the ins and outs of the enterprise. Although such divisive thoughts remained tucked away between his own two ears.

Mitch was already seated at the head of the conference table when Aura entered the room. Joint lab meetings were their thing, considering no other professors in the department were married to one another.

"Interview went that well, huh?" he said with a scathing undertone.

"Eh. It is what it is." She kept moving.

"Well, that's comforting."

The rest of the lot would be arriving at any moment. Mitch looked into the reflection of his laptop and adjusted his mane with the slap of a paw.

He pushed the conversation forward. "What did Bryan say about the interviews?"

"Nothing. He's acting like we have three competitive

applicants."

"Well, don't we?"

"Hey, Aura," said one of the grad students as she pranced into the room, interrupting the couple. She circled the table before finding her spot next to Mitch, who looked at the rest of the room, the empty chairs surrounding the table.

"Hi, Mitch," she added. "We still doing professional development today?"

"Yeah," said Aura. "We'll cover everything that needs to be written into your diversity statements using the appropriate language. Hopefully, we'll have time for some of you to practice inclusive introductions, too."

A few more students trickled in, claiming their spots at the water's edge, propping open their computers in a silvery wave.

"Perfect," said the first student. "I've really been struggling with what to say when introducing myself. I wanna make sure that I'm being mindful of everyone in the room."

"As you should," said Aura. "Your talks should be a safe space for everyone involved."

The room drifted into silence, everyone absorbed by their reflections—cell phones, laptops, and the like. Not a dark screen in the room.

"Alright. Before we get started," said Aura, "we have a quick announcement. This isn't to leave the room, though, since it isn't official yet." She stood up and moved to the door, pulling it shut after dipping her head into the hallway. Then she paced back to her seat. "It looks like we'll have a new adjunct in the department sometime soon. In addition to teaching our Ecology course, I'm hoping we can get him on board with some of our DEI work, too."

"Well, he'll be an adjunct," Mitch said. "So there's no guarantee that he'll be doing anything other than teaching. *If* he's hired."

"So, he'll be able to help out with the Outreach Institute, then?" the student asked Aura, in complete avoidance of Mitch's input.

"That's what I'm hoping," Aura said. "Maybe we can all get together over lunch once he's settled."

"*If* the department brings him on," Mitch repeated. He might as well have been talking to a brick wall. An oblivious one.

"Speaking of outreach," his wife continued, sidestepping his comments, "I'm thinking of pulling one or two of you off the morphology study and having you work on the Outreach Institute for the time being. The research can wait. I'm gonna be more tied up with my responsibilities as chair, so I'll need some help with planning the individual activities for the Institute."

Suddenly, it appeared, she had their attention.

"Isn't the morphology work time sensitive?" one student asked—the boy whom Mitch had rarely heard speak.

"Yeah, but we can deal with a smaller sample size if we have to. We'll just aim for a smaller journal," Aura said. "What we can't handle is a half-assed outreach program."

"So, he has a lot of experience with DEI work, then?" the first student asked.

"Who?" Mitch said.

The girl addressed Aura. "The new adjunct."

"I'm guessing probably none," Mitch gabbled to himself, accepting the fact that he was in his own little world.

Aura turned to her husband. "Do what?"

"Huh?"

She turned back to the student. "I don't think he has a great deal of DEI work under his belt, but we'll figure it out. Just because he's an adjunct doesn't mean that he can't help."

The other student spoke up, voicing his concern. "I'm not

sure a smaller sample size for the morphology study is gonna cut it. We're already dealing with a small number of individuals across treatment groups. Anything less is really gonna mess with the stats. Most importantly, the reliability of the results."

"So . . . what?" the girl said. "We don't help?" She looked to Aura. "I'm sure we can do both. There's no reason we can't stay on the project and help organize the DEI work as well."

Mitch leaned forward, his hands flat on the table, fingers outstretched and tensed. "No. I don't think that's a good idea. Y'all need to stay on the research. We need to make sure y'all have enough chapters to defend." He looked to Aura.

She sat back and crossed her legs, pulling her shins in close. "They're my students, Mitch. And I say they can help with the outreach."

"No, *one* of them is your student. The other is jointly advised. We can talk about this later. We need to get started."

How dare she. Mitch was all about the DEI work. Outreach was *the* work, he had come to realize. But prioritizing Kole's involvement before he was even in the department was rubbing Mitch a bit too deep-tissue. A little rough. Forget the outreach. If his students were to end up working with Kole, forget it. Interim chair or not, it wasn't happening. Hell, *wife* or not.

"Besides," Mitch continued, "the morphology study is a collaboration between our labs. But we'll figure it out later."

Aura's student looked down at the table. She spoke with a slight cut in her voice. "So, research comes first, then?"

And the room looked at Mitch.

23

THE HIGH BEAMS FROM Deborah's car floated across the driveway and pierced the windows of Hunter's home, Drake whimpering from inside.

Both anxious and saddened to be there, Deborah walked up the stairs and onto the front porch. The fact that she needed to take a step back from Hunter, to reevaluate their relationship, pushed her forward. She knocked on the door. A single yellow light to the side of the porch hardly illuminated the front of the home, the pup scratching the metal square at the bottom half of the storm door.

As hard as it was, she had no choice but to follow through with her gut. Footsteps thumped from inside, growing louder, until Drake turned to meet his owner.

Deborah had considered it while in the car, but it was too late to walk away. She was committed—to the break-up.

"Hey," Hunter said with a lack of carbonation as she swung open the door. She stepped aside and held open the screen.

"Hi," Deborah responded. She knelt just inside the home. "And hi to you too, my big guy," she added, her baby voice in full effect. The dog's ears slapped noisily from side to side as she scratched his chin. His eyes closed in apparent delight.

Hunter let the door go, and it slammed shut. The flimsy

metal frame rattling with an aftershock. She walked into the kitchen and resumed her ritualistic washing of the dishes. Deborah could see that it was her attempt at avoiding the situation altogether.

"Your things are in the bedroom." With a soapy hand, she pointed the short distance to the doorway. "Feel free to get what you need." She looked back down at the sink.

Deborah sensed that her presence was nothing more than a distraction. Hunter had gone from ninety to nothing in no time at all, the flame pinched out as if it had never been lit.

"Do you wanna talk at all?" she asked, standing in the foyer. "Stop slaving over the sink for a little while?"

"I'm actually pretty busy. I gotta get these done."

"Yeah, those dinners for one sure do rack up some dirty dishes."

Hunter dropped a plate into the sink, the water splashing up and over the counter like a wave against granite shores. She looked at Deborah, leaning forward with both hands against the countertop. A popping sphere of bubbles rested on the edge of her shoulder.

"Sorry," Deborah said.

Was breaking it off clean and clear the way to go? Nothing further to be had? Maybe stopping to talk at all would only deepen whatever pain was left wedged between them.

Deborah pointed to the room. "I won't be long, then."

The boxes were neatly organized and stacked in a single tower, their edges perfectly aligned, stupidly flush. Each one was labeled in black permanent marker: *clothes, bathroom, other*. She was astonished how easily, how quickly, Hunter was ready to move on. Sure, it was what Deborah wanted. What she had asked for. But it only turned the retrieval into a guilt-ridden walk of shame as a result.

Hunter appeared in the doorway. "You need a hand getting those out to the car?"

Deborah pushed her phone into her back pocket before leaning over and grabbing the stack from the bottom. "Nope." She walked back into the kitchen and paused at the center of the room. "It's fine if you don't wanna talk," she said. "I get it. But I don't wanna end things on a sour note. This isn't easy for me either."

"I'm sure it isn't," Hunter said. "But it is your choice."

A rattling knock shook the front door.

"I'll get out of your way, then," Deborah told her. "You clearly have company anyways."

Hunter moved toward the door, her neck reaching out. Curious. "No, not really."

She opened the door. David stepped inside.

"Deborah," he said with a nod. "How's it going?"

Hunter looked at her ex, straight-faced. Deborah's gaze darted between them. Was it a drive by? An unexpected visit? A scheduled hangout?

"Good," Deborah said, walking to the door. "I'll let y'all get to it, then." She put her back to the screen and pushed her way out.

Hunter followed. "Hey," she called out from the top of the stairs. "Just so you know . . . I had no idea he was stopping by. You're more than welcome to hang out if you want. There's no need for you to make this into a thing."

Deborah placed the boxes onto the ground and opened the back door of her car.

Who randomly stopped by a colleague's house at this time of the night? Someone who was comfortable, that was her guess. Perhaps someone who was more than a colleague.

The yellow moon lay suspended behind the home, steeped

in a deep fog, matching the hue of the porch light flawlessly, albeit a touch larger. Hunter's silhouette stood framed in the foreground.

"Thanks. But you look pretty busy," Deborah said. She placed the boxes onto the back seat and shut the door. "I hope you have a good night."

She watched Hunter's shadow, backlit by two canary spheres, rest on the porch as she backed out of the lot. As she threw the car in drive, she realized that her decision had only complicated her life even further.

How does one take a leap of faith if the fall is straight down from the Golden Gate? Like the old days, with no net.

For the first time, she was at odds with her decision.

24

ADJUNCTS WERE FED LEFTOVERS when it came to office space. Scraps not desired by the tenured. And deans rarely assigned offices to faculty of any caliber, but Bryan was willing to make an exception.

Kole wasn't just a teacher, a low-level professor brought on to cover an unfortunate situation; Bryan saw him as a tool. And he was going to use him—as he saw fit.

The automatic door opened as he gestured for Kole to walk ahead. "You first."

Kole entered the biology building with his new boss not far behind.

"Usually, we set up adjuncts next door to the grad students in the Computer Center," Bryan said, "but like I mentioned before, maybe we can work something out in the long-term if everything goes well. So I'm putting you here in the biology building, where most of our faculty members are."

The building was an elderly two-story square structure. The white cinderblock walls showed the building's age, holding one coat after another of fragile paint. Surely the base layers were steeped in a heavy dose of lead. The labs and offices were virtually smothering one another, on par with the size and finesse of a shared broom closet.

"Well, I appreciate it," said Kole. "I know I'll be coming and going quite a bit, but it'll be nice to have somewhere I can put my feet up before and after class."

"I figured as much. Here it is." Bryan pointed to a door in a corner of the first floor, flanked by two other rooms—a janitorial storage cupboard and a faculty member's office.

He shoved the key into the lock, looked up to Kole, and lifted his chin to the other professor's door as he shook the metal. "Not only will you be surrounded by other faculty members over here, but one of your ole pals from grad school will be right next door."

Kole walked over to the door and peered at the blue-and-white name plate, his hands deep in his pockets. *Dr. Mitch Olivier, Associate Professor, Biological Sciences*, the sign read.

"It wasn't all that long ago that y'all were back here in the same department," Bryan said. "It's funny how things work out."

"Yeah," Kole said as he turned back to his office and walked into the room. "Once upon a time."

"It isn't much, but it's all we have for the time being. I figure you'd rather be in a smaller office over here than something larger but surrounded by students."

Kole huffed a short burst of a breath. "You got that right."

The room was a cramped eight-by-ten space with no window, one power outlet, and a banged-up metal desk. Nothing more. Nothing less.

"Technically, it's supposed to be a postdoc's office for whoever has the lab space next door. That's Mitch, but he wants all of his postdocs in with his grad students to 'promote equity.'" Bryan held up a hand. "His words, not mine. All I know is it'd piss me off if I had just gotten a brand-new postdoc position and then I was forced to shack up with a bunch of students. But hey, that's his business, not mine."

"Ha. Well, this'll work just fine. I have a bunch of space over at LSU, but it's lab space that everyone shares. It'll be nice to have something to myself over here."

As he handed Kole the key, Bryan caught a whiff of something sour. The AC rumbled to work from above. By the look of it, Kole had recognized it too.

"Now that's a mighty fine odor," Bryan said with an apologetic tone. "I'll have to put in a work order to get that looked at."

The scent was about 90 percent carcass, 10 percent formaldehyde—an unmistakably powerful combination. For sure not enough preservative, Bryan mused. Years of animal research, botched dissections, and work with mammals had trained his nose well. "Sorry," he added. "I'll get to the bottom of it."

Kole looked up at the vent, which was rusted with condensation. A shimmering char. "That ain't no lab work if you ask me."

Bryan looked at the postdoc. Kole's chin was pointed up to the ceiling. "Yeah. I get the same feeling," he said. "Let's get out of here and get you over to the main office so you can wrap up that paperwork, huh?"

Kole nodded.

They walked into the hallway. Then Kole turned to lock the door, inserting the key into the doorknob.

"It's not often we see you over here in the slums." Bryan heard the voice from behind. He turned to see Mitch walking toward them.

Impeccable timing.

"Mitch," he said in greeting. "How's it going?"

Bryan moved out from in front of Kole, to the center of the

hallway. In no time at all, Mitch's face drooped to a kind of suppressed irritation.

"You remember your old collaborator, huh?" Bryan said to the professor.

Kole turned to greet Mitch, his smile extended to a handshake. "Oh, I wouldn't say he's that old. Long time no see."

The anticipation ravaged Bryan's stomach as he noticed the broad grin smeared across Kole's face.

It took him a moment, but Mitch shook the man's hand. "It's only been a few years." He looked at Bryan. "It looks like someone is pretty good at negotiating."

Even for Bryan, the handshake seemed too long.

"It's a nice place you got here." Kole leaned his head toward the office.

Mitch pulled the keys from his pocket and turned to his office door. "I'm glad you like it. Just don't get too comfortable. I'll need it back come the fall semester." He turned to Bryan. "New grad students and all."

Bryan jumped in headfirst. "As it turns out, Kole might be sticking around for a while. But I'm sure we can work something out."

"Of course." Mitch pushed open his door. "Kole's really good at working things out. How's LSU, by the way?"

The postdoc leaned against the wall and folded his arms. "Couldn't be better."

"Oh, I'm sure," Mitch said. "According to Google Scholar, you're thriving." He walked into his office.

"Still chasing those numbers, aye?"

"Always," said Mitch. "Better than running down a career."

They stood across from one another—Mitch in his office, Kole on the outside, the threshold keeping them at bay.

Bryan poked at the coals. "Well, I don't know about the two

of you, but seeing y'all together again just lights a fire under my ass to get back to work."

"Yeah, that sounds like a good idea. Enjoy the space," Mitch said.

"Always." Kole lifted a half-baked goodbye hand in the air.

They walked down the hallway and out the door, and Bryan was the first to break the silence. He looked down at his phone. "So, Jessica's waiting for you in the office. She'll take care of your paperwork. Let me know if ya need anything."

"Thanks, Bryan. I appreciate it."

Bryan turned to walk away.

"Oh, before I forget," Kole continued. Bryan turned back. "Is there any way we can set up a meeting sometime later this week? I'd like to sit down and pick your brain for a minute or two. I'm working on an NSF grant and could use your thoughts on something."

Bryan didn't meet with postdocs. That wasn't a dean's thing. This whole arrangement, as a matter of fact, was beyond the call of duty. He belonged up in his office, delegating and doing dean-like things. But he needed Kole. A wounded department needed Kole.

"Sure," he said. "As long as it's quick."

"Well, you gotta stop to eat at some point. How's lunch tomorrow?"

Bryan lifted his phone as he turned away. "Putting it in the calendar now."

All considered, it was a reasonable favor.

25

Several hours had passed, and Bryan needed to step away from the computer before his double vision graduated to a migraine. He texted the wife, one single-fingered tap at a time.

"I'm heading over to biology," he said to the receptionist. "If I'm not back before you head out, have a good one."

"Thanks, Bryan. I'll see you tomorrow."

It was already nearing 5 p.m.—closing time for the department. He figured that Jessica was waiting for him as usual, so she could lock up and they could head out together. On occasion, he would remain behind and work late into the evening. Contribute to the academic cause.

He walked into the biology office as Jessica was shutting down her computer for the day.

"Hey, you about ready?" she asked.

He dropped himself down into the seat in front of her desk. "Nah. I think I'm gonna stay behind and get a few more hours in. I have a last-minute meeting tomorrow at lunch, so I need to wrap up a few things so I can get ahead."

"Oh. Okay, then."

He never got used to the disappointment on her face when he was unable to go home. It was a balance they had weighed before he took the job: having a personal life versus the unmatched opportunity of presiding as dean over an entire college. Bryan knew he had the support of his wife. He always had—always would, he suspected. Still, the sacrifice was no less painful.

"Should I make your favorite for dinner? We can eat together when you get home." Jessica walked around the desk and threw her purse over her shoulder, then leaned over for a subdued kiss.

"No need to wait up. Why don't you enjoy the evening?" He smiled from his burning, vascular eyes. "Order out, and I'll see you in bed tonight." Looking at his watch, he took a deep breath in. "It's gonna be a late one."

She ran her hand across his chest before leaving his side and walking to the door. "Hit the light on your way out?" she asked.

"Sure thing," he called over his shoulder.

Bryan crossed his legs and released the day's burden through a heavy sigh. Then he opened his sports coat and removed a minuscule stainless flask from the inside pocket, the opening stitched as if it were made to fit. He glanced back at the door. Simply wetting his lips calmed the nerves, and the mere act of lifting the tin skyward sent a warmth between his legs.

He needed to get back to the office. A new bill had been passed, and the boss had fires to extinguish. Finally, the lawmakers were finding some sense in their efforts. Certain admissions into select Ivy League colleges had been deemed unconstitutional. Apparently, it was poor taste to admit students based on their race.

He chuckled to himself. "Who would've thunk it."

Alanis Morissette's "Ironic" came to mind.

Double standards are a bitch, he thought. He looked to the invisible man on his left shoulder and tucked his chin in to his collarbone. Eyes angry. Voice stern. "Of course we can't deny students based on their race. Everyone knows that." Then he looked to his other shoulder, doe-eyed. Speech innocent. "But we can admit them based on it."

He stood up and walked out of the office, then locked the door. He left the building and bounced on the balls of his feet down the sooty stairway, singing in a shrieking pitch about ten thousand spoons and a knife.

• • •

It was late enough, and eyedrops were no longer soothing the sandiness behind his eyes.

Jessica had already texted him twice before he decided to call it a night; the picture was what did him in, though. Thigh-highs were his no-questions-asked.

He grabbed his coat from the back of the chair and draped it over his arm. As he walked to the door, he realized that something had to give, sooner or later. He couldn't continue to mediate all things political for biology. He had other departments to serve. And he was tired of playing high school principal.

Shit. His phone. No photo left behind. Bryan returned to grab his cell. Snatching it off the desk, he turned back to the door.

He hesitated.

It was closed, but it had been open only a moment prior. A void seeped from the crack beneath, the space outside no longer lit.

Bryan opened the door, delicately, and stepped toward the reception area. His foot had hardly breached the doorway when the scalpel slipped deep into the top of his abdomen, then glided downward like an unhindered zipper—releasing his entrails to the floor.

The dean felt the blood drain from his head, gurgling, like

the water from a warm bath when the rubber stop is pulled.

And the cold brought with it an old friend—a drunken blackness.

part two

A PICTURE'S WORTH

26

BODIES WEREN'T MEANT TO look that way.

Hunter was incapable of pulling her eyes from the mangled corpse, the pieces no longer connected. She thought of high school and the frog dissection, each leg pinned to the metal tray. Then freshman biology and the rats, bathed in a stenchful liquid.

None of it came close to what she was standing in front of. A pure sickness. Criminal, even, but not in the legal sense. No, the scene was morally unjust. Some murderers killed in what they believed to be justified acts of self-preservation, out of an innate need to survive. This was something more. Something sinister, in her mind.

The dean's corpse lay on his desk, each wrist and ankle tied to the nearest leg of the table with a coarse hemp rope. His body face up. An open bottle of Jack nearby.

A single incision ran from the base of his sternum down to the pelvis, exposing what should have never been seen. The contents of his abdomen lay strewn across the desk, hanging to the floor.

"So," Hunter said. Then she turned to Parker. "You think the flies are relevant now?"

Sure, the scene disturbed her, but she felt that the two cases were one and the same; the body was only one frame of the reel.

Her hypothesis was slowly evolving into a theory.

Parker crouched next to the desk, near Bryan's head, where a glass vial lay, capped and filled with a clear liquid.

He squinted and looked to the single fly at the bottom of the glass ampule. Submerged in what looked like diluted ethanol, preserving the specimen.

"How can you be sure it's the same fly?"

"It's what I do," Hunter said with unmoving confidence.

Parker gloved up, then lifted the vial to his eye with a delicate grasp, holding the miniature jar between his thumb and middle finger.

"They have a tell-tale look," Hunter continued. "They're dorsoventrally flattened, and like I said before, wingless."

Her mentor turned to her with his regular, confused brow. All too often she was surprised by how naïve he was when it came to entomology. It was a primary subfield of pathology, after all. Hence, her employment.

"Like a pancake." Hunter motioned with her hands, slapping them together. "Top to bottom?"

"Yeah, I think I got it." Parker placed the vial down onto the desk and stepped back, looking at the scene as a whole.

She pointed to the near-empty body cavity, open to the arctic indoor air. "I guess liver temperature is off the table?" She nudged him with her elbow. "So to speak."

He shook his head and rubbed the crease at the bridge of his nose. "You have one sick-ass sense of humor, you know that?"

"You're welcome."

Parker pointed to the forceps next to the vial. "Why leave the tool behind?"

"Aren't there some questions we leave for Homicide? I wouldn't exactly say that that falls under Pathology."

"Sure it does. Is the fly relevant?"

"I think we've already established that."

"Okay, then. Presumably, the forceps were used to handle the fly. The fly is relevant to the decedent. Therefore, the forceps are relevant. Besides, you said it with the last one—it's too particular. It's calculated. They were obviously left behind for a reason."

"Well, it does feel like a setup, out in the open. But I'd say they were left behind as part of the message. All of it's a message. Although it feels a little . . . off."

"What do you mean, 'off'?"

"Messages. From repeat offenders. Again, I feel like this is a job for Homicide, not Pathology. But if you ask me, anything obvious at the scene of a crime—at the scene of a murder, in particular—should be taken with a grain of salt."

"Meaning?"

"Don't fall for it."

Hunter walked to the table, careful not to disturb what parts of Bryan lay on the floor. Then she turned the bottle of whiskey toward them. A gentle rotation. "But for the sake of collaboration, I'd be asking what's up with the Jack."

Parker offered a grunt. "And the answer?"

She shrugged, unable to look away from the bottle. "Ditto."

• • •

Hunter gasped as she exited the building. A free diver breaching the surface.

The untainted lakefront air was a nice change of pace from the rancid atmosphere inside—from the taste of decomposition. She pulled a pack of spearmint gum from her pocket; it was a two-piece kind of morning.

"Should I borrow some of that ahead of time?" Deborah asked as she walked up the steps toward her.

"If you plan on getting anywhere near the second floor." Hunter held out the pack. Then she turned and looked up to the building. "I've got watermelon, too."

Deborah peeled back the foil from one of the sticks. "Leaving so soon?"

"No, not really. We've been at it all morning. I'm surprised you're getting here as late as you are."

"Yeah, well. As it turns out, if you wanna get ahead in journalism, you need to do more journaling." She handed over the pack. "I've been sitting in front of a computer since 6 a.m."

They both looked around, the only sound emanating from a group of freshmen roughhousing in the distance.

The one aspect of human interaction that came anywhere close to the discomfort of eye contact was silence, and Hunter was having none of it. She began walking down the steps, but Deborah stopped her.

"Hey." She pointed a thumb over her shoulder. "Sorry about the other night. I was a bit caught off guard and . . . I, uh . . . I didn't know what to do."

Hunter was unsure what to make of it. Deborah? Caught off guard? The claim felt a little backward.

"It's fine. Like I said, I had no idea he was stopping by." Hunter looked down, fiddling with the packet in her hand. She pushed the hair that was hanging over her eyes to behind her ear. "You could've stayed. David and I are colleagues, Deb. I don't have anything to hide."

"Yeah, that's what I keep hearing. Like I said, I apologize."

The quiet returned.

"The coroner's already gone," Hunter said. "But Parker's still around. Maybe he'll give you a word or two." She began to walk away.

Deborah walked down the steps toward her. "Or maybe

you can."

Hunter stopped and turned back.

"I'm on a time crunch and could really use a break on this one," she continued. "Maybe I can ditch the scene altogether, and we can go for a bite to eat?" She held up her hands, the gesture of a hostage. "I'm willing to take whatever you have to offer. No pressure. I swear."

"Supplemental material?" Hunter suggested.

"Of course."

She looked around, checking the surrounding area for any eavesdroppers, any stragglers. Then she moved in close, cheek to cheek, the mintiness drifting from her ex's mouth. Her glimmering lips shining in the day's wetness.

Hunter exhaled a soft breath into her ear. "You look nice." She let it linger for a beat before backing away. "You'll get closer if you go up from the back door," she said as she walked to the parking lot, glancing over her shoulder.

Deborah's eyes appeared to stumble over an ounce of guilt.

27

HUNTER RETURNED HOME FOR an early lunch with the hope of grabbing a catnap to ease the thoughts. Drake's song and dance, echoing from inside, drowned out the end of a relationship that waxed and waned in the back of her mind.

As she unlocked the door, she noticed that the old-timey slot mailbox on the wall was overflowing with more than the usual allotment of junk. Peeking from the top of the opening were her monthly subscriptions—the guilty, gossipy pleasures for when she needed a break from the pile of true crime on the coffee table.

She grabbed the stack of envelopes and magazines and placed them under her arm before pushing open the door with her foot. Drake crawled between her legs, then rolled onto his back. His open season for tummy rubs.

"Seriously, dude? Right in the middle of the doorway?"

He flopped upright and barked an apparent objection, moving his spectacle into the kitchen once the belly show had gone unaddressed.

Hunter looked at the clock on the oven. It was 11 a.m. She hoped to get back to the office by twelve thirty.

"What do ya think, bud? We should be able to get about forty-five minutes in, huh?"

He growled in return, an ostensible agreement.

She reached above the stove and grabbed his box of Cheerios from the cabinet, then his bowl from the floor. More times than not, the snack knocked him out cold.

They walked the few steps to the living room and sat side by side on the couch. Hunter placed Drake's bowl on the arm of the sofa and filled it with cereal. Then she lay back and pulled a few Os from the box for herself. The daylight fought its way through a crack in the curtains and divided the floor in two as the crunch of Drake's appetite played on loop in the background.

Hunter shuffled through the stack of novels on the table beside her, but nothing commanded her attention. Nothing that looked likely to both interest her and put her to sleep at the same time, if that was possible. The pile of mail interrupted her thoughts.

People Magazine, *Louisiana Sportsman*, *Forbes*—the usual stuff.

Then she saw it. Peeking out from beneath the bills she planned on avoiding for days to come. The gambrel hanging from a rafter. A dim yellow light, motionless but with an apparent swing. She pulled the magazine from under the pile— *MurderoUS Weekly* across the cover.

She sat up and brought the title nearer to her eyes. The subtext brought with it an acidity, perched at the top of her stomach. Ready to erupt.

This Week's Issue: How a Hunter Became the Hunted.

She turned to the content page, finding the appropriate page number, then flipped hastily to the cover story at the cardstock centerfold of six dreadful pages. The magazine cover only got bigger, more detailed, once she turned the coverage sideways and opened it farther.

"And there it is," she stuttered aloud.

A clear shot of the scene, minus the bodies, printed front and center for the nation to see. But how? It had been monitored by local law enforcement, the address undisclosed.

She turned to the next page of the article and attempted to read, but the text was coming at her in pieces.

Drake nudged her elbow and let out a slow whimper.

"No. Forget the nap, dude. Forget the nap."

Hunter grabbed a bookmark from one of the novels on the table and placed it horizontally at the top of the article, then moved it down the page at a speed that prevented her from stumbling over her own ambitions. Even then, she only caught a glimpse of words here and there as her mind wandered through the possible ways the article had gotten published. Legally published?

The words grabbed her in broken phrases and refused to let go.

The decedent, Steve Daigle . . . professor and chair of biological science . . . survived by his wife and daughter.

The writing only twisted the knife as it continued.

Throat laceration . . . hung . . . no leads.

But how?

Hunter turned back to the four photographs at the beginning of the article: one of the camp from the road, one of the backyard from the driveway, one of the skinning shed from a distance, and a close-up of the scene itself—the gambrel hanging beneath the shed, illuminated by a small light from above.

It was the lighting that jolted her curiosity more than anything. The only photograph taken in daylight was the first one of the camp, from the roadway. The rest of the pictures were from the night.

She stood up and paced to the kitchen counter, then

shuffled through her work bag, which held her computer and paperwork. After returning to the couch, she placed a binder onto the coffee table and flipped through pictures of the crime scene. Copies of the original photographs, supplied by Homicide.

They clearly weren't the same frame. But what stood out was the angle of the prints. The three nighttime photos appeared to have been taken at similar angles to comparable ones provided by Homicide.

Hunter removed one of them from the clear sleeve of the binder and placed it next to the magazine. It was a picture of the crime scene itself. She inched them closer to one another, scanning the edges. Then she moved the edge of the magazine over the top of Homicide's copy. The edge of the shed side by side across the two photos.

The backdrop of trees at the edge of the skinning shed matched perfectly between the two images—between the magazine and Homicide's original. They weren't similar, or taken around the same time, even. They were exact copies, only cropped differently. The branch of a cypress hung over the edge of the structure in just the right way.

Homicide's photography was on the loose.

David's photography.

28

ASIDE FROM WORKING IN their respective offices, academia was forbidden in the house. It was a near impossible feat, but Mitch had insisted on the agreement from day one. Of course, the occasional slip-up was inevitable—Aura's fault, mostly.

The separation of church and state ensured a pristine academic reputation that didn't leach into the home, an organized lab producing high-impact papers from a subordinate staff.

No marriage dare ruin that eternal paradise.

They ate breakfast across from one another at the dining room table for two, as formal as an at-home meal could be. The silverware set appropriately, napkins in lap, plates sparkling.

Every meal reflected their lives together—planned and executed with a harrowing sense of organization. That was how Mitch needed it. To maintain the textbook image, he required the picture-perfect home. And that meant everything, and everyone, had its place.

At the university, Aura was interim chair. His committee member and mentor, once upon a time. A professor who was always one step ahead of him. But at home, he made sure that was not the case.

The doorbell, too dignified for the square footage,

ricocheted from wall to wall. The voice of a mansion, trapped in a two-bedroom body.

"You expecting someone?" he asked, his gaze on the plate before him.

Aura looked at the door. "No."

He placed his fork down on the table, back in its rightful place, an equal distance from the plate as the knife was. Then he stood and walked to the door, adjusting his collar along the way. He unlocked the keylock and deadbolt, followed by the chain above. Then he swung open the latch at the top of the entrance.

"What's up, little bro?" he greeted his brother, Paul, as he stepped aside and held open the door. Mitch watched as Paul removed his shoes and placed them on the doormat in an orderly fashion, next to their own.

"Nothing much. Sorry to stop by unannounced. Hope I'm not interrupting."

"Of course not." Mitch shut the door behind him and repositioned each lock from the top down. "Coffee?"

"Yeah. Black and sweet'll do."

"Still no sugar in the house."

"I figured as much."

They walked through the dining room and into the kitchen, passing Aura en route. "Hey. How's it going?" Paul said as he leaned down for a cheek-to-cheek welcome. A rarity between the two of them, to Mitch's eyes.

"Oh, I'm hangin' in there." Aura appeared unimpressed by Paul's effort. They put on an unconvincing show. Their interactions were a simple tolerance of one another and nothing more. Their relationship, or lack thereof, had been a stalemate for Mitch's attention. A modern-day World War I.

Mitch poured a cup and added a single packet of Splenda to the piping brew. Then he handed it to his brother, along with a tiny square napkin fit for a bar top. "Wanna sit outside?" he asked. He looked to his wife but ignored her frustrated twist of the lips.

"Sure," said Paul.

Mitch ran a hand over Aura's shoulder as the brothers headed out to the back porch. She gave him a look of apprehension—or maybe just emotional fatigue. He knew how she felt about backdoor conversations. Especially with Paul. But the chair had no upper hand in the home.

Church and state.

"I'll get straight to the point," Paul said once the door was shut. Then he pulled an obnoxious, gurgling sip from the cup as he looked out to the elaborate backyard garden the couple had planted from scratch. "You have any idea who that was creeping on the fence line the other day?"

"Creeping?"

"When you were visiting. You were talking to someone down at the property line. Remember?"

Mitch looked off to the side before responding. "Oh, yeah. I told you already—it was someone looking into the homicide. But once someone else showed up, I didn't feel like getting roped into the drama. So I ducked out."

"'Roped into the drama'?" Paul copied, looking through the window as Aura stared back at them. He moved out of view and spoke in a cautionary tone. "He was your boss, for fuck's sake. Don't you think it would've been helpful for you to talk to 'em? You're acting like it's some sort of inconvenience."

"Look," Mitch started in, "I don't need any more theater than what I already have to deal with at the university. It isn't my job to speak with anyone about what happened. Not to mention, I have nothing to say. I don't know anything." He walked into the yard and began pacing from fruit to fruit, checking their readiness. "If they need to talk that bad, they know where to find me."

Paul scratched his color-neutral five o'clock shadow. "I hope you know how that looks, Mitch. From the outside looking in."

"Yeah, well. As a great philosopher once said, 'Do I get bonus points if I act like I care?'"

• • •

They were only outside long enough to knock back an eight-ounce drip. But after returning indoors, Mitch could see that Paul had overstayed his welcome, based on his wife's murderous expression.

Paul set his cup onto the counter. "Well, I better get going. I'm sure y'all have a busy day ahead of you."

Mitch looked to Aura but got nothing in return. "Yeah. Thanks for stopping by," he said, and walked his brother to the door.

He returned to the kitchen and leaned against the counter, occupying his wife's line of sight, waiting for her usual disapproval. "After all this time, you're still *that* annoyed by your brother-in-law, huh?"

Aura pulled a napkin across her mouth and stood up before walking her plate to the sink. "It has nothing to do with being annoyed." She kissed him with an open mouth on the cheek. "Sometimes, I wonder if the two of you should've gotten married—with as much time as you spend over at his place."

"He lives alone. How well-off would you be if you lived by yourself and never had any visitors?"

Mitch had developed a sweet spot for his brother ever since he had become a widower. He might not have been a people magnet, but when it came to family, a brother in need was a priority.

"And besides," Mitch continued, "you know that you can come over there with me anytime you want. Right? He's said from day one that you're always welcome."

"Yeah, I know. I just wish we'd spend more time together is all." She scrubbed the plate with a particular ferocity.

Mitch cut in. "Here, let me get that."

Each and every dish, every utensil, was cleaned before being placed in the dishwasher, but only with the soft side of the sponge—steel wool was sacrilegious. Mitch was adamant about using non-scratch only, after the dreadful Teflon incident of 2020.

Aura stepped aside, and he happily took over.

"Look, if me spending so much time over there upsets you that bad, then I'll make it a point to be here more often. I mean, we're working 95 percent of the time anyways."

"No, no. I'm sorry. I don't mean to be so pushy. It's fine. I know you're only looking out for him."

After placing the plate into the dishwasher, she turned off the water and centered the faucet over the sink. Aura folded the towel in two, then once more before placing it to the side, flush with the edge of the counter. The sponge was rinsed again, wrung out, and placed dryly in its holder, the bottle of soap set evenly against the backsplash. Lights off.

Mitch looked on. Everything in place.

She continued. "So, what did he need?"

"Nothing, really. He was just wondering who someone was. Someone who's looking into Steve's death."

"Oh, really? Is everything okay?"

"Yeah. Nothing more than people being overly nosy."

She ran her fingertips along the divot of his collarbone, then down his chest before tugging at the bottom of his shirt.

"I think I'm gonna head upstairs and work in the office for

a bit," Mitch said.

"You want some company?" She nudged his lips with the tip of her nose.

"I wish, but I have a lot of work to get done."

Aura's tongue left a faint, wet trail from his chin down to the lump in his throat.

"You sure about that?"

Her nose backtracked up the dampened path.

"Yeah, I'm sure." He placed his hands on the sides of her arms and stepped back, holding her in place. "No one makes full professor working nine to five."

29

DAYTIME SLEEP WAS ILLUSIVE.

The article was pulling Hunter in like she was a pair of gliding wings from above, circling and drawn to the hunter's reed that called from the cattails below. Zigging and zagging, wings cupped, orange feet out to the water. Bracing. Pitching like a fighter pilot.

She entered the lab and promptly noticed the light from beneath Parker's office door, the blinds closed but holding back a moony glow from within. She began walking toward the room but then thought twice, turning to her own office across the way, second-guessing, unsure of the article's lure.

Teaching assistant, academic researcher, med student, lab technician, part-time pathologist. A new job was always a peculiar thing for Hunter—walking the line between proving herself and getting the job done. Her first case in forensic pathology was proving no different.

On one hand, she could keep quiet. Keep the whole thing to herself, cuddle up in the freshness of a new job; after all, she was the fresh meat on the block. A toddler standing at the edge of the sofa, holding tight, legs trembling, working up the nerve to let go.

For Hunter, the prospect of falling face-first was always an adrenaline rush.

On the other hand, risks were her game. And getting ahead meant taking chances. Perhaps bringing the article to Parker was a moral obligation. A necessity, even.

She hung on to the thought, testing the waters.

No more than a second had passed after entering her office, and she had made the decision to go for it. Hunter dropped her bag on the chair and circled back to Parker's side of the lab.

She knocked on his office door while listening to the shuffling of papers from inside. It was as simple as that. She had committed.

"Come in."

She entered the room with the magazine in hand, rolled into a tube like a delicate piece of fine art. Parker's office was one of a kind—the desk of a child, seafoam paint peeling from its edges, centered in the room and surrounded by four bare walls, other than a wooden cross hanging behind him.

"Hey," Parker said. "What's up?"

Hunter took a seat off to the side of his desk and rested her chin on the end of the rolled paper. Her mind wasn't in the right place for the formality of small-talk greetings. "You ever read any of the true crime coverage?" She spoke as she unrolled the title, then held it over the desk, leaning forward.

Parker grabbed the magazine as he offered up a response. "Oh yeah. I've read a few of these." He scanned the cover art, which he apparently didn't recognize, then hurriedly flipped through the pages. "It's not really my cup of tea, with the dramatic writing and all. Everything's always printed so much more urgently than it really is. But, yeah. They put out a good article here and there."

"I thought you might have. Turn to the centerfold," Hunter said. "She's a beaut." Leaning back, she crossed her legs. Her chin rested in the L of her thumb and index finger.

Parker didn't speak, only looked over the top of the pages as he held open the magazine on end.

"Look familiar?" she asked.

His response wasn't as dramatic as she had expected, and less than favorable.

"One thing to remember in this line of work," he said with a deprecating tenor, "is that someone's always gonna be champing at the bit to get at what you're doing. Whether it's right, wrong, or a flat out lie, there's always gonna be some reporter or news coverage looking to make a quick buck."

She grabbed the article from his grip like he was handing her a disease. In her mind, his reaction was nothing more than objectionable.

"Sorry, but don't you think Homicide, or someone else, should look into how this got released in the first place? There aren't many people who have this information to begin with."

Parker lifted his hands up in a shrug. "Well. You are right about that. But one thing to consider is that once something like this is out there, it's out there. There ain't no bringing it back. Besides, our department, and Homicide for that matter, are already spread thin enough as it is. This type of thing happens all the time, Hunter. It's something you're gonna have to get used to."

She opened the title and flipped to the article, shaking her head with a bite of the lip. "So the fact that some of these pictures perfectly match Homicide's photos doesn't concern you?"

Parker stood up from his desk. "Like I said—what's done is done. Yeah, it sucks. But all we can do is be careful with our work. And if the images are similar to Homicide's copies like you say, then it really doesn't look good for us, either. Don't we have the same photos? Here." Parker walked over to a filing cabinet in the corner of the room, behind his desk. He unlocked the top drawer and shuffled through a dense row of manila folders. Then he pulled out a thick packet of forms, held together by a black clip. He handed them over.

"What's this?"

"The same confidentiality protocol that you should've received during your intake appointment. It covers everything. Data encryption, password protection, preventing internal leaks. You name it."

"And you're giving it to me because . . ."

"Because of that." He pointed to the magazine folded under her arm. "Because you seem to be concerned with a story written about the case you're working. Like you said, only so many people have access to the information covered in that column. Including you."

Hunter removed the journal from under the grip of her bicep and held it up. "You think *our* department had something to do with this? Or me? Parker, I've been here for all of a few weeks. You really think I'd be that careless with my first case?"

He walked back around the desk. "No. I don't. But you seem concerned, and as your supervisor, I wanna make sure that you have all the resources that you need."

Was his response warranted? He seemed considerate, concerned maybe, but was also hinting at the idea of a slip-up. She didn't know how to take it.

"Okay. Well, thanks. I'll be sure to give it a look."

Hunter figured it best to leave it at that. She turned to see herself out, her concern not fully quenched by the conversation.

"If you're that concerned about it . . ." Parker said. He held out a hand, curling a finger toward himself while looking at the magazine. "I'll take care of it."

She rushed back to the desk and handed it over as a wave of reluctance washed over his face.

"Thanks, Parker. I know it isn't our number-one priority, but I think we should—"

"You just focus on what you already have on your plate. Okay?"

As she turned to leave, he opened the centerfold again.

30

To Meaux, the biology office felt like a no-fly zone. Forbidden territory that was almost sinful to enter. Sacred ground that wasn't to be seen without her husband.

As small and petty of a task as it seemed, she needed to return Steve's keys to the university. Admittedly, her ulterior motive was to check in on Jessica. Meaux knew good and well what it was like to experience not just the loss of a husband, but the murder of a loved one. An experience that had yet to fade.

Meaux walked into the first room of the office—the one that served as a buffer for incoming guests before they entered the remaining space, including the primary office where Jessica worked. The woman's assistant greeted her before she made it any farther.

"Oh my gosh. Hey, girl." The oldish redheaded woman walked from around her tall corner desk and embraced Meaux with an unusual bear hug, trapping both of her arms at her side. A peculiar greeting for two women who were hardly acquaintances. Then she leaned back and placed her hands on Meaux's shoulders. "How are you holding up? Are you okay? I'm sorry, I don't mean to pry. Are you okay, though?"

All Meaux could do was fashion a not-so-warm smile. The kind of grin that she suspected anyone would hope to see from a woman who had gone through such recent trauma. "I'm good. And you?"

"Oh, I'm doing just fine," the woman said with a wave of the hand. "But we're not gonna ramble on about me. Have a seat. Please. Have a seat." She pulled over a chair from the waiting area, which held a coffee pot that looked as if it had received nothing more than a mediocre sponge bath since it was purchased in the '90s, several containers of powdered creamer of questionable age, and a few dusty mugs turned upside down on an old brown cafeteria tray. "Take a seat, hun. Please, take a seat."

Was she temporarily strung out, or was she always so much like a Tasmanian devil? Meaux had only run into the assistant on occasion, but she couldn't for the life of her remember her name. Or the fact that her demeanor was beyond exhausting. The building's signature bleachy aroma, however, convinced Meaux to keep moving.

"I won't be long," she said. "I'm just here to turn in Steve's keys. Is Jessica around?"

The assistant returned to her stool behind the podium-like desk. "Sorry, but she's been out ever since . . . you know. I can help you, though." She held out her hand. "I'll be sure they get back to Access Control."

"Yeah, that'd be great." Meaux handed over the large gold keys. "Any idea when she'll be back in? I mean, I don't expect her to be working or anything. I was just hoping to touch base with her and see if she needs anything."

"I'm not sure, hun. Oh, there is something that I have for you, though." The assistant walked into Jessica's office, taking her time, looking tired from inheriting a role that was a bit too responsible compared to her usual door greeting. She lifted two large cardboard boxes off the floor and set them on the desk. "I went ahead and put these together for you. I hope you don't mind. But Jess said that you, or someone else, might be coming by for everything sometime soon."

Meaux walked over to the boxes—one labeled *Paperwork*, the other *Personal*.

"This looked like everything of importance, but you're more than welcome to double-check if you'd like. Again, I hope you don't mind."

Meaux lifted the lids and peered inside.

"No, no. I don't mind at all. I appreciate it. Yeah, I'm sure I'd like to head up to his office and look around at some point." She ran her hand over the row of papers, then looked at the other box of assorted items. "But I think that's gonna be a job for another day."

"Of course. I'm sure it's all still fresh." The assistant grabbed a piece of paper off Jessica's desk and wrote a short message at the bottom. "Here. This is a list of everything inside. I'm not sure how long Jessica will be out, but if you have any questions, feel free to give me a call. My number's at the bottom."

"Yeah, thanks again. I'm sure you're busy enough without this on your plate, too."

"Really, it's fine. I promise."

Meaux pointed over her shoulder. "I'm gonna step out into the hallway and make a call real quick. You mind helping me down to the car with these when I'm done?"

"Yeah. Of course."

"Thanks."

She pulled her phone from her pocket and dialed Jessica as she walked out of the office. After the fourth ring, Meaux knew she wasn't going to answer, so she waited for the voicemail.

"Hey, Jess. It's Meaux. I stopped by the office today, but

you weren't here. I was just calling to see if you wanna get together for dinner sometime. I know it's last minute, but I—"

A call waiting beeped over the line. She held out the phone, Jessica's name flashing across the screen.

"Hey, I was just leaving you a message."

Meaux stepped one brief stride at a time down the hallway, looking at the bulletin board and department calendar on the wall.

"Yeah, sorry. I was just getting inside after running some errands. What's up?"

She noticed a somberness in Jessica's voice, a tone that conveyed exhaustion and a mere necessity to go about the normal workings of everyday life. What more was there to do following your husband's death?

"Not much. I was just wanting to check in on you. See if you need anything."

Meaux passed the department's bulletin board. *Congratulations Dr. Olivier on your promotion to Associate Professor!* was printed at the top across multiple sheets of paper in large, artsy block lettering. A picture of the department faculty, gathered in celebration, was stapled beneath the notice.

"Thanks. I'm okay, I guess. As good as I can be. What about you?"

Her eyes moved across the board to a series of grant award notices. A list of professors and their corresponding funding for the academic year. As she stepped back and looked at the board in its entirety, from a distance, she found it peculiar that, in a department with so many contributors, there was no credit or celebration of the graduate students or postdocs. Only professors.

"And life goes on," Meaux whispered to herself.

"Do what?"

"Oh, nothing. I was wondering if maybe you'd like to grab dinner sometime? I'm sure you have a lot going on right now with . . . everything. But I think it might be good for the two of us to get together. Maybe you need someone to talk to?"

Meaux could hear Jessica wavering. Nothing but a tearful sniffle from the other end of the line.

"Sorry. I don't mean to upset you. We don't have to. I just thought I'd offer."

"No, it's fine. I'd like that a lot, actually. I could use a break. How's tonight?"

There was no need to acknowledge the obvious. Two murders, back-to-back, in the same department. Both leaving a wife behind to pick up the pieces. The phone call itself was the acknowledgment. Repeating the evident would only invite unnecessary pain.

"Tonight sounds great. How's six o'clock?"

"I'll see you tonight."

• • •

No sooner had Meaux walked out of her house to unload the boxes from her car than Jessica was pulling into the driveway.

Meaux could see her through the windshield, teary-eyed as she parked her car and slid from the driver's seat. She walked to Jessica with open arms, attempting to find words, something to make the greeting more normal. She failed to string together a noteworthy sentence, and Jessica greeted her with nothing more than a prolonged hug, which conveyed just how appropriate a lingering silence was in the moment.

Jessica finally released her grip. "Thank you," she said.

"For what?"

She looked around as the water welled in the far corners of her eyes. The tension of the liquid kept the tears from pouring over, but only briefly. "For this. Inviting me here."

Meaux pulled her in again. "Of course, Jess. Of course."

They turned and walked up the driveway before Meaux reached into the trunk of her car.

"Do you need a hand?" Jessica asked as she wiped the trailing saline from her cheeks. "Here. Let me help."

"Thanks, girl."

After walking inside, they set the boxes down onto the dining room table.

"These from the university?" Jessica asked.

"Yeah. Steve's belongings from his office." Meaux removed the lids and sat down in the nearest chair, looking at the seemingly bottomless containers. "I need to go through them at some point, but I'm not sure I'm ready for that just yet."

Jessica's attention wandered over the contents. "What is all of this?"

Meaux hesitated. "Like I said, I picked it up from the—"

"No." Jessica's eyes began to flood yet again. "This." She looked around, her hands rising then falling helplessly into her lap. "None of this makes any sense. Why in the world would someone do this? Why Bryan?" She pointed to what remnants of the chair's career lay organized on the table. "Why *Steve?*"

Meaux leaned forward and held Jessica's hands with a tight, caring grip. "I don't know, Jess. I have no idea. What I do know is that they'll figure this out. There's no way something like this goes unresolved. They'll figure it out. Okay?"

Jessica nodded, looking over at the boxes, a picture peeking out from within. Then she gave an upward nod to the photo.

"Who's that?"

Meaux looked over. "Who?"

"In the picture. Next to Steve."

Meaux stood up and grabbed the frame from the box. "Oh. That's Rob Hebert." She handed it over. "He and Steve were good friends. They hunted together all the time." She smiled for the first time in a while. "He would come down to the camp with us almost every weekend during hunting season."

"The name sounds familiar."

"Well, he did work with Steve here and there. That's how they knew each other. Bryan probably knew him, too. Or at the very least had heard of him."

"What does he do?"

"He's a professor over at LSU."

"Huh." Jessica ran her hand over the glass as another tear dripped from her chin, splashing against the edge of the frame.

"Everything okay?"

She looked up, then back down at the photo.

"Yeah." She placed the frame back into the box, face down. "What's for dinner?"

31

IT WAS NO LONGER an itch. The flies were an evident connection between the murders, a slap in the face to whoever had found the bodies—and Parker was beginning to acknowledge exactly that. Hunter needed to double down and triple-check what was relevant, now that the flies were more than just a shaky hypothesis.

The rookie now had a leg up.

As she sat in the center of the lab, poring over everything she had come to know about hippoboscids and deer keds in particular, there was a concern brewing in the back of her mind. Hunter recognized that she was unlikely to fall victim to the mistake. But nonetheless, the idea of it festered like the specimens she knew and loved all too well.

Hunter worried that she would make the same error that ran rampant in the medical world. Patient presented with gut-wrenching chest pain, nausea, vomiting. The nurse practitioner was certain of the diagnosis. Stress and anxiety belonged to everyone. But no worries—diet and exercise cured all. The cardiologist knew it was a heart attack. No questions asked. Textbook case. And the GI on call said to go home. A simple antacid would take care of the reflux. Test? What tests? Specialists needed no confirmation.

The problem with serving a specialty was the fact that you already had the answer in your back pocket. You knew the diagnosis. All you needed was the problem.

Unfortunately, the same was true for the science of criminal investigation. Pathology included. Hunter was well aware of how it looked—an entomologist putting the entomology front and center of a murder investigation. It was too obvious, too good to be true. Like a serial killer who calls from a payphone to turn himself in after convincing himself he's about to be caught. Only in a perfect world. Right?

But the second murder was a tell-all—the killer's mind on a silver platter. *Here is the specimen you are looking for. And some alcohol for safekeeping,* she thought, her mind playing in the morbid voice of a Post Toasties killer. His tone deep as he dropped the fly into a vial of ethanol.

Or as *she* dropped it?

Hunter knew she had a reason to follow the entomology, but a pestering whisper from the corners of her conscience said otherwise.

She pulled the two case files from the cabinet beneath the lab bench and placed the photos side by side. The entomologist within her already had the answer in her back pocket, but the pathologist needed to dig further. Consider the scenes as a whole.

In short, she needed to be the GP. Not the specialist.

Even if the entomology was key, that was for Homicide to take to the streets. She needed something on the pathology end. Something in the front pocket.

Hunter pulled two of the photos closer together. One decedent hung, one tied up, restrained at the wrists and ankles. Both cut and displayed, but in different fashions. Memorable fashions, certainly.

In addition to the flies, the other obvious connection was the university. A dean and a department chair. Again, it was too obvious, though. Too "back pocket."

Her mind naturally wandered over to Homicide's area of expertise. But she needed to stay true to her role as a pathologist. Perhaps a report on the entomology was all she could offer.

Was that enough?

Parker entered the lab and walked to his office, unlocking the door as he looked to Hunter. "Hey, Romero."

"Hey. You got a minute?"

"Yeah, just let me set my stuff down."

As he entered his office, all she could do was fidget. She had been advised to explore other areas of the homicides, to look at something other than this, and yet she was about to push forward with it. As a newcomer with something to prove, who wouldn't take the opportunity and run with it?

Hunter ground down on a stick of spearmint gum, then folded the shimmering wrapper until it could bend no more. She drew a bottomless breath and savored the coolness that vented its way to the back of her sinuses—a distraction that robbed her mind of the conversation ahead.

"Alright. What we got?" Parker asked as he approached the bench.

Hunter slid the photographs in front of him, along with the specimens from both scenes. "Well, I'm at a standstill," she said. "You already know that I think the flies are important. And I think we can agree that the second homicide proves that, since the specimen was practically handed to us. I'm just hoping Homicide is taking that into consideration. It's pretty obvious they're both murders. And unless something comes at us from left field, the cause of death will be straightforward with this one, just like it was with the last one."

Parker pulled the photographs in closer. "Okay. So what are you asking me, exactly?"

She looked up at him and shrugged.

"Alright." He took a seat on a neighboring stool, then looked over the table at the photos and specimens. "I think you're doing just fine, Hunter. Your report on the previous homicide was great, which included your findings on the deer keds. And that's something you should include in this one as well. I think Homicide will put two and two together and use that to do what they do best. Like you said, we have a clear-cut manner and cause of death, unless the coroner's office finds something else with the autopsy. And that's our priority. Unless something else important jumps out at you?"

Hunter pulled her lips to one side while scanning the material. Silent.

"You don't look satisfied," he said.

"It's not that. I'm just unsure about where our job begins and Homicide's starts. I have more than enough evidence to think that the deer keds are the key to everything at this point. But like you said before, we need to consider the pathology as a whole. I guess I'm just hoping that Homicide will actually do something with it."

Parker's eyes agreed. "Of course. Like I've said before, Homicide works far more closely with the coroner's office than they do with us. But they see our reports just like the coroner does. Besides, the specimen was there for everyone to see with this second one." He pushed one of the photos toward her. "They're gonna move forward with it. Trust me. The team over there doesn't miss a beat."

"Okay. I'll wrap up the report and get it over to the coroner. They should have the autopsy report by now. That's something else that drives me crazy."

"What?"

"That our office is separate from the coroner for the most part. You'd think that we'd be one and the same."

Parker rose from his seat and pushed the stool back across the aisle with his foot. Then he snickered. "Don't get me started on the organization of our departments. Every state and city has their own thing going on. They're all a bit different."

"Fair enough."

"Don't be too hard on yourself. The cause and manner of death are our main priority. The coroner takes care of the autopsy, and we help. Any additional information goes in the report and is passed on to Homicide. I'll be sure they get it after I look it over."

"Sounds good. I appreciate it."

"As far as the flies go, keep it up. I'm sure Homicide will appreciate the expertise. That's why you're here, after all."

"Copy that."

The wink that followed conveyed a bit of support. It was the only approval Hunter needed.

32

GRANT REVIEWS WERE 25 percent science, 75 percent politics. Mitch handled rejections about as well as undergrads coped with seeing red ink.

His most recent NSF grant had been not only rejected but declined on the grounds of "insufficient DEI efforts." Although not mentioned by any one of the six outside reviewers—who all gave the grant "good" or "excellent" ratings—the internal NSF panel had found that the grant was deficient in broader impacts.

Too much scientific discovery. Not enough push-our-agenda.

But Mitch didn't mind. Not one bit. Agendas were his game. And he was on point to push it whatever way led to a summer salary and the title of full professor. A title he knew for a fact he deserved more than anyone else in the department.

As far as shitty news was concerned, it was the bottom of the barrel. The chalky sediment that had settled at the bottom of his mocha while tending the flock every Monday, Wednesday, and Friday at 9 a.m. But there was plenty of crap news to go around, and one way to unload it was to share it with his Co-PI.

"Got some bad news," Mitch said, greeting his wife as he walked into her office.

"Oh yeah?"

"Our grant got rejected. I was gonna forward you the email from the program officer, but I thought I'd just walk over here and tell you myself. Bad news is always a bit spicier in person."

"Wow. Thirteen months of waiting for a six-month decision, and that's what we get? Now I'm curious to see what the reviewers and program officer had to say."

"Well, if the timeline has you upset, maybe it's best you wait to see the reviews. Let's just say the panel had different thoughts than the reviewers."

Aura pulled back her hair and tied it in a tight, angry ponytail. "Give it to me straight. At least if I know now, I'll have a few days to process it."

Mitch folded his arms and leaned against the wall, looking up at the ceiling. It was painful to repeat. "Six reviewers—all good or excellent ratings. Not a single negative critique of the broader impacts. The panel, however, felt that our DEI efforts were"—he let it linger for effect—"insufficient." One side of his face winced at the phrasing, his eye closed. The other eye was open to gauge her disdain for the news.

His wife let out a cackle that Mitch equated with that of a wounded hyena. A spotted cub, cornered and separated from the pack, surrounded by the threat of zero funds.

"*Our* labs? Insufficient outreach?" Aura spoke as if learning a new language. As if she was uncertain what the words really meant. "Did they even look at the proposal? I mean . . ."

"Apparently, we're just recycling what we've already been doing instead of coming up with a program from scratch. I guess continuing to do what's already been proven to work isn't good enough anymore. Although, I can't say I'm surprised."

Aura began stroking the keys of the PC. Her lips were pursed with determination.

"What are you doing?"

"Being productive," she said. "I can't sit here and think about that grant right now. If I do, it's gonna be the one and only thing that singlehandedly ruins my day. I've gotta sit on it for a while."

Mitch leaned down to the desk, his head floating in front of her, above the laptop.

"Can I help you?" she said.

"I'm sorry for the shit news."

She continued banging away at the already-faded alphabet.

"I was hoping you could take a break for a minute so we can talk," he said. "What are you typing up anyways? Those poor letters haven't done anything to you. At least, not that I'm aware of."

"I'm sending out an email to the lab. I've been wanting to set up a meeting specifically for the women in my lab group. Sort of a workshop on being a successful woman in academia. With everything that's going on nowadays, I think having a conversation that's open and free of judgment might do 'em some good."

"That's a great idea. Let me know if I can help."

She didn't look up in response. "To be honest, I'd like to start the conversation without any men, but if we meet again at some point, you're welcome to join us. Especially since you're mentoring women in your lab. It might do you some good, too."

"Speaking of women in the lab, I was hoping to get your thoughts on the recruitment day that's coming up."

"You have some prospective students coming down for interviews, right?"

"Yeah. I invited one guy who's finishing up his master's at Southeastern and one who's here as an undergrad. They contacted me a while back, but I formally invited them after I met with Bryan."

Aura finally looked up from the priority-one email. "Okay. Isn't that a good thing?"

"Yeah. But since things have changed, and you're technically chair now, I wanted to see what you thought about inviting some other students."

"I really don't think you have the time or space in your lab for four more students, babe."

"No. Not more students. *Other* students—to replace the two guys I had invited. Tell them that something came up. We no longer have the room."

"And why in the world would you wanna do that? I thought you and Bryan came up with a plan to bring in the best students you could find."

"We did. But given this whole thing with the NSF grant getting rejected, I thought it might be a good idea to take some initiative and bring in two female students who are more representative of a minority. The PhD student wouldn't have a master's, but she's been working as a lab tech and she's already middle author on a few papers. The master's applicant has a rough GPA, but I think I can write a letter to the GPO explaining why she's a good fit. We've done it before. Hell, if it had been left up to my GPA and GRE scores, I never would've gotten into grad school."

Aura appeared interested in the idea, offering up a suggestive frown. "Are you sure there isn't anything you wanna talk about? Losing Bryan hasn't been easy for any of us. And needing to talk about it isn't something to be ashamed of. There's a lot going on right now."

Talk? Who wanted to talk about such a thing? If anything, keeping it bottled up was the way to go. Not talking about it was the one and only way to make it go away.

"The last thing I need to do is talk about it. What I need is to fix this grant. We should be able to get it turned around pretty quick. What do you think?"

"Yeah, I guess. You know, what we could do is include the Outreach Institute as part of the broader impacts. Technically, it's the first semester we're doing it, so it could be considered a new program."

"Oh, that's good. That's really good."

"As far as the two students for recruitment day, that's your call. Personally, I think any opportunity to bring more women into STEM is a smart decision."

"Then it sounds like we're on the same page. I'll go ahead and reach out to the other two and let them know that the spots are no longer available." Mitch made his way to the door, a new pep in his step.

"Hey," Aura called out. He turned back. "Let the women in your lab know they're invited, too."

"Invited?"

"Yeah. To my lab's meeting for the women. It's only fair. You didn't think I was gonna leave 'em out, did you?"

33

AS FAR AS ROBERT was concerned, most professors didn't belong in the lab. Or at the very least, not within an arm's length of anything remotely carcinogenic. That was for the hired help.

His experience had taught him that by the time most professors received tenure, their efforts were best spent writing grants, editing the papers that their students had written, and growing their lab group. The endless nights at the bench, banging your head against the monitor to run a single line of code was for those who still had something to prove. The ones with remaining aspirations.

But Robert was of a different breed. Although Kole's research was far from his PI's area of expertise, Robert did what he could do to give his postdocs a leg up, in hopes that they would be among the 10 percent who landed tenure-track faculty positions.

He could never remember where the statistic had come from, but 10 percent sounded a bit on the high side.

"You ever try to cut a one-millimeter-long organism under a microscope using nothing but a thick-ass razor blade?" Kole asked Robert as he sat hunched over the lab bench, peering through the two eyepieces of the dissecting microscope.

"Nope. A better question is why you'd wanna work with

copepods to begin with. You're trying to dissect them? Really?"

"Not dissect them. Just cut them in two for some sample prep. As simple as that sounds, it ain't so simple."

Robert walked over to the other end of the lab bench, opening drawers and rummaging through the contents. "Well, the easiest solution is to use something that's a bit more precise. More effective. Although, you could argue that scalpels are better used on something with a bit more meat on the bones. So to speak."

He walked over to Kole and handed him a thin silver packet, a fresh scalpel vacuum sealed inside.

"You know . . . like a mammal," Robert added.

Kole tossed the razor blade onto the table, then began unwrapping the new blade. "What are you talking about anyways, 'why would I want to work with copepods?' You work with parasites. Isn't that all under the microscope?"

"No. I work with cervids—which *have* parasites."

"Tomayto, tomahto."

Robert chuckled on the inside at how thin the line was between calling himself a behavioral ecologist versus an entomologist. In the past, he had adopted both titles at different times, depending on who asked, or what job was on the line.

The postdoc mated the blade with an old handle, the sharpness hitting Robert's eyes in broken flashes of steely gray.

"Trust me. That'll get the job done better than some razor blade," he said.

"You sure about that?"

"Everyone thinks they're holding something sharp until they see what a surgical blade can do. Give it a go." He pointed to the sample beneath the microscope in front of Kole. "It's a thing of beauty."

Kole turned back to the sample, placing the blade nearer to

the copepod in the clear petri dish. Robert moved in close and kept a watchful eye over his shoulder.

"I be damned," said Kole. "Now that's clean."

"Makes all the difference in the world, huh." Robert huffed and shook his head.

"What?" Kole asked.

"Nothing." He raised his hand to the microscope. "It's just funny how the right tool makes so much of a difference. Even with something that small."

"Well, I appreciate it. I've been going at it the hard way this whole time."

"No problem. That's what I'm here for."

After prepping the specimen, Kole reached for a small glass vial labeled in black permanent marker. Then he grabbed a glass pipette in the other hand.

Robert liked to keep the air of his lab relaxed, stress free, but it was also his job to watch out for his mentees and their inevitable mistakes. "Be careful with those glass vials," he said in a thick English accent. "We don't need another *bloody* accident. I only have so much funding for cleaning supplies."

Kole dropped his head with a laugh. "Haha. At least I clean up after myself, aye."

Robert tossed a pair of latex gloves next to the microscope. "Speaking of funding," he said, "I'm working on a new grant and was wondering if you wanna be included as the postdoc."

Kole set down the glass vial with the anterior half of the copepod inside, sunken to the bottom in a clear solution that would fix the tissue in place for future microscopy work. He turned to Robert.

"I guess that depends on what the grant is and what I'd be doing."

"Well, it isn't color biology, but I could use someone with

some stats experience. Someone who knows their way around R—mostly some mixed modeling."

"So, I'd be responsible for all the data analysis?"

"In part. The other half of the role would be the broader impacts. As you already know, NSF requires a broader impacts section on all their IOS grants that outlines the outreach initiatives, DEI work, and how the research will impact society as a whole. So you'd be heading up the outreach projects more than anything else. But I think we can write it up so that you're Co-PI on it, too, if that helps."

Kole turned back to the lab bench. "Thanks. But I'll pass."

Robert had expected Kole to be hesitant, perhaps because of the time commitment or even the logistics of writing a grant while finding a professor slot somewhere else, but the last thing he'd predicted was a speedy rejection.

"No? Really?" he said.

Kole continued working while talking in the opposite direction. "Sorry. I appreciate the offer and all. I'm just getting to the point where I need to focus on the science. That's not what I spent the last ten-plus years going to school for."

"What do you mean that's not what you went to school for?"

"Just like you, my degree is in biology—not the social sciences. I totally get it that you have to include a broader impacts and outreach section in the grant, but that's not something I can take the reins on."

"And you think you're gonna be competitive on the job market looking for an assistant professorship? It's a game you're gonna have to be willing to play, whether you want to or not."

"Well, after all this time, I'm still sitting here as a postdoc, so . . ."

Robert was certain that he was watching Kole commit

academic suicide, and he wasn't sure whether there was anything he could do about it.

34

THE PHRASE "NEVER JUDGE a book by its cover" was out of control, a hard-and-fast rule passed down not only as haphazard reading advice but life advice, too. As far as Hunter was concerned, it was about as sound as "the first sentence of a novel should tell you whether it's worth reading." Weren't books meant to be discovered? Explored?

What was she supposed to do when searching for her next fix? Find the appropriate section in a bookstore—which was apparently a direct challenge in Pillet's stockpile—and read the blurb and first paragraph of every title available? Absurd!

The cover was front and center in Hunter's decision to purchase a novel, followed by the back cover copy. She had no problem swallowing her approach to finding her next read, as unpopular as it might have been. After all, if the contents of a book were *that* good, then the author should have taken pride in its presentation. No?

Covers mattered. Even if that did pin her as literature enemy number one.

She scanned the true crime section in Pillet's shop. None of the artwork jumped out and grabbed her, so she moved on to the psychology section, which included three small stacks of books that hid the baseboards. One of these appeared to contain more forensic psychology than anything else. Hunter knelt and shuffled through a few of them.

One cover in particular forced her to crack open the page. *Criminal Interrogation and the Art of Suggestion*, the title read. The cover was the ideal combination of intrigue and visual pop—a metal table sitting at the center of a white cinderblock room, a two-way mirror in the background. A Styrofoam cup of coffee steaming next to a '70s tape recorder at the table's center. An *Unsolved Mysteries* type of feel. Simple, but also effective.

"Perhaps one day," she mumbled to herself.

Hunter flipped through the frontmatter to the opening page of Chapter One. "Criminal interrogation is just as much an art as it is a science," she read. Then she turned to the middle of the book, a random chapter, and continued to read. The blurb was last.

She trusted that her career trajectory would somehow lead to an investigative role. Perhaps a chance at working more closely with Homicide. But she knew that such an opportunity would take time, and her current job in pathology would only aid her chances in the long run, so she had accepted the position with a focus on the future.

"Entomologist turned investigator" had a nice ring to it.

She heard Pillet call from behind the front desk, "If you're looking for the mysteries, you're getting warmer." Hunter turned to see a wide-open grin smeared across the owner's face.

"I thought the mystery was in finding the next read," she responded.

"You're getting colder," he said.

She wondered how such a hidey-hole of a store could harbor a hidden mystery section but, given her fondness for Pillet, figured it would be best to entertain his game.

What if there was no hidden section? What if he simply got

a kick out of watching people search for something that wasn't there?

Hunter held on to her new book and stood up, moving closer to the bookshelf running down the center of the store.

"Warmer," Pillet said.

She stepped to the other side of the row, glancing back to the counter.

"Colder."

"You realize he's fucking with you, right?" Hunter heard from behind. She turned to the back corner of the shop.

She recognized the voice, somewhat of a deep, flat tone. A blank type of register. She couldn't place it, but she could feel it. Watching.

As Hunter turned toward the voice, it came rushing back— the flies swarming amid a sticky heat, a thick brush along the fence line, falling to a muddied ground beneath barbed wire.

"Is he really?" she responded.

The man pulled back the corner of his mouth and looked over her shoulder toward the front of the store. He raised a hand to Pillet in a silent greeting.

"Well, I don't have any solid evidence"—he looked around the room—"but I don't see anywhere in here to hide an entire section of books. Do you?"

He stuck out his hand, a book in the other. "Mitch Olivier. I don't think I formally introduced myself."

Hunter spoke before returning the gesture. "Hunter Romero." Then her palm met his. His hands were rough, but with a delicate grip.

"So you're looking for the infamous mystery section, huh?" Mitch asked.

"Maybe. I'm entertaining the idea at least."

He finally released her.

"Sorry—you had said before that you worked for Mr. Daigle? Is that right?"

"Yeah, sorry about that. I had family waiting for me, and I've already been getting bogged down with Steve's passing as it is. Plus, I didn't wanna get in y'all's way over there at his place. It's been quite a shock to all of us. I'm a professor in the biology department over at UNO. Steve was the chair."

He seemed calm. Put together. A stark contrast to how he had come off previously. The woodiness of cedar wafted her way, surprising her senses. Was it the hair? An aftershave, perhaps?

"No worries at all," Hunter said. "I work for the city of New Orleans, and I've been assigned Mr. Daigle's case. Have you spoken with any of the law enforcement yet by any chance?"

"No, no. Not yet." Mitch's eyes wandered across her from head to toe, backtracking to the book in her hand. "Interrogation, huh?"

She looked down, then raised the book. "Oh, yeah. Forensic pathology by day, law enforcement by night. It never really turns off, I guess."

Her eyes nodded to the book he held in his own hand. "Entomology?"

He chuckled silently, only his shoulders and chest acknowledging the irony. "Same. Evolution by day, bugs by night. It *can't* turn off."

"Oh, I get it. Trust me," she said. Then she pulled a card from her back pocket, holding it out for the taking. "If there's any information you have regarding Mr. Daigle's passing, feel free to reach out. Here's the number to my department. They'll be able to connect you with Homicide if need be."

"Homicide, huh?"

All she could do was stare. Only, at his feet.

He held up the card to his eyes. "Thanks. I'll be sure to reach out if anything comes to mind."

She heard Pillet again, calling from the register. "It doesn't take an entire search party, you know."

Hunter pointed over her shoulder. "I guess I'll get back to the hunt. At this point, I don't think even he knows where the whodunnits are at."

As she stepped toward the back of the store, Mitch cut her off. He inched forward, just enough to invade her personal space.

"One piece of advice," Mitch said in a quiet grit. "Stay in your lane."

Then he stepped aside.

35

FOR DEBORAH, HER CAREER was the end-all, be-all of self-fulfillment. Nothing was more rewarding for the middle-aged journalist than climbing the ranks as a soloist with no rope. Bootstrapping her own career from the bottom up. And that meant doing whatever it took to plant her flag at the summit.

Snow or shine.

The reddish morning ball was stealing its way over the skyline. Deborah's fiery hair blew across her face as she sipped her tea, eyes lax in the dawn's chill.

The morning's meetup was everything if she was going to move up in the world and abandon base camp.

As she drew a sip from the small ceramic cup, she saw a woman appear from around the corner of the eatery. High heels, black skirt, white button-down. A black binder was the only item she carried as she strutted toward the outdoor dining area. She was a poster cutout of the businesswoman cliché. It wasn't long before they locked eyes, and the lady approached her with an affable greeting.

"Goddamn legs for days," Deborah said out loud to herself.

"Hi. Deborah Doucet?" The woman reached out her hand. "Lauren Williams."

She was definitely something to look at. Her skin a medium

roast, teeth cut straight from a Crest ad, and posture fit for English royalty.

"Nice to meet you," Deborah said. "Thanks for reaching out."

Lauren sat across from her as the waitress approached the table. "You're very welcome."

"Hi, can I get you anything?" asked the server.

"A water would be great. Thanks," Lauren said, before looking to Deborah. "So, I have some good news," she continued. "The editor thought that the information you provided for the journal was fantastic. The story went off without a hitch, and it's already getting more attention than she thought it would. So . . . great job. Really."

"Well that's great, then." Still, Deborah had reservations about the seemingly positive feedback. "I really appreciate it. What I don't understand, though, is the need for meeting with me in person."

The waitress returned with a water, placing the green bottle in front of the representative. "Let me know if you need anything else," she said.

"Thanks," Lauren responded. "Well, as you already know," she continued to Deborah, "our main office is in New York, and Cadence thought it would be best for you to meet with someone from our local office instead of getting another phone call from herself, halfway across the country. It's good, though. Trust me. If she's asking you to meet with a local representative"—she pointed to herself—"that means she's serious about bringing you on as an editor."

Deborah took a sip of tea as she thought, waiting for the rep to move the conversation forward. The honey soothed the catch in her throat.

"Okay. So where do we go from here?" she asked.

"You have two options. One—you can provide some more information to Cadence directly, and we can follow up with a second article. Or two—you can piggyback off the article from *MurderoUS Weekly* and write one of your own—which I think you would be hesitant to do, if I'm not mistaken. And for good reason."

"So, she's wanting more?"

"The way we work? More crime equals more coverage. If a single murder is getting as much attention as the Daigle case, then a second murder means a second article. Either way, she's hoping to see that your first assignment wasn't a fluke. She wants to see that you'll do whatever it takes."

"Well, like you said, writing the article myself would only draw attention. So that's off the table." Deborah straightened her back and looked out to the sidewalk, watching the morning strollers meander by. "Is there anything in particular she's looking for, or just more?"

"There was another murder, no? She's looking for insider information. Just like before." The rep leaned in. "If it were me, I'd make it worth your while. She wants to see that you'll go out on a limb for the publication—no matter how many times you're asked, or for what reason."

Deborah had already gone out on a limb—a rather decaying, unsteady one at that. And apparently, her face showed it.

"Look, if doing this again, multiple times in a row, bothers you, then this gig might not be what you're looking for," said Lauren. She stood up and took a sip of water. Then she grabbed the binder, pulling an issue of *MurderoUS Weekly* from inside. She held it out across the table. "Here. This is the last article that Cadence wrote up on a repeat offender. If you're looking to land the job, you might wanna start with getting her everything that she covered in there. Just remember, you're being given a chance for a reason."

She placed the binder under her arm. "Best of luck." The woman walked away, looking even better than when she had arrived.

• • •

It was like carrying the key to her future life in her handbag—a roadmap to writing the article that could solidify the career Deborah had only dreamt of for years. The only remaining question was whether or not she could do it.

Her first rodeo wasn't a problem. Sources were a dime a dozen in the journalist community—quid pro quo, a friend of a friend, a debt owed. The prospects were endless.

But the dilemma was her personal life.

She walked through the back door of her home and set her purse down onto the marble kitchen island, her eyes on the potential prize. Sitting on one of the three barstools, Deborah stared a hole through the magazine that was peeking out from the top of her bag. But all she could see was Hunter—her chestnut hair falling across the bridge of her dotted nose, her dampened cheeks shimmering with the sting of an abrupt end. The spice of seafood returned to the journalist as clear as the memory itself.

It wasn't until the second murder, not long ago, that Deborah had realized she might've saddled up more than she could handle. If her ex was working the serial homicides she had fed to the New Yorker, could she still do it? Could she continue to put her career first?

Perhaps the break-up was meant to be after all.

Or was it?

She grabbed a piece of printer paper from the drawer across the kitchen. Then she pulled the magazine from the bag before flipping to the editor-in-chief's article.

It was the type of story every crime journalist aspired to write: worldwide coverage, gruesome slayings, a killer's signature left to interpretation by anyone willing to take a crack at it. It had every hallmark of what had inspired Deborah to become a crime writer in the first place.

The years of college and menial office assignments were finally paying off.

Signature? she wrote on the paper.

A repeat offender meant a likely pattern and, if she was lucky, a calling card. If there was anything the public devoured faster than a serial murderer, it was a killer's obsession with ensuring their crimes were linked.

After all, who didn't want credit for their work?

36

"SO HOW DID A crime writer and a pathologist get involved anyways?" Parker asked. "Wait. Don't tell me." Then he closed his eyes with a tight, over-the-top squeeze and held a finger to the wind.

"You mean, how *were* we involved?" said Hunter.

He flung open one of his lash-lined lids. "Were? Please, do tell."

"It's a long story."

Parker looked around the lab before exciting a single brow. "Okay." He folded his arms and sat back against the lab bench.

It could have been worse. Her mentor could have been a complete jerk and not opened up at all. He could have been a problem instead of merely peculiar. Hunter considered keeping her story to herself, but only for a passing second. The way she figured, if she was going to move up in the world of all things criminal, it would behoove her to oblige the right people—in the right positions.

Strange or not, she needed to go with it.

"Well," she started in, "we met a while back, when I was a research assistant in the entomology department over at Southeastern. Deborah was finishing up the fourth year of her English degree. She had a story to find, and I was it."

"A story?"

"Yeah. The final exam for her journalism course was to write up a story on someone at the university. Anyone. And for any reason. I had just landed a research fellowship for my master's work. We met up, discussed my thesis, and we became close friends. The rest is history."

"Well surely that kind of history can't be thrown away in such a short amount of time. That was quite a while ago, no?"

Hunter wasn't one for plastering her personal life all over town, much less around her job. But Parker was silently insisting. Waiting for the details.

"I agree," she said. "But it wasn't me. I mean, it wasn't me who . . . you know."

He waited.

"Or maybe it was me. I don't know."

"You don't know?"

"I mean, I do know why. I guess I just wouldn't have done anything differently." Clearly, such an answer was unsatisfactory. "She's the one who ended it," Hunter added.

Her eyes scanned the lab bench, working their way down to the floor.

"Ah. There it is," Parker said. "You don't agree with her reasoning."

"I can't fix what I can't help, and I can't help who it is that I work with."

Parker winced. "Now that's a tough one," he said with a sympathetic shade of voice. "Well, there aren't many people in our department." Then he looked off to the ceiling's empty space, searching for the answer he apparently was going to pull out of her, whether she liked it or not. "Homicide?"

A simple tilt of the head provided her response. She looked at Parker to gauge his reaction, hoping he wouldn't push the matter any further. She should've known better.

His focus shifted to her wrist, to the unmoving *A* stamped in scarlet just above her palm.

Hunter pulled her arm beneath the table.

"You know," Parker said. "I don't wanna test my luck any more than I already have, but there's a great group of people that meet every Sunday who'd love to have you around. I'd be glad to introduce you."

She didn't know how else to say "no, thank you." It wasn't that she didn't appreciate the offer. Or that she had anything against Parker. There were simply some aspects of her life she felt were best sorted on her own, in the privacy of her own space. Some ideas were too personal to share.

"Thanks, Parker. I appreciate it. But like I've said before, church isn't really my thing. No offense."

"None taken," he said in a welcoming manner. "I just hate to see whatever it is, or whoever it is, affecting your work. It seems like you could use some good company is all."

Hunter felt no need to respond. She had said all she had to say at the moment.

"And besides," he continued, "just because you're 'at church'"—he accentuated with air quotes—"doesn't mean anything other than you're in the company of those who care."

She couldn't have disagreed more, and she fought to hold back her contempt for the conversation. To bite her tongue yet again.

"I don't agree, really, but I'll give it some thought." She forced out the words, although they tasted a bit rancid. A day or two past their expiration date, curdled and impossible to swallow.

Parker's expression downshifted from curiosity to a disappointed frustration.

"How so?" he asked. "It's nothing more than an offer to be a part of something positive. It's just a chance to try something new. Something good."

"You sure this is something you wanna get into at work? I don't wanna make things awkward between us. Really."

"Of course I'm sure. Things will be just fine. They are fine."

So she eased into it. "Okay. Like I've said before, church just isn't for me. I was raised Christian. I went to church for nearly twenty years. Every Sunday, I was front and center. But things change. People change."

"Sure they do. I'm not arguing with that at all. But believing in something bigger than yourself can do the mind some good. You know, give thanks to what brought you here in the first place."

"And what's that?" Hunter asked.

Parker opened his hands, holding an invisible answer. "God."

She hesitated to say more, to push back against something that had no intention of moving.

"Well . . . respectfully, Parker . . . I'm very thankful. But I feel like the universe is magical enough in and of itself—without inserting something else where my understanding falls short."

"So, why not hedge your bets? What's it gonna hurt?"

"Because I refuse to be a pawn in some cosmic chess match."

Based on his dull expression, Hunter considered that maybe Parker had not been denied in this way before.

37

THE COUPLE SAT NEXT to one another at the head of the conference table, waiting for their lab groups to arrive. The professors' grant had been rejected, which meant anyone and everyone in the lab had been summoned for damage control.

Mitch looked down at his watch, then to the door, his foot tapping in an off-beat rhythm beneath the table.

"Who are we waiting on?" he asked Aura. "It's already five till."

Her eyes systematically scanned the table. "There's still a few who aren't here. I'll text them now and see where they're at."

He was desperate to resubmit the grant and avenge his loss. Get his reputation back to a shining polish. A flawless reflection of the professor and academic he had always known himself to be. Mitch didn't see rejection as a possibility, and he certainly couldn't accept it as an outcome. His work was flawless. His writing seamless.

And it became the flock's duty to pick up the pieces—as long as his name was listed as PI, of course.

A few more of the lesser-minded trickled in.

"That looks like everyone," said Mitch.

"No. We're still waiting on one more." Aura checked her

phone, just before the door opened.

She stood up and moved at a hurried pace toward the entrance. "Dr. LeBlanc. I'm glad you could join us."

Mitch turned his attention to the door. Surely, his ears had failed him.

Kole strutted with an erect swank around the table and sat across from the professor. "Mitch"—the postdoc nodded—"how's it going? Thanks for the invite, by the way."

"The invite?" said Mitch. Then his mouth transformed into a Cheshire grin, although he fought against it tooth and nail.

Kole returned the sentiment. "Let's fix up this grant, shall we?"

"Everyone, I'd like to introduce you to our newest adjunct professor," Aura said, "Dr. Kole LeBlanc. He's joining our lab meeting to help us out with some revisions on our NSF grant."

Mitch couldn't object without making it obvious that he had been omitted from the loop. Second in charge to the grant's Co-PI, of all people.

His own wife.

"Good to be here," said Kole.

What was done was done. Aura had clearly fucked up. But as far as the kids were concerned, Mitch was just as much on board as anyone else, so he went along with it—albeit with his hands shackled at the waist.

"Yeah, let's get going," said Mitch. "So we submitted this NSF grant over a year ago, and we just found out it was rejected because of the DEI work, even though the reviewers didn't seem to have a problem with it. What we're looking for is feedback on the broader impacts so we can get this turned around and sent back in, hopefully by the end of the month. So if anyone has any comments on the—"

"Yeah, I got something," Kole said.

Mitch stared at Aura. Then he spoke from the side of his mouth. "I wasn't really done explaining the—"

"The broader impacts don't really look like they would affect anyone other than a few prospective freshmen."

Wasting no time with his response, Mitch interjected, "Well the broader impacts were written to—"

"And there's nothing new in the outreach initiatives," Kole continued. "It looks to be all recycled programs and events that the department already has in place."

"Like I was saying, they were—"

"Kole has a good point," Aura cut in. "That's exactly what the internal review panel had to say."

"*Sure*," Mitch said in a slightly heated note, "but like I was saying, the broader impacts were written to continue with what has already been proven to work here in the department. NSF pretty much wants to see that a proposal is guaranteed to work before it's funded. There's zero room for uncertainty."

Screw the kids, he thought. *It's between us now.*

"So why not use those programs as a springboard to launch something bigger and better?" said Kole. "Besides, the way to increase our reach as scientists is to work with high schools and middle graders. Not try to appeal to incoming freshmen who already plan on entering a STEM field. Broader impacts are about society at large, not recruitment."

"Oh that's beautiful, Dr. Leblanc. Maybe we can offer a balloon animal to the best in class," said Mitch.

A few chuckles seeped from the otherwise silent crowd as Kole adjusted his fallen stray locks. The truth of the matter was Mitch didn't think the idea was half-bad. But Kole had wandered into the wrong pride, and all roaming cubs carried the same fate.

"Okay, I think we're clearly getting off track," said Aura. "Why don't we try incorporating that with something new that we've already been working on. We're planning an Outreach Institute for next semester, which can involve high school students and possibly middle school as well."

Mitch dropped his pen on the table and folded his arms.

"That could work," said Kole. "I think the important thing is to reach beyond the collegiate level. But if the Outreach Institute is something new, that's even better."

"So we should forget about recruiting underrepresented groups to our labs?" Mitch asked.

He glanced at the rest of the room. At that point, the students looked hesitant to step foot anywhere near the conversation.

"Well," Kole started in, "broader impacts aren't meant to be about recruiting lab members of any group. It's about exposing students to STEM careers and disseminating our research to the rest of society. Besides"—he looked around at everyone else—"who is it that's underrepresented here?"

• • •

A few hours later, Mitch leaned against the gray stone of the building's edge, just outside the double doors of Milneburg Hall, where Kole's lecture would soon let out.

Two more minutes and a flock of hangry freshmen would stampede in the direction of the University Center. But for Mitch, lunch could wait.

He refused to have his lab meetings hijacked, and by a postdoc of all people. By some dud from the past. Mitch had built a life for himself. A career, where he was respected by his peers for what he had accomplished—for what he had built from the ground up. One paper at a time. And no one, including his wife, would undermine that reality.

The first of too many students busted through the doors and turned toward the smell of fried chicken in the distance, scattering faster than a herd of wildebeest from the Nile. The weak abandoned in the dust.

Mitch approached the double doors as Kole exited the building, the adjunct lifting the strap of his leather computer bag over his head and adjusting it across his chest. "Hey, hey," said Kole. "Long time, no see."

Mitch stood at the center of the walkway, hands at his side, shoulders taut. "What the hell, dude? What are you doing?"

Kole looked around. "Teaching. Or at least I was. Now it's lunch."

The postdoc began walking away, as if Mitch were nothing more than a wounded calf, left to the devices of what monsters lay in wait within the muddied waters.

"It's common courtesy," said Mitch.

Kole turned back. "I'm sorry?"

"To ask permission before attending someone's lab meeting. It's common courtesy to ask before you just show up out of the blue. I know you're new to the whole professor thing, but our meetings aren't exactly an open hall."

"I was invited."

"Oh, is that so? By whom, the president?"

"No, the chair . . . Is that all?"

"Leave," said Mitch. He could feel the heat flush through his cheeks as he wiped the sweat of his palms back through his oiled hair.

"I'm trying. But apparently, you feel the need to ambush me on my way out the door."

"That's not what I mean, and you know it."

Kole gave him a two-fingered salute before turning away. "Give Aura my best," he said as he strode in the opposite direction and disappeared into the drove.

• • •

Hunter only had ten minutes before the start of Mitch's class. And the last person she had expected to run into on the way there was Mitch himself—speaking to Kole.

She stepped behind a large cycad at the corner of the University Center, shielding herself from their view. It was a short exchange, but it looked like a run-in gone bad. Mitch was standing alone, watching Kole fade into the moving crowd.

The postdoc began walking down the sidewalk, which led straight to Hunter. Her curiosity alone pulled her out from behind the bush and into his path.

"What happened? LSU got too big for ya?" she asked as they nearly collided.

"Adjunct," he replied. Then he looked around as if he had suddenly realized where they were. "And you're here because . . ."

In that moment, Hunter recognized that she may have stepped onto the wrong side of her ambitions. Into a steaming pile of "oh shit."

"Because . . . I work for the city, remember? There's this thing going on. A double murder. A professor, a dean. You may've heard of it?"

"Yeah, I get that," said Kole in a downy whisper, stepping to the side of the path. "But I thought you were looking into Hebert."

"You worry about the academic side of things, and I'll take care of the legal stuff. Yeah?"

She looked over his shoulder to Mitch, who had finally turned away and walked in the opposite direction.

"You know Olivier?" she asked.

Kole's eyes were otherworldly, glowing as they burned orange in the day's heat.

"Of course. It's impossible to work here and not know who Mitch Olivier is."

38

"Are you sure you're okay?" Meaux asked, her daughter framed in the rearview mirror. Their car was stopped in the middle of the highway. Meaux hesitated to make the turn down the driveway.

"I promise," said Angie. "It's what Daddy would want."

Meaux knew how it would've appeared to anyone else—a mother bringing her daughter back to the property, back to the scene itself, where the girl's father had been brutally murdered. No parent in their right mind would've contemplated such a thing. Her heart was torn, though. She had a wild, innate need to protect little Angie at all costs. But she had also watched her, day and night, as she stared out of the kitchen window of their broken home, asking if her father would ever again pull into the driveway. If he would ever honk the horn again and wait for his little girl to greet him at the car door.

It shattered Meaux's soul into the tiniest of pieces she had never known existed.

When she had told Angie that she was returning to the property to gather a bouquet of flowers for her father's grave, the girl had insisted that she tag along. Against the better part of Meaux's judgment, she gave in. Between the innocent tears and bedtime questions, she had developed a soft spot for her daughter's requests. And when it came to Steve, Meaux could never have denied her the memory of her own father. The memories of her childhood.

She nodded at Angie's reflection in the mirror. "Okay, love."

She turned into the drive. The scene was still taped off, blocking the entirety of the backyard and rear entrance to the house. Meaux parked alongside the shed behind the driveway, which effectively blocked the view of everything the mother considered even remotely provocative to the seven-year-old.

As she stepped out of the car, Meaux caught a wave of crimson clover in the distance, swaying across one of the food plots in the day's gentle breeze. A single road ran from the front of the property to the back, where a bayou separated solid ground from marshland. Three small food plots with a single hunting stand at each lined the path, which led to a rickety wooden bridge over muddy waters.

Angela pointed. "Can we go over there, Mommy?"

Meaux held out her hand, which was filled in no time by little Angie's touch. Mr. Snugglesworth rested in the crook of her daughter's other arm.

It was a brief walk to the first field. An old plywood shooting house shaded in forest-green spray paint sat in the back corner, tucked away on a trail that was hidden from the main road. Steve had explained to her more than once why the box stands were set where they were—why it was on the backside of the food plot and not the front. Something or other about being downwind.

They tiptoed into the field of clover and wheat. The timbery scent of pine, mixed with a subtle hint of cypress, floated across the field that swayed in waves just above their feet.

Meaux could remember her husband's advice when out on

the property. "Always be quiet," he used to say in a muted register. "We're in their home now."

She stooped to one knee, tugging Angie's hand down with her. Then she covered her daughter's lips with a single finger.

Meaux pointed to a group of the blood-washed flowers, waving this way and that. "What about these?" She spoke as delicately as the wind across her throat.

Angela nodded as a smirk snuck out from beneath her pale vanilla hair. "They're perfect." A few sunflowers, some strands of wheat, and an iris or two completed the mission. Without convincing one another, they dropped to a sitting position and admired the beauty of it all. Feeling the appreciation for what Steve had left them. A little touch of nature.

As Meaux shifted her weight to one knee and began to stand, she caught sight of a doe and her fawn. She rested her hand on Angela's lower back and raised her finger to the deer in a slow creep, ducking beneath the top of the rolling red tide.

"Look," she said. "Look at the mommy and her fawn." Angie's face lit up—as wildly as her father's excitement on opening day, Meaux remembered.

"Where's her daddy?" the girl asked in a tender voice.

In that moment, the fragments of Meaux's heart were tested yet again.

"He's around," she responded. "He's watching them. Protecting them if anything were to happen. But he's around."

Angie cracked a smile.

They crouched below the brush and made their way back to the cover of the woods, where the girl paused and grabbed the bouquet from her mother. She pressed the flowers to her nose and closed her eyes as Meaux fixed her hair, which had been ruffled by the wind.

"It smells like him," Angie said.

Meaux nodded with a smile of comfort and exchanged the teddy bear for her own hand.

As they approached the camp, Meaux could see the girl's expression change from happy to what looked like saddened memories. Meaux crouched in front of her, then held her tight.

"He misses you, too," she said.

Angie's eyes moved a small distance to the side, focusing over her mother's shoulder.

"What's that?" she asked.

Meaux turned and looked behind her. "What?"

"That." Her daughter squinted.

A small box was strapped to the trunk of a cypress tree, a bit off the beaten path at the back of the camp. Meaux stood up and walked over to the tree, then grabbed the item while unhooking the bungie cord that held it in place.

She popped open the hinge and saw nothing inside but a blank screen, the battery seemingly dead. "I think Daddy used these for hunting," she said.

Meaux closed the box and turned it over—to some faded writing in black permanent marker. She ran her finger over the words but could only make out a few of the letters. It took her a moment, but she finally recognized the worn and jagged name.

"But this isn't Daddy's."

39

HUNTER WAITED UNTIL MITCH had entered the lecture hall before she slipped through the side door and found a seat in the back row of the arena-sized room. A bone-numbing cold and an eerie silence put her on edge from the moment she stepped inside.

Even so, she was reminded of her teenage glory days. Countless times, she had snuck into the movie theater with her boyfriend during the summer between seventh and eighth grade, when she had been dating the principal's son. Snacks tucked away deep in their jackets, hats down low, a pocket flask filled with some of her mother's red liquid courage. Creeping behind the curtain.

Her days of minor espionage were in the distant past, but they were memories that she clung to tighter than a newborn to a mother's scent. In the moment, she realized how unhealthy it might be—thinking back to nothing more than some puppy love over a dreamy summer so long ago. But it kept her warm during the frigid, adulty nights.

She sat at the end of the row, her shoulder against the wall, watching from the corner of her eye as the students trickled in. Her black hat and aviators were sure to keep her hidden in plain sight, she thought. The sunglasses may have been a bit much, but she decided to roll the dice and go with the hungover-kid-in-the-back kind of appearance. The look was bound to show up at least once per period. All she had to do was think back to a few years prior, while she was at Southeastern.

To her surprise, the room was half-empty. But the students who had shown up looked borderline terrified. Over the seemingly infinite number of minutes before the class began, no one spoke. Once seated, no one moved. No one dared get up and leave—as far as the attendees were concerned, there was no restroom. Rules had evidently been laid out from day one, and that was a vital glimpse into the persona of Dr. Mitch Olivier.

Hunter couldn't put her finger on it, but there was something in the room that made her shift in the cold, hard plastic of the seat. Something about *him*, perhaps.

The professor set up his laptop, then began his PowerPoint without bothering to address the class. The show had begun, as if it had never broken from the prior lecture.

"We left off in our last lecture with the physiological evidence for evolution, some of which is more or less evident," he said.

His command of the class was as perfect as the knot in his skinny black tie: confident and down the center. His flow of lecture was a seamless transition from one topic to the next. Professor Olivier paced from one side of the room to the other, talking as if consumed by an in-depth conversation over a cup of morning mocha. To Hunter, it was quite the show. Almost artistic. It also seemed like where he was most comfortable.

Hunter remembered that, according to her new book, how someone acted in your presence versus how they moved in your absence could say a great deal about not only what they thought of you, but their guilt or lack thereof. And the one thing that stood out to her—like a ripple across the watering hole—was the professor's eyes.

She removed her shades and rested the tip of her chin on her hand. Hunter wanted to see for herself, unobstructed, how he commanded the room. He spoke to the slides projected onto the big screen. He talked to his computer. Hell, he even spoke to his feet as he walked from side to side. But the one thing he seemingly avoided was the crowd.

The last person Hunter had expected to find commonalities with was Mitch Olivier.

"For example," he continued, "we see that some traits are merely the byproducts of the evolution of other traits, as opposed to selection itself. Stephen Jay Gould and Richard Lewontin adopted the term 'spandrel' in reference to such traits, a name they borrowed from the architectural world."

She removed a crumpled pack of spearmint gum from her skin-tight jeans. The wrapper might as well have been a pen dropped to the floor in the front row, and everyone within a ten-foot radius stopped and turned as she unpacked the green stick.

It was clear that he wouldn't speak, but a boy behind her tapped her chair with his foot and held out a hand. *I'll take a piece* was implied by the silent gesture.

Hunter handed him the pack, which slipped from his grasp and hit the floor with a ringside slap.

"Excuse me, is there a problem?" Mitch called from the front of the room.

You son of a bitch, Hunter thought. *I'm about to get thrown out of a class I'm not even taking. At a college I don't even go to.*

The professor took a step down the center aisle and toward her row.

Or better yet, charged with stalking.

"No, sir," said the gum-dropping kid behind her. "Sorry."

She kept her head down, the rim of her hat blocking her

view of his face.

"If I'm interrupting something, I can put the lecture on hold," Mitch continued from the aisle.

"I apologize," the kid said. "It won't happen again."

Hunter watched the professor's feet as they shuffled back to the front of the room. "I'm glad we're on the same page, then," he said over his shoulder.

The boy picked up the pack of gum, grabbed a piece, and handed it back to Hunter.

"Moving on," Mitch continued, "we see rather obvious evidence with examples like the recurrent laryngeal nerve in animals such as giraffes." He clicked to the next slide, which contained a cartoonish diagram of giraffe anatomy next to a photograph of a dissection.

"The nerve originally evolved in our fishlike ancestors, linking the brain and gills not far from the heart. However, millions of generations later, in the development of the neck in mammalian ancestors, the nerve gradually lengthened—one small step at a time." He pointed to the long path of the nerve from the giraffe's brain, down around the aorta, and back up to the larynx. A trip of approximately fifteen feet to cover a span of mere inches. "If we take this to be intelligent design, then maybe we're not as advanced as we think."

It was an interesting story, Hunter thought as she formed a thinning bubble at the edge of her lips. Just the line of thinking that had led her to science in the first place. To an understanding of the world that was worthy of appreciation, all on its own.

"So as you can see," Mitch continued, "the evidence is often hidden in plain sight."

Then the bubble popped like a gun at the starting line, forming a smothering film across her nose and mouth.

40

THE CLOCK WAS TICKING, and Deborah shuddered at the breath of her future, panting down the back of her neck with its driveling teeth, waiting for her to trip and fall over the wrong career move. One false step, and she would be nothing more than a writer of misdemeanors and suicides. It was enough to keep her head above water, but in the end, she craved the stories that would keep her awake in the dark.

Murder was the only game she was after.

She rested on the brick steps of the sizeable five-story building and waited for David to emerge from his office. The reporter knew better than to step inside. Past experience had taught her she wasn't welcome—especially after her heated run-in with Homicide's lead detective. Apparently, reporters only "blurred the lines" between truth and entertainment. So she had decided to bother one of the detective's colleagues instead.

"Really?" David said as he stepped outside and strode down the staircase. "I'm gonna go out on a limb and say that Hunter doesn't know you're here."

Deborah held out a peace offering—a double espresso with almond milk. No whip.

"I won't keep you long," she said.

"You're right. Because I'm walking away." He turned in the

opposite direction.

"David, I need your help."

The man paused and looked back with an irritated shrug. Deborah held out her arm, suspended between them, her hand gripping the cup. He accepted the drink but wasted no time pushing back.

"Deborah, you're asking me for information I can't give you. You do realize that reporters, crime writers included, are meant to cover the facts of a case, right? Not report on privileged information that may or may not be the key to putting someone behind bars."

"I'm not here for a lecture, but thank you. And what makes you so sure that I want information for a case? Maybe it's something else entirely. Maybe it's personal."

The tech gave her one of his don't-bullshit-me looks. The corners of his mouth tensed, his eyes glancing up from a downward gaze.

"Because I've worked around writers and reporters my entire career, and as much as you might not admit it to yourself, criminals are your three meals a day and snacks in between. I can't say I blame you"—he looked back to the building—"but there's lines in the sand for a reason."

He sipped the coffee, his face changing from a whitewashed anger to a tolerable, mild annoyance.

Deborah huffed from fluttering lips. "What the hell is that supposed to mean?" Although she had attempted and stumbled pathetically over the friends-come-first approach, she felt that David was clearly making this about something other than work. He'd been on the defensive from the get-go.

"It means that I'm not willing to risk my career for one of your columns."

"Look, all I need is one more story, and I'm in the big

leagues. One more, and I'll never ask you for information on a case ever again."

"Oh come on, Deborah. You're a crime writer. You know all about addicts and where they end up in the long run. 'One more' is their signature line. If you really want something from me, then take my advice. What you need is to stop getting information you shouldn't have in the first place, or you're gonna end up on the wrong side of the story."

"Goddamn, you're a buzzkill. It's a magazine story, David. Not a deposition."

"I don't care what it is. But what it's not is my problem. And what about Hunter?"

She'd had a feeling the conversation would eventually go there. Straight to the personal. Bypass friendship—do not collect your promotion.

"What about Hunter?" Deborah asked.

"What about her? Really? You're just gonna ignore the fact that if you write up the wrong thing, from the wrong person, you can sink everything she's been working on? She's just now getting a leg up with her pathology position, and you're gonna risk that on some magazine article?"

"This has nothing to do with Hunter. I'm coming to you for a favor, not her."

"But you do know that she's working the case, don't you? I'm sure that's something you've already gotten from one of your more reliable sources."

"I don't need a source to figure out what Hunter's up to, and I'm sure you're well aware that we're no longer seeing each other. It's interesting, though, that she's the first thing you wanna talk about."

"Wow. You really are something else."

"Excuse me?"

"You think that just because you're not involved with someone anymore, you can screw 'em over to further your career and satisfy your own needs?"

Something had clearly changed with David. Deborah had a hunch as to what it was, and it wasn't her ex's newfound career.

"Look, are you gonna help me out or not? I came to you because you're on the case. Not because you are or aren't Hunter's . . . whatever."

David set the coffee down onto the steps before taking a seat himself. He folded his hands in front of him and looked down the city street. His heel played with the gravel as it tapped at an anxious pace.

"You need to stop playing games with her, Deborah. What she and I had is in the past. Neither of us can help the fact that we work together from time to time. Don't put that on her."

She fidgeted with the strap of her purse, which clung to the edge of her shoulder like a soloist to the icy edge of a mountainous pass, her pick digging into the melting frost of what little relationship she had with David. "I'm sorry, come again?" She spoke in an icy gust of words.

"Hunter—just because the two of you aren't involved anymore, like you say, doesn't mean that you can play around with her career like this."

Deborah cringed at how easily he twisted the facts to fit his own narrative. Not only was David the reason for the break-up, he was throwing it back in her face.

"That's a mighty big claim coming from the very person who split us up in the first place."

She could tell she'd struck a nerve, the very pathway that controlled his attention, which snapped under the weight of her words.

"Walk away," he said. "Walk away now before one of us

regrets it."

"No. If I don't get what I need from you, I'll move on to the next. You're not the only one with an iron in the fire. Just remember, David—sources are a dime a dozen."

"Maybe," he responded with what appeared to be sympathy. As if maybe he really did care. "But relationships aren't. Especially the loyal ones."

"What? You're gonna hold a grudge now? Come on, I thought you were better than that."

"I don't hold grudges, Deb. I just don't forget the way people treat me and the people I care about. There's a difference."

"Oh, so you care about her now? From what I heard, there was nothing to care about."

David stood up, orphaning his cup on the steps. Lonely at the bricks' edge.

"Unlike you," he continued, "I don't need to get something in return in order to be loyal."

Then he walked away, this time without turning back.

41

IF THERE WAS ONE thing Hunter had learned while navigating her professional life, it was that great rewards came from even greater gambles. If an idea made her stomach churn and form knots fit for a docked warship, it was probably worth pursuing.

So the start of a new career called for new risks. Calculated risks. Sure, it might not have been the best of ideas. But perhaps the clearest window into the mind of Mitch Olivier was through the panes of his wife.

In searching the literature, Hunter had noticed that Olivier's name was almost always accompanied by someone else's—Aura Theriot, from the same department. During her stay at Southeastern for both her undergraduate and graduate degrees, Hunter had been steeped in academia enough to notice that it was nearly impossible for spouses in the same department to separate their work from one another. This was an observation she had made while working with other universities more than anything. She had found that more departments than not had at least one married couple.

From the outside looking in, one would have thought that such an arrangement—"let's talk about an idea over breakfast before we leave home, and I'll put you on as middle author"—would violate some sort of ethical clause. But the pyramid was built from the inside out, and a signed disclosure meant asses covered.

Dr. Theriot's office door was cracked, but Hunter knocked with a light one-two tap of a knuckle.

She heard a voice from inside. "Come in."

With a smile, she stepped into the room. As much as it hurt, she sucked it up and met the professor eye to eye.

"Hi, can I help you?" the woman said.

Hunter held out her hand in greeting.

"Hi. I'm Hunter Romero with the New Orleans Pathology Department. Do you have a minute?"

Dr. Theriot's touch was welcoming, her hands buttery smooth. "Oh," she said. A surprised confusion crossed her face. "Sure. Have a seat." She gestured to a chair off to the side of the room. "What can I do for you?"

The office was on par with an operating room. Immaculate would have been an understatement.

"My office is working the recent homicide cases here at the university. Well, one of them was on campus, at least. I'm just asking some questions here and there to get a feel for the cases and collect any information that may be useful in the city's investigation."

The woman rolled her chair over to the minifridge in the corner behind her desk. "Something to drink?" she asked.

"Sure."

She handed Hunter a sparkling water.

What was it with the Pellegrino, anyway? Was that part of a professor's contract at every university? *Sign right here on the dotted line, just below the sparkling water clause.*

"Thanks," said Hunter.

"Well I'm glad to help in any way that I can. Is there anything in particular you're looking for?"

Hunter offered a guilty grin and lifted her shoulders.

"Okay, then," Dr. Theriot responded.

"To be honest, my office is fairly certain in assessing the cause of death for both of the cases. So, we're looking to help out our Homicide department with their investigation, looking into *why* they occurred. It's sort of an all-hands-on-deck kinda thing. Is there anything prior to the murders that we should know about? Anything that may have happened?"

"Not really," Dr. Theriot said. "They both came straight out of left field and were a shock to everyone. All we're trying to do is pick up the pieces and keep the department running. My husband and I were working pretty closely with Bryan on some outreach stuff we have going on, and of course, Steve Daigle was our chair. That's the only reason I'm in the position I'm in now."

"So nothing has happened lately with a student or anything? Nothing out of the ordinary?"

The professor looked as if she were about to break down, to confess and spill it all about how overwhelmed she was. An innocence teased her lashes and threatened to spill over from the edge of her vision.

Hunter didn't feel the need to push her any further.

"Well, the reason I'm here to see you is that I ran into your husband next door to Steve Daigle's residence. His family camp, where he was murdered."

"Mitch?" She pulled her head back, away from the conversation. "Why would Mitch have been next door to Steve's place? I mean, they worked together. We all did. But I don't . . . I'm sorry. I'm a bit confused."

"Do you have any relatives that live out that way?"

Hunter snatched a tissue from the corner of the desk and passed it to the owner. She could see Dr. Theriot running the names in her head.

"Mitch's brother, Paul, lives in the area. But he's all the way out past the oaks."

The tunnel of oaks was a city landmark located on the outskirts of town, where fluorescent lights met solid woodland. Centuries-old oak trees formed a tunnel of Spanish moss on both sides of the road for nearly half a mile. It marked the gateway to what locals called "the hardwoods."

"That wouldn't happen to be down off of 39, would it?"

"NOPD covers Braithwaite? That's all the way out past Poydras."

"With cases like this, we do. Both of the victims lived and worked in New Orleans, even though Steve Daigle was found at his family camp out in Braithwaite. Which, if I'm not mistaken, is next door to your brother-in-law's place."

Dr. Theriot's cheeks turned from a pinkish tint to a haunting flush. "Next door? Mitch has never mentioned that. We've been out there several times over the past year. I'm sure he would've said something."

"Have you been out there recently?"

"No. Not lately."

Hunter pulled a palm-sized notepad from her back pocket. "You mind?" She pointed to a pencil on the desk.

"No, not at all."

Hunter crossed her legs and rested the booklet on her knee. "So, where is your husband's office at again?"

Her words alone seemed to cut the air between them.

• • •

Hunter knocked, but her effort rang hollow down the open hallway. The adjoining door was shut to within an inch of closing.

A steady stream of alcohol made its way into the hallway and drew her into the room, from nothing more than her own curiosity. The lights were on, but was anyone home?

"Hello?" she said as her foot crossed the doorway.

The room was eerily reminiscent of her Southeastern days, the not-so-distant past. Faux wooden cabinets, black workbenches that remembered a handprint with ease, and stained drop tile ceilings. The smell was somewhere between Katrina aftermath and teenage bedroom. It was clearly Mitch's lab according to the sign on the door, albeit a few decades behind on its renovations. Messy for a clean-cut guy.

She walked farther into the lab, peeking her head around the corner and into what appeared to be a stock room.

"*Hello*," she said again. "Dr. Olivier?"

The only response was a deep buzz coming from the clear tubes above her head, a soft white glow bouncing from one end to the other. In need of replacement.

As she turned a second corner, Hunter entered a room that sat between the lab and what must have been Mitch's office, given the location of the bordering door. A complete one-eighty from the outdated mess of the lab itself. The room jarred something deep within her, something a bit déjà vuish. And then it hit her.

She was also infatuated with the curation of her work.

The room was stacked from floor to ceiling with cabinets and drawers of glass vials, showcases, and cabinets of the professor's collected work. Specimens on top of specimens. Hunter saw a piece of herself reflected in his obsessive habits of organization. She even recognized the samples themselves, skillfully preserved with a sense of perfection.

She ran her hand across the wooden drawers. The labels were hand printed in a fine felt tip: *Ixodes scapularis*, *Amblyomma americanum*, *Rhipicephalus sanguineus*.

And there it was. *Lipoptena mazamae*.

She pulled out the drawer. Inside were rows of glass shell vials, the caps labeled with various dates going back more than a decade. The older writing faded.

Her finger moved to the newest lettering, forming that year's date.

So many choices.

The last date recorded, Hunter noticed, was none other than the day before murder number one—Steve Daigle. No other dates followed.

A total of three vials were recorded from that day in particular.

Hunter plucked one of the cylinders from the row and held it up to the light. The wingless flies dotting the bottom of the vial, swaying in what she knew was ethanol.

Then she closed the drawer before pushing the vial down into the small watch pocket at the front of her jeans.

She had an idea, but the flies weren't it.

42

IT WAS DAY ONE of the three-day event. The one-off chance for Mitch to bait his prospective students and show them why they would be mad to consider any other lab for their graduate programming. Feed them exactly what they wanted to hear: if they joined up, they got a TA salary of $21K a year; full access to his wife's advisement—after his own mentorship, of course—and the opportunity to have a letter of rec from the one and only Dr. Mitch Olivier upon graduating. Terms and conditions applied.

The offer was nothing more than pure fame among the flock, as far as Mitch was concerned. The department called it recruitment day. But the professor called it divine opportunity—for the potential recruits, that was.

The two girls sat across from the couple at the conference table like they had just seen Medusa herself, frozen in a naïve fear of the unknown. Two recruits, seemingly hopeful at the chance to add their own stone to the academic pyramid. Eager to drink the punch.

Mitch was willing to take full advantage of the fact that they had no idea what they were signing up for. After all, some of the tenured members themselves were oblivious to how the academy *really* worked.

The goal was cheap labor that would drive the construction of his monumental image. For the grad students, it was a privilege to carve the stones and inch them to the top, one laborious heave at a time.

The foundation: undergrad. Level one—grad school.

"So, we start in August, right?" one girl said. Mitch could tell she was the overachieving type. The one who sat in the front row, hoping she had what it took to answer the next question. The one who sought out extra work to prep for the exam. The kid who was too busy reading to dress appropriately for an interview.

Her blanched, bird's-nest hair and red-hot eyes told Mitch that she was about a 9.5 on the insomnia scale. She had every reason to be nervous. She was sitting in front of the judge, jury, and executioner of her academic future.

And Mitch ate it up.

"Well, this is more of an interview than anything else," he said. "It's really for y'all to get a feel for the department and for us to get to know you. See if we're a good fit for one another."

The girl's eyes adopted the primary Texan attribute. "Oh. Okay." Her posture slipped.

"But Dr. Olivier invited y'all here because he thinks you're the best candidates for the department," Aura added. She gave Mitch a sideways glance.

"Sorry, but I'm a bit confused," the other girl chimed in. "Would we be in *your* lab?" She pointed to Mitch.

"Yeah, well, it can be a bit confusing," Mitch said. "You have options. Most people who join either of our labs end up being co-advised by both of us. But who you end up asking to be on your graduate committee is ultimately up to you. Although, we'll give you our suggestions based on who we think would be a good fit for your research."

The second girl was a bit more together. Her hair flowed over her shoulders, as straight as could be. Her eyes were pure white and innocent.

Mitch rated her low on the no-sleep scale but just as anxious as the other applicant. Her fidgeting feet and inability to stop blinking were making him itch on the inside.

"Since we work so closely with one another," Aura said, "you'll have access to all of the same resources, regardless of whose lab you join."

Like hell was she going to poach one of his prospects. Or two, for that matter.

"Well"—Mitch looked to his wife—"y'all are here because you're interested in joining *my* lab. I think what Dr. Theriot is trying to say is that she's here to help, should you choose to join my lab group."

"As chair," Aura said, turning to the girls, "I'm here to tell you that recruitment day is all about getting to know the professors in the department and seeing who's the right fit. You may be here to interview with Dr. Olivier's lab, but that doesn't mean you can't dip your toes in the water elsewhere." She gave them a wink. "As a matter of fact," she continued, "we have a lab rotation program for that exact reason."

"Of course," Mitch said to the applicants. "But like we've already discussed, y'all are looking to join a lab that's active with outreach opportunities. Our labs, and my lab in particular, are always involved in outreach programs. So if that's what you're looking for . . ." He held out his hands, palms up.

The couple had an agreement, and Aura suggesting that his recruits could join either of their labs wasn't it. In Mitch's mind, the logic was simple: he takes on more female grad students, current students are listed on the grant, NSF is all about diversity. So . . . Mitch gets funding to bring in more lab members, female students beget female students. He gets famous, rules the academy.

Simple.

But his wife, apparently, was taking full advantage of church and state. And Mitch was being reminded that Aura had a leg up as department chair and full professor. It was every faculty member for themselves, and time to hit eject.

"Well, it's gonna be a long day. Why don't we talk some more on the move. Let's give y'all a tour of the lab, shall we?"

Mitch stood up and gestured to the door.

"Oh, that's exciting. Y'all share a lab space?" said the tired one.

"Not exactly," Mitch said. "Some of our students work together, but we still have our separate labs. I'm sure Dr. Theriot is willing to show you around hers when we're done."

As they walked out of the room, Aura began to reassure them that she would be around.

"Let me know when y'all get done, and I can—"

But her husband drew a grand divide between them, as he pulled the door shut.

• • •

"So, this is where the magic happens," Mitch said as he opened his lab door. "It isn't much to look at, but it gets the job done."

He pointed to a set of benches off to the side. "We have some workspace over here. Plenty enough for the two of you. Offices are in back." Then he pointed to a room off to the other side. "Inventory is over there." Then to another door at the opposite end of the room. "And the specimen catalog is this way."

He opened the only closed door in the lab, a sign reading *PI Only*, laminated and duct-taped to the door. After entering the room, he pulled a frayed white string that hung from the ceiling.

"Oh wow," the orderly girl said as the lights flickered on. "Organized. I like it."

"I don't show this room to everyone, but I have a good feeling about y'all joining the group."

The truth was, he did show the room to everyone. He got off on it. It was his life's work, his magnum opus. Whether anyone else understood its glory was completely irrelevant.

"Any parasite found in or on the cervid family is in this room." He turned to one of the cases and pulled out a drawer. "Bot flies." Then he pushed it back in and moved to another, tapping the label. "Hard ticks."

Then he pulled out a drawer that was twice the size of all the others. "And perhaps the most noteworthy of all—hippoboscids."

The girls moved in closer, stretching their necks to see the collection.

Mitch ran his hand down the rows of vials. An arousing twinge snaked its way down the center of his back.

"This is everything we've ever worked on, dating back to your grade school days. If it's in one of our publications, it's here," he said. "Including our most rec—"

His finger stopped.

The girls looked to one another.

"What is it?" the disheveled one asked.

"You okay?" the other added.

Mitch looked over, his finger still in the drawer. "I'm not sure."

43

DRAKE WAS HUNGRY. AND so was she.

Hunter grabbed a bowl from the corner cabinet and filled it to the brim with Drake's Os. A small splash of milk hardly disturbed the mountainous wheats. To no surprise, the pup barked in clear objection at the violation of his personal stash.

"Oh, calm down," she said. "I'm the one who had to deal with the crazy lady at the checkout who thinks I'm an addict, and I'm the one who paid for it. So they're mine, too."

Drake circled his tail and let out a frustrated growl.

"Yeah, yeah. You're next."

She walked over to his bowl and poured the snack in a three-foot cascade from above, some of the circles dinging from the dish and rolling across the floor.

"There. Happy? I'll be up top," she said, pointing to the roof. She grabbed some paperwork and her laptop from the counter and began walking up the claustrophobic staircase that led to the rooftop patio, but Drake started barking before he ever touched his food. "I love you too, big guy." She continued up the creaky staircase.

Lunch usually consisted of a scheduled nap with Drake or, at the very least, a good book. But today, Hunter was eager to get the ball rolling on what she had snatched up from Mitch's lab. It had been almost too easy, though—too come-and-get-it.

The killer had left a convenient present at the scene of the Guidry murder, and it just so happened to point straight to her suspicions? To the vials stocked to the ceiling in the professor's lab?

Maybe.

Either way, ruling out the possible led to the probable.

Hunter had decided to work from home for the rest of the day. Her at-home office was not only more convenient than trekking into the city, but it was away from everyone and everything distracting—something she was learning to hold closer to her heart as the years went on.

She opened the hatch at the top of the stairway and let the door fall to the roof before walking out into her own little piece of heaven. The rooftop was paradise itself, as far as she was concerned. A slice of beauty, galaxies removed from the earthly world below.

A lawn chair and end table filled the space, along with the endless array of plants that circled the rooftop patio. It was a continuation of the garden sprawled across the deck below. A slice of happy. Contentment, even. It was the place that held Hunter's soul—and somewhere no one could touch.

She dropped the papers onto the hand-painted blue table and sat back in the chair, looking up to the cloudy, late-afternoon sky. The peach fabric skipped across the atmosphere like buttercream over the softest of cakey layers, spreading in a consistent pattern until it was lost to the distant horizon over the world's edge.

In the moment, it was all she needed.

Hunter had always found solace in being alone. Relationships were one thing, but she valued her isolation and sought it out on a regular basis. From a young age, she'd been a self-induced loner, choosing books and sunsets over Friday-night lights and ballgames. The drama and drinking had always faded, other than the hangovers. But the stories stuck around in the background of daily life, especially when absorbed over a good falling sun.

She could hear Drake clawing his way up the stairs before he burst onto the rooftop with a satisfied, slobbery grin—almost a leer—that told her he was full. He wasted no time trotting over to her and nudging her leg, the cold wetness from his nose smearing across her calf.

"Cut it out," Hunter demanded, but he kept pushing.

"Just chill, dude." She pointed to the view. "Take it all in. Relax, why don't you."

But Drake insisted. He nudged and nudged until his twitching tail knocked her paperwork from the table beside her.

"See. Now look at what your insistent, cute face has done."

As she bent over to pick up the mess, she realized that she had grabbed the mail from the counter by accident—her subscriptions included.

Hunter paused, glaring at the pile. Then she looked to Drake and his puppy dog eyes. He let out an anticipatory grunt and wobbled to her, licking her cheek.

She pushed aside some of the mail, and there it was, all rushing back. The corner of the *M* in a font she recognized all too well.

He nudged her yet again.

"What if I don't want to?" she asked.

He only whimpered.

She picked up the magazine and flipped to the inside page—to the Updates section. Then she ran her finger down the list of columns.

Page thirty-two . . . Trouble in the Academy.

Hunter turned to the back, her fingers slipping between the sheets of paper. Creasing the edges.

She scanned the article, unable to start from the beginning. There were no photos this time. Only words.

The article was two pages, not much compared to the original. Maybe the first story was a one-time deal. A one-off leak that she could put behind her, tuck away in the off-limits region in the corners of her subconscious. Suspects weren't really her thing, anyway. At least that was what it said on paper.

Or were they?

"Alright, boy. I guess we're doing this," she said with a shaky intonation.

As she read the story, it seemed harmless enough—a bit about UNO, some words on Bryan Guidry's background and his work as dean of the College of Sciences, a general description of the scene. Not nearly as detailed as the previous write-up. But then came the last paragraph.

Parasitic flies . . . a possible calling card.

She slapped the magazine shut and tossed it onto the deck. "Well that's enough of that." She spoke to Drake, but really to her own worries more than anything.

Hunter looked out at the skyline, running her options through her head, double-checking that she wasn't crazy. That she wasn't overreacting to something that wasn't a problem in the first place.

Then she turned back to her pup.

"Do I have to?"

He barked an "of course" that she simply could not ignore.

"Wait here," she said.

Hunter ran back down, inside the home, and pulled the small hand safe from above the fridge. She opened it and removed the glass vial before jogging back out to the rooftop.

She patted the dog's head and flipped open her computer.

"You're always so supportive, you know that?"

After a quick search of Electron Microscopy Sciences' website—a vendor she'd used while in grad school—she found what she was looking for. Glass shell vials came in every shape and size imaginable. A million different iterations in design: screw cap, pop top, black cap, white cap, clear, amber, 2-ml, 8-ml. The options were absurd. But one thing was for sure—any scientist who did microscopy work, who was worth their salt, used EMS for their supplies.

Nothing was certain, but ruling out Mitch Olivier was a start. And if the suspect really did have the nerve to start a catch-me-if-you-can game with investigators, they should be fair in their use of clues. They should use hints that could lead law enforcement directly to them, should the law be bright enough to put two and two together.

She unscrewed the cap and looked at what information was etched into the bottom of the black plastic. *EMS – 4 ml – #60992-04.*

It was all she needed.

Hunter didn't want to call him—she had to. She pulled her phone from her pocket and hit the dial button. Three rings was far too grueling of a wait.

"Hello?" David answered.

"Hey, how's it going?"

She held the vial up to the sky, watching the flies wash back and forth in the clear fluid. A small rainbow reflected from the glass, bouncing in and out of existence as she rotated the cylinder.

"Oh, it's going. It's good to hear from you. What's up?"

"You have access to what was collected from the Guidry murder? I think I might need a favor."

44

ROBERT PREPPED HIS MICROSCOPY samples in the microtome room—a dungeon of a space in the basement of the science building that was cramped, dark, and desperately humid.

It was ground zero in the war of the academy and college sports. Orangish cabinets harbored chemical solutions that were nearly seventy years old, a white crust foaming from the caps. The faucets and drains of the sinks below were rusted and stained with only god knew what. Peach paint peeled from the walls and fell to even peacher floors, sparsely illuminated by weak amber lighting that flickered more often than not, like a fire slowly scorching the walls.

The room was an enigma—no one knew who was really in charge of it, and no one asked, so the chemical catalogue was never touched. Janitors only paid attention to the trash if it was put out in the hallway, and keys were passed down from one occupant to the next. A complete one-eighty from how Robert organized and cared for his lab space above.

No one made a fuss, and no one was the wiser.

Robert had heard that only a handful of faculty knew where the room was located. Take a left through the main door of the basement, go through the third door on the right, which was an old faculty break room that nobody used, and it was through another door at the back corner of the lounge. Hidden away along with the festering mold problem that had become a worse health hazard than the outdated chemicals.

He was surprised to learn over the years that, according to the time log, he was one of only three people who used the room, including two professors in chemistry who hardly stepped foot on campus.

He was supposed to meet Kole down there to mull over ideas for data collection while Robert helped with the sample prep for one of their co-authored projects. But so far, Robert was alone.

Signing his name on the log sheet, he lifted the clear plastic cover from the pristine machine. It was a thing of beauty, really. A twenty-thousand-dollar piece of equipment sitting in a pure shithole. A diamond in the dust. And another mystery for another day.

Robert found it fascinating—what an ultramicrotome could do. To say it cut tissue would have been an understatement. He was helping Kole prep their copepod samples for microscopy work, which meant cutting the preserved specimens thin enough for the transmission electron microscope to image.

The width of a human hair? Eighty-five thousand nanometers. The width of tissue sections cut by the diamond knife of the ultramicrotome? Eighty nanometers. At least that was the sweet spot for the microscope.

He removed the thumbnail diamond knife from the instrument box next to the machine and locked it in place beneath the eyepieces for viewing. Rule one of using the microtome: always check that the three-thousand-dollar diamond knife wasn't chipped. His professorial wallet had learned that the hard way, after assuming one of the microtome's previous users had been responsible and honest.

The door flung open, hitting the counter behind it.

"Jesus," Robert said with a jolt, tripping over his own feet. "A heads-up would be nice."

Kole froze, looking at him with uncertain and apologetic eyes. They moved to the knife. "Well it's only, what, two or three thousand dollars?"

"It's a budget I ain't got—that's what." Robert pointed to a second chair behind the microtome. "Take a seat."

Kole sat down in one of the two rolling chairs.

"So what's your sample size on the project?" Robert asked. "You remember how long it takes to cut a single sample, right?" He spoke in a forewarning tone.

"Yeah. Too long. I'm shooting for five copepods per group, five cells per individual. Although, with the way my current schedule is, teaching over at UNO a couple days a week, it might take me a little longer than I had planned."

Robert grabbed one of the golden resin samples from the petri dish and screwed it into place above the diamond blade. "How's it going over there, by the way?" Then he filled the minuscule trough with water to catch the sections of tissue as they were cut. The tension of the liquid caused the water to bow, creating a silvery sheen across the surface, reflecting the blade at its edge.

"Eh, it's alright I guess. The teaching is going great, but the department seems to be more concerned with outreach and DEI work than they are research. Or teaching. But it's just a stepping stone to something bigger and better, really."

The professor could sense that Kole was at a crossroad. Scientists had a job to do, and the job involved the dissemination of their work to the greater community—and recruiting members of the community to careers in STEM. But the problem for Kole, he sensed, was that the academy was no longer making the science a priority. That, he could sympathize with.

Robert felt his face forming a sarcastic grin.

"What?" Kole asked.

"Nothing."

"What? I can take it."

He considered what he was about to say before making it a thing, but he decided in favor of making the point clear. "Like I said before, you know you're gonna have to play the identity politics game if you're gonna get a job as a professor in academia, right?"

"Play the game?"

"Yeah. DEI work comes with the territory. I mean, look at me. I'm not the biggest fan, but I do what I have to in order to get the funding. It's a game you're gonna have to be willing to play."

Robert finished adjusting the sample and started the machine—one gradual drop of the sample at a time as the holder advanced toward the blade, cut by cut. Increments so incomprehensible, they were undetectable to the naked eye.

"And what if I'm not willing to play? It's a rigged sport for people like us, aye."

"No one said anything about the match not being rigged." The professor lifted the edge of his mouth. "Like a trout in bear country, academia is a cutthroat business."

45

ROBERT KNOCKED ON THE sparkling glass door of the home. He could hear the pitter-patter of little feet scurrying across the floor from inside.

The towering door inched its way open, a tiny someone tugging at the other end.

"Hello," Angie said in a cute morning voice. Her yellow-white hair still staticky from what looked like a good night's sleep.

"Hey, you," said Robert. "Is your mommy home?"

She turned back to the inside of the house. "Mommy, someone's here!"

Meaux walked down the hallway, dressed in nothing more than a pair of not-much-covered black shorts and a white V-neck T-shirt. She sipped her coffee with two hands cupping the ceramic mug.

"Oh, hey Rob. What's up?"

"Sorry to stop by unannounced, but I just wanted to see how you were holding up. If maybe you need anything."

"Yeah, come on in."

They walked through the living room and into the massive kitchen, where Steve's wife had set up shop. All of the man's belongings, personal and work related, were strewn across the dining room table and floor.

"Can I get you anything? Some water? Coffee?"

"Oh, I'm good. Thanks, though." Robert nodded to the pile of effects. "What's going on here?"

She poured herself another cup from the beeping pot. A translucent steam coughed from the top of the vessel and fogged the wooden cabinets above.

"You know—just going through what I can. The longer it sits around, the harder it's gonna get. I figured I might as well get started sooner rather than later." Meaux turned around and leaned back against the counter. "Ever since the funeral, I just can't keep still."

He let out a sympathetic huff. "Uh-huh."

His eyes moved across the room, from the mountains of paperwork and bills on the table to the stacks of books and clothing on the hardwood floors.

"I know how it looks." Her voice was defensive.

Robert scrunched his chin. "No, no. I don't think it looks any kind of way. Other than a wife who just lost her husband, trying to sort things out. Like you said, it's gotta get done sooner or later."

They stood in silence for a moment, Angie playing in the background.

"Can I ask you something?" Meaux said, looking down to the floor.

"Of course."

She paused for a prolonged moment. "Did anything happen leading up to this? I mean, I know I'm his wife and all. Hell, we lived together. Had a kid together. But he was also really close to you. Y'all hunted nearly every weekend for months on end, even spent time together outside of hunting season, and had worked together in the past. Was there anything . . . weird going on with him that maybe I didn't pick up on?"

Robert wasn't sure how to respond. It was a question he'd known he'd be asked sooner or later, but his forethought didn't make the ask any easier. The problem was this: Steve had been an academic pariah. He spoke his mind when others wouldn't. He kept his head down but wasn't afraid to stand up against his peers when he needed to. Many of Steve's colleagues spoke poorly of his no-bullshit approach to science and mentorship, putting his productivity and students before his own reputation, or that of the college. So it was no surprise that he had enemies—professional, at least.

It seemed best to tread lightly.

"I can't say that there was," Robert said. "He was chair of the department, so he was working nonstop, putting out fires and trying to balance his research and students with everything that came along with the title. But I can't say that it was anything out of the ordinary."

"Yeah, that's what I figured. It just doesn't make any sense. And what happened with Bryan Guidry makes it even worse. I mean, you'd think they'd be able to make some sort of connection by now, with both of them being from UNO, in the positions they were in. You think it'd be obvious, no?"

He tried his best to ease her worries. "Well, I'm sure they'll come up with something soon for that exact reason."

"And as far as I can see, the university is just going on like nothing ever happened. Classes, research. Everything. Just another day of business, you know. The wheel just keeps on turning."

Meaux's chin began to tremble as she flashed her eyes up to the ceiling, fighting the wave of saline Robert could see welling in the foreground. He stepped toward her and put his hand on her arm.

"Something'll come up," he said. "As painful as it is, these things take time. But you've got Angie to keep you company, yeah?"

Looking to the living room where her daughter lay on her back, singing along with a cartoon on the television, Meaux closed her eyes and bobbed her head in agreement. "Yeah. I do." And she pushed forth an expression of hope. Then she pulled a tissue from the box on the counter and blotted the black that had begun to trail down the side of her nose.

"Oh, before I forget." She turned to the dining room table. "I think this is yours. We found it out at the camp, a ways back behind the shed, off to the side of the trail." Opening a cardboard box, she rummaged inside. "Here." She handed it over.

"Yeah, Steve borrowed it a while ago." The memories came back like the sun over a morning frost, melting the ice so that it flowed freely yet again. "He used to tell me all the time that he was sure, he was positive, that there was a buck walking the trail back there. 'You should see the size of the damn tracks,' he used to say. 'It's like clockwork, every evening hunt, right at dusk. I'd see him right there along the wood line as I walked back from the food plot.' It was after shooting time, of course. I don't think he ever got the picture he was looking for."

"Well, I know he'd want you to have it back. Put it to good use."

Robert unlatched the cover and turned it on end, running his finger over the SIM card protruding from the side, clicking it out then back in.

"Thanks, Meaux. I appreciate it."

He closed it and snapped the latch back into place, then wrapped the bungie cord around the camera.

Meaux pointed to another box on the floor. "I collected his

paperwork from the university, too. I know y'all had collaborated from time to time, so I think you'd get more out of it than anyone else. It's yours if you want it."

"Yeah. I'd hate to see it thrown out."

46

HUNTER FLOUNDERED AROUND THE house, trying her best to keep busy. But the phone followed her around like a bad daydream, staring at her with its black, glassy screen.

Hunter had never cared for favors. They balanced relationships on unsteady ground—one person waiting for the other to come through, then the first person has to figure out a way to repay the favor, even though the second person insists that it's fine.

It was never fine.

Several hours had passed since she had spoken to David, but he was known for his catlike work ethic—lazy by appearance, but he got it done when the time came to chase down a lead on the open plains of the Crescent City. Homicide didn't mess around.

She grabbed her interrogation book from the counter, then called Drake over to the couch. As she split the pages and removed the dried magnolia petal that served as her bookmark, the oaky, wooded trace of freshly cut paper massaged her senses. Dropped her shoulders a little. For Hunter, nothing else compared to the smell of a fresh paperback. She pulled the book to her lips and closed her eyes, drawing a deep breath. The tip of her nose touched the inside margin.

Her body fell limp as she descended down into the cushions, and she let out a subdued moan that carried with it the day's worries.

Drake barked. Hunter's heart skipped a beat as she looked to the porch—the outline of a man at the storm door, unmoving with his hands at his side.

Then a knock.

A knock? How long had he been standing there?

She sprang to her feet and immediately stumbled over Drake but managed to catch herself on the arm of the sofa.

More knocking.

"Yeah, I hear ya. I'm coming, I'm coming."

Hunter regained her footing, waving her hands in front of her. "Come on. Move, move, move." She shooed Drake away and into the few feet of kitchen.

She flicked on the porch light, only to see David outside, waving a hand in greeting.

"Oh, shit. Sorry." She opened the door. "I thought you were gonna call."

He stepped inside and greeted Drake with the usual head rubs. "So, I took the information that you gave me, and—"

"Is it a match?"

Hunter was doubly surprised. One, she'd been expecting a phone call. Not a visit. Two, his sudden arrival had opened the floodgates. All of the pleasure-laden memories flooding back. The thing between them had never been labeled. It was never a full-fledged relationship, per se. But damn, did it feel good. And for whatever reason, his unexpected arrival brought it all back. The way his arms filled out the sleeves of his shirt just right, accentuating the vein running down the center of his bicep. The way his scruff blended perfectly against his throat. His eyes, always managing to find a shimmer even in the darkest of shadows. All of it a slippery slope.

David cocked his head to the side and widened his eyes. "It looks like it."

"I knew it. I knew that I—"

"Don't get ahead of yourself. This doesn't prove anything. Tens of thousands of those vials are sold month after month. I passed it along to the rest of the team, and they're gonna look into the alcohol dilutions and see if there's any similarities. Maybe see if they can match the supplier. The only problem, and I'm guessing here, is that you didn't exactly get your hands on that the legitimate way."

Hunter leaned forward, her palms bracing against the counter. Arms locked out, straight. "I can work on it. Just give me a day or two, and I can tell you if they're a match. We can even run DNA on the flies and see if they're—"

"Hey, we got it," David said in a reassuring voice. He reached out and grabbed her finger with his. "They'll figure it out. You forget that we have our own department as well. We'll handle it. You focus on what y'all already have, and we'll take care of the rest."

He stepped toward her, closing the distance.

There was something about the raw, nature-burdened scent that he had always carried around with him. Not even a cologne, she suspected. Just . . . him. The last time she had breathed it in was still fresh in her mind, her eyes closed, head buried face down in the pillow of his king-size bed. Their bodies slick from the heated night between them.

Hunter looked to the pile of paperwork on the counter. "You keep up with any of the big crime journals at all? Any of the national magazines?"

She walked over and picked up the last two issues of *MurderoUS Weekly*.

"No. Why?"

Hunter dropped them onto the counter in front of him. The high-pitched slap caused Drake to bow down and brace himself, preparing to pounce.

David leaned over, his forearms resting on the countertop. He thumbed his way through the articles.

She continued. "Because there's only so many people involved with these investigations who have access to the photos in those articles."

"What articles?"

"The ones I have dogeared, David. Those look familiar?"

His eyes looked up and met hers as he turned to the first story.

"You recognize those? Homicide's pictures? The pictures that *you* took at the scene?"

He grabbed the second issue and turned to the start of the column, marked by the bent corner of the page. Then he shook his head and tossed the title aside.

"I don't see what you're getting at, Hunter. Sure, I took the photos, but I'm not the only one who has access to them. Hell, you have the photos, too—and everyone in both of our departments."

"Wow. You sound like Parker, you know that? It's all just one big coincidence that no one needs to look into. Isn't it?"

David's head hung down low, his gaze refusing to leave the counter. Hunter could see his mind working through the glint of his stare. The gears turning. But it wasn't clear if he was fumbling for an excuse or trying to think of a legitimate explanation for how the pictures could have slipped through the cracks.

"Someone needs to start coming up with some answers, because privileged pieces of evidence and crime scene photographs don't just up and hit the streets by accident."

He stood up, folding his arms. Then he leaned against the counter and looked over to Drake as the dog rolled onto his side, his hopeful tail doing its usual song and dance.

"Nothing? No response?" Hunter spoke with a bit of a whip in her voice. The inside of her cheek was turning raw from her incessant chewing, from the nerves—a result of dreading the very conversation in which she found herself.

"Deborah approached me."

Hunter threw up her hands. "Oh. So that's where this is going? You're just gonna change the topic and shift all the blame over to someone else? She's an easy scapegoat right about now, isn't she?"

"I'm not scapegoating anyone, Hunter. She came to me looking for information on the second murder."

"When? *Where?*"

"A couple days ago."

"And you're just now telling me this? Really?"

"Hell, Hunter. I didn't know if I should tell you at all. I'm sure the last thing you want is me, of all people, running to you with dirt on Deborah. Of all people."

"Okay. But Deborah asking you for information isn't a complete surprise. Is it? I mean, she's a reporter. They snoop. Besides, how in the world does that link her to these?" She picked up the magazines and dropped them back onto the counter.

"It wasn't just snooping, Hunter. She was pushing to get more out of me than I could've given her."

They stood in silence, mulling it over. Hunter wasn't sure what to believe. And it was the exact reason that she regretted favors. Now, she wasn't convinced one way or the other if David was telling the truth or if he was using Deborah as a pawn to work his way back into her personal life. What had been meant as a simple ask had turned into a hailstorm of emotions—an ex, and an almost ex but more of "thing." Careers on the line. Stories that didn't add up.

"I'm not saying that it links her to the articles for sure," David said, "but you and I both know that she hardly ever comes to me for anything, much less a story. Not to mention, if she was working on one, where's it at?"

"Maybe you should leave," she said.

"Leave? Hunter, I'm trying to help you. I took what you gave me, and I'm using it." He walked over to her and leaned against the counter, grabbing her hand and interlacing his fingers with hers. Dragging the tip of his thumb across her palm, down the center of her weakness.

She fought it tooth and nail, but to no avail.

Then, a smile. He spoke warmly. "I was waiting to tell you because I didn't wanna hurt you. I think you've had enough of that lately. Don't you?"

He ran his lips across the top of her hand. The edge of his mustache pricked her skin, but in a begging, needing-to-be-touched kind of way.

"David—"

He looked up at her, but she said no more. She didn't need to.

Hunter felt his hand slip into her hair, grabbing the back of her skull. Pulling her in. A kiss that was anything but gentle. Not a subtle suggestion, no—it was everything she needed. And she knew that, in the moment, he had her right where she wanted to be.

David grabbed her waist and pulled her in, pushing himself onto her and moving her back at the same time, against the counter's edge. Then she returned the favor. Thrusting him backward into the wall. A canvas print of the lakeshore falling to the floor.

His hands slid from her hips down to the tops of her thighs, picking her up with no effort at all.

She hit the light switch as they passed the door. David carried her to the couch, where he laid her down on her back. Her legs wrapped around him, her ankles interlocked.

He sat up and removed his shirt from the bottom up, his arms crossed, her hand running down the center of his chest.

Then he paused, if only for the briefest of moments. "Wait." He grabbed her wrist. "Are you sure?"

Hunter sat up and held her arms above her head. Attempting to rationalize it would only ruin what she had already decided. It was going to happen, one way or another.

"No," she said. "I'm not."

He lifted her shirt as she felt the warm air run across the small of her back. Her hair fell to her chest, brushing the edge of her nipples.

47

IT ATE AWAY AT him, piece by fleshy piece, from the inside out, any time he woke up before his wife. Waiting for her to spring back to life and return with his breakfast. He rolled over. Her eyes were just then beginning to twitch.

Mitch looked past her shoulder at the red numbers of the alarm clock—a quarter past seven.

Nearly half an hour he'd been waiting. Lying there. Staring at the faces his imagination had discovered in the popcorn of the ceiling. Some of them were familiar, some not.

"Morning," Aura slurred as she pried open her eyes, their color not yet visible under the shadow of the room. A small puddle of dribble lay on the pillow below the corner of her mouth. A strand of her fading cocoa hair traversed the bridge of her nose, snaking its way across her naked lips.

"Is it?" said Mitch. His blood began to boil, one irritated bubble at a time, as he checked the clock yet again.

His wife lifted her head and pulled her pillow in closer, bunching the misshapen ball of cotton into a tight sphere before dropping her head back down. Her eyes disappeared as she eased her lashes together.

"You been up long?" she mumbled, her voice fading back into oblivion.

Mitch grumbled. His restless leg rolled from side to side. "Long enough."

Aura opened her eyes once more, at a slothful pace. He could feel the heat throbbing, radiating from his forehead. His insides slowly turning a cooked crawfish red.

"Long enough?" she asked.

"Just listening to my stomach. That's all."

Mitch's time was far too valuable to sit around waiting. For anyone. When would she manage to drag herself out of bed? Get dressed? Do her million and one morning things that she needed to do before she could run for breakfast? None of it would get done with her head on the pillow—that, he was sure of.

"You need some help?" he asked.

"Help?"

"Getting up."

She was slow to respond. Slipping in and out of consciousness. "No."

He would have to wait another twenty minutes, at least, before she would return.

Aura rolled over and put her back toward him—the unspoken flag of the wife, fleeing from the conversation like the flashing white tail as the deer hopped off into the wood line. Spooked by the hunter's movement.

Every husband knew the feeling of the silent "fuck you"— like the white-tailed deer's snowy, departing message.

"So. How'd you sleep?" she asked, speaking in the direction of the alarm clock.

"Fine, I guess," Mitch said as he slung the comforter across the bed and swung his legs out to the side.

"What are you doing?" she asked.

He trudged to the bathroom and brought to life the blinding lights above the sink, the Edison bulbs cutting across the room like a blade, splitting the top half of the master suite from the bottom. The yellowy-white rays flooded every corner of the landscape that sat above the mattress. Aura rolled over and faced the other way, her head assaulting the pillow in nonverbal cues of frustration.

"Seriously, Mitch? It's too early." She spoke while kneading the pillow, failing to adjust it just right.

"Is it?"

"Where are you going?" Her voice was more awake now.

He ran the water and soaked a face rag until it was scorching hot, then wiped his face clean of the nightly sweat.

"Going to get breakfast, I suppose. It doesn't look like you're getting up anytime soon."

His wife sat up, bracing herself with locked arms.

"What's up? You seem a bit off," she said.

Mitch walked out from the bathroom, his hair slick, a fresh shirt on. "I'm just hungry. That's all."

"Hey," she said. She paused, looking down, fumbling for the next word. "Do, uh—do you . . . never mind."

"What?"

Aura dropped herself back onto the linens, an airy bubble flowing beneath the sheet, escaping at its corner as if it had never existed.

"Nothing. Can you get me my usual?"

Mitch sat on the edge of the bed, his hands folded. "What is it, Aura?" he said in a monotone type of speech. "I know it isn't nothing. What's wrong?"

She stumbled over her words a bit more before arriving at a complete sentence. It was clear to Mitch that she was struggling to come out with it. Something that would lead to nothing more than a disagreement. She wasn't good with words like he was. Most people he had met didn't come close to having his way with the English language. A good scientist, an academic above all else, should be careful in their speech. Precise in their language.

"Why—why didn't you tell me that Paul lives next door to Steve's camp?"

He could feel the warmth deepen, working its way through the corners of his empty gut.

"I thought you knew. You've been over to Paul's several times. I mean, it's . . . Steve's place is—Steve's camp isn't exactly right next door. There's quite a bit of woods that separate their properties."

The question had seemingly appeared from thin air. A T-bone at fifty miles an hour, dead center of the massive, four-way intersection of Hangry Street and What the Actual Fuck Boulevard.

"Well, have you talked to Paul?" she said.

"About what?"

"About the fact that he lives next door to a murder, Mitch. The murder of someone you knew. Your *boss*."

He jumped up from the mattress and slipped on his shoes at the foot of the bed. "No, Aura. I haven't. Living next door to someone doesn't make you an accessory to murder. Or guilty, for that matter."

"Calm down, okay? I'm not saying anything like that. I just wish you would've told me, is all."

"Well, now you know."

She continued staring a hole straight through him, her glare thick with something more to be said.

"What, Aura?" Mitch asked while picking up his keys from the nightstand.

His wife scrunched her brow, a bottomless crease appearing across the center of her forehead. Then she pursed her lips, forming the start of a word that had yet to escape her mouth.

"What?" he repeated.

"Have the police talked to you yet?"

Mitch shoved his keys deep into his pants, followed by his phone in the other pocket.

"And why would they do that?"

Aura pulled the sheets up to her chin.

"Isn't that the weekend you were out there? At your brother's?"

48

THE LAB WAS BRIGHT—almost too much so. But Hunter didn't mind, not that morning.

She walked through the room and unlocked her office before tossing her bag onto the chair and propping open her laptop. Unlike the lab, this space needed some visibility—something other than the tabletop lamp. She revived the ceiling lights, and they flooded the room with the purest of white. Her giddiness in plain view, on her sleeve for the world to see.

"Well hey now," she heard from across the lab. Parker's voice echoed throughout the room, reaching her office across the way with a resounding tenor. "It looks like someone decided to forego the darkness this morning, huh?"

Hunter felt the autonomic pull of her cheeks as they tugged at the corners of her lips, the winged flutters dancing at the top of her stomach from the night's memories.

"Oh yeah," she said. "I think it's time for some light in here."

Parker leaned against the inside of her office doorway, his arms interwoven.

"Come on," he continued in a prodding voice, "what is it? I can see it smeared all over your face like a kid caught in the fridge at 3 a.m." He drew a circle around his own expression with a single finger. "Let me guess—you . . . grabbed breakfast on your way in? You got beignets, didn't you? Extra powder?"

She ran her hands down her figure, from her ribs to her legs. "Really, Parker? Fried dough? With this body?"

"Nope. Nope." He waved his hands. "That's not it. You . . . found some money on the sidewalk and decided to share it with your newest friend." He bounced his eyebrows in a suggestive manner.

She gave him an "oh please" look, accentuated by a sardonic scowl, hand on her hip.

"Okay, okay." He nodded with a smirk, like he was finally going to get it right this time. As if he knew Hunter as anything more than a new employee. "I got it. I got it. You've decided that Sundays are for—"

"Whoa, whoa, whoa," Hunter said, throwing up her hands in surrender, "let's not get crazy with the conspiracy theories."

Parker stepped farther into the room. "Wait a second." He narrowed his eyes to two pinpoints, looking her up and down, left to right, front and back. Then he inched even closer. "You were sinful with a special someone last night. Weren't you?"

Hunter could feel the blood rush to her dimples faster than a crab dropped into the pot at a full, rolling boil. She stepped back and turned to her computer.

Parker let out a slow, crawling whistle. "Well, well, well. I'm happy for you," he said. "I mean, I can't say that I approve morally or anything. That's a little above my pay grade. But, you know, I'm glad. Speaking of happy," he continued, "I heard that Homicide has a lead they're looking into. They think it might be the key to a suspect they've been lookin' at."

Suddenly, the butterflies—flapping and gliding at the top of Hunter's gut, fluttering in circles, giving her all the warm fuzzies of something fresh, dipping and diving in the springtime sun, floating from flower to blooming flower—hit the floor, their wings crushed beneath the weight of uncertainty.

"A suspect? What suspect?"

"No clue," Parker said. "They didn't say. All I know is that they stumbled across something that they think is worth pursuing. But they can't risk it, so they're keeping it quiet for the time being."

"Well, is there anything we can do?"

"Not really. Like I said before, our job is primarily cause and manner of death. Anything else, we pass along to Homicide."

Maybe she did do it right. Maybe calling in David was the best thing she could've done. Leaving Parker out of the loop might not have been the best call, but hey—the information was with Homicide, and that was all that mattered. But was that really it? Was the vial that important? Or did they have something else?

"What about the coroner?" Hunter said.

"They need to be kept up to date too, but it all goes back to Homicide either way."

"Can you keep me in the loop?" she asked. "Let me know what the lead is, or whether or not anything comes of it. That is, if you find out?"

An urge to know more, to be on the front line of the investigation itself, pushed Hunter forward, nudging her in the direction of something more than mere lab work. She couldn't place it—the need to prioritize what was supposed to be the concern of the Homicide department. But whatever it was, she craved more.

"Yeah," Parker said, "I'll let you know. And uh, be sure to give Deborah my best, will you?" He winked a congratulatory eye.

"Deborah?" She spoke the name as more of a suggestion

than a question.

"Oh. So . . . not Deborah?"

Her dimples grew deeper. "I never said anything about Deborah. Did I?"

"Nice," Parker said. "Don't worry, though." He grabbed the handle and began easing the door shut. "Supplemental material."

He pulled his thumb and index finger across his lips.

part three

A THOUSAND CITATIONS

49

NICKELBACK'S "WOKE UP THIS Morning" blared from the radio as Mitch barreled down the highway with breakfast in the passenger seat. The windows were down, air shearing its way through the cab of the truck. Aura's avocado toast and his double-smoked bacon sandwich bounced with each flaw in the road. Their coffees splashed in the cupholders of the center console as Mitch's gut crawled with contempt for the early-morning run.

It was one thing for Aura to throw her weight around at the university. To act like the interim chair that she was. Pushing him to his limits, testing his qualities as a tenured faculty member who hoped to one day climb the pyramid to full professor. But pulling that shit at home wouldn't fly.

He couldn't let it.

There was a reason he had banned discussing work in the house, and it wasn't so that his wife could treat him like an employee.

Mitch spun the volume knob on the radio, launching the music into a deafening register. Then he eased the gas pedal nearer to the floorboard, driving as if the speed limit were nothing more than a trying distraction, an afterthought not applicable to hardened husbands.

It was time to hit the reset button. To reiterate the fact that their home was a place for husband and wife—roles with clear expectations that couldn't be muddled by academic titles.

Mitch hit the brakes, and the truck slid into the driveway, rocks flying from beneath the pickup and pelting the metal garage door. A plume of dust floated into the face of the home. He pushed open the truck door before snatching the soggy bag of food and dripping cups.

"I ain't got the patience for this crap," he said to himself. "Like I'm an undergrad or some shit."

He balanced the cups, one on top of the other, and held the bag between his teeth as he struggled to unlock the front door.

"Come on, man," he said with a mouth full of oily paper. The bag tasted of cardboard soaked in grease, submerged in a fryer that had failed its last several health inspections. Burnt chunks of flour floating to the surface. The occasional roach crawling along the edge of the basket, slipping into the oil but overlooked by the kitchen staff. He kicked open the door, but he didn't make it far before the bag fell from his teeth.

He attempted, out of habit perhaps, to set the coffees down on the foyer table, but his arms felt divorced from the rest of his body. Like he was looking down at his perfectly parted hair from above, stumbling head-first into a horror-ridden daydream from which he could not escape. A nightmare in which there was no hint as to what was reality and what was an illusion.

Mitch took a single step forward but froze once he realized it was too late, his foot slipping in a pool of his wife's blood. He threw up his hands in an attempt to back away from the situation. To deny what he couldn't manage to look away from.

Her body lay slumped over the back of the couch, a broken stream of red dripping from her throat into a puddle that was impossible to avoid. He stepped back, his hands bracing against the doorway, unaware of what he was doing. Of what was unfolding before him.

Then he felt it.

The stickiness across his palm. He looked down at his hands. His slick, radish fingers, gliding together. And the wall, painted in a cerise mist.

The last time his hands had felt that way was when he had field dressed his final kill of the season—a doe he had taken with his bow. But this was different. His wife's blood had a strange feel. It was a little more . . . viscous. He swirled the ends of his fingers together, his breathing shallow, rapid.

He looked back to the body. Back to the corpse his wife had once inhabited, now a lifeless shade of crème.

It didn't make any sense. He had just been here, talking to her in bed.

Mitch pulled his phone from his pocket and punched in his code on the screen, but his fingers did nothing more than slide across the glass. He entered the numbers a second time. Then a third. Pressing harder.

And that was when he heard them. The sirens.

The phone slipped from his grasp and landed in the doorway. He turned around to the front porch. One car sped into the grass of the manicured lawn, skidding to a stop. Then three more. Then five. The lights flooded the lawn in a wash of blinding flashes. He looked back over his shoulder as he put up his hands.

And there Mitch stood, his bloodied phone at his feet, dropped from his red-handed grip as he stood in front of his wife's body. It was draped over the sofa in his living room, her throat severed, still dripping onto the swirling marble floor below. All of it, framed in the doorway of his own home.

• • •

The back of the cop car was a hot box, and the tinted windows did little to mask the Louisiana sun, beaming into the back of the cruiser like a toaster oven, cooking Mitch's sanity one ticking, stifling second at a time.

All he could do was watch from the hard, unpadded seat, his hands cuffed behind his back, the steel digging into his wrists, pinching his skin against the bone, as they unrolled foot after foot of yellow tape across the front of his home. A bead of sweat rolled down his temple and past the outside corner of his eye, down his cheek. The itching was unbearable in the suffocating humidity of the car. He leaned his head down to his shoulder and wiped the saltiness.

Cops were scattering like ants, running from their cars to the house, and back to their cars. Pointing to the home, writing on their clipboards. Talking on the radio. In a split second, Mitch's life had been transformed into an absurd spectacle, and all he could do was watch.

But then, causing him to flinch in the seat, the same cop who'd arrested him opened the driver's door and rolled down Mitch's window. Another officer approached him, leaning against the top of the cruiser, peering in. His black sunglasses were as deep and dark as the nightmare that Mitch had yet to wrap his head around.

"You ain't gonna be here much longer," said the officer. "Is there anything else you wanna tell us before we bring you in?"

"Sure. You wanna tell me what the hell is going on?" said Mitch.

"Officer Briggs has already read you your rights. I think the rest is self-explanatory."

"This makes no fucking sense. Y'all have no idea what's going on, do you? No more than I do."

"Well, what we do know is that we received a phone call for a domestic disturbance. And, as luck would have it, it just so happened to be the same address that we were already headed to. I think that tells us quite a bit about what's going on."

"What the hell are you talking about, 'already headed to'? Who the hell called you?"

"Are you sure there isn't anything you wanna tell us? Maybe something about the letter your wife left on the kitchen counter? Or the luggage she has sitting by the door?"

Mitch looked behind the officer, to the front door of his home. Only then did he realize he hadn't even made it past the foyer, past his dead wife, before he was handcuffed and thrown into the back of the car.

"Look, I have no idea what you're talking about. I left home to go get breakfast, and when I came back, everything was exactly how you see it. I have *no idea* what the hell is going on."

"Uh-huh," the cop said, clearly not buying any of it. "And the fact that your hands are covered in her blood, her blood is on the bottom of your shoes, and she was packed up and ready to leave, a goodbye note and all, is just one big coincidence, right? And the phone call for a domestic disturbance, saying that y'all were screaming and fighting, is just a big misunderstanding. Yeah?"

Mitch clenched his jaw, hoping one of his teeth would shatter, distract him from the pain and uncertainty of it all.

"I want my lawyer."

The cop pushed off the cruiser, then adjusted his sunglasses at the bridge of his nose. "Yeah. I think that might be in your best interest."

The arresting officer got in the car, looking in the rearview mirror. His eyes were steeped in disgust. Mitch couldn't see the rest of the man's face, but from the eyes alone, he could envision his scowl.

Mitch's window began to crawl up until the outside air was stifled.

The officer outside his door slapped the roof of the vehicle. "Safe trip."

50

DEBORAH HAD RECEIVED WORD of someone's arrest only that morning—a professor from UNO.

In the past, she had learned that her best bet for landing an interview from someone at the station after an arrest—or at the very least, getting some sort of information on the case—was to bring gifts: coffee and diabetic food, in particular. But not the healthy, low-sugar, rubbery junk. What she needed was the snacks that led to *being* diabetic. The grainy, get-you-high, feel-the-sugar-between-your-teeth type of stuff.

She had never served on the law enforcement side of the equation, but she knew from experience, from covering enough cases late into the night, that no one in the precinct cared to slog through hours of interrogation or paperwork without the proper sustenance. And she knew for sure that stopping off at Randazzo's Bakery would do the trick. So she did.

When Deborah arrived at the Homicide department, she was quickly reminded of how frigid the building was. Her heels echoed across the marble floors of the massive lobby as she made her way to the four steely-doored elevators. She pressed the glowing arrow on the wall while balancing the drink carrier and bags of breakfast in her hands, her computer bag swaying at the edge of her shoulder.

"The things I do for a story," she said to herself, her arms burning under the weight of it all.

After a brief ride, she stepped out of the dangling box and onto the even colder, white tile of the Homicide unit. The first person she saw was David, and she locked eyes with him from across the room.

She held out the coffee and food as she walked toward him. "I come bearing gifts."

"Really? What are you gonna try to pull out of me this time? A rabbit?"

Deborah continued to extend the offering, the burn worsening. "Please. I'm not cut out for this type of manual labor."

He grabbed the carrier and bags from her hands. "What do you want, Deborah?"

"Actually, I'm looking for Hunter. I figured she might be hanging around, given y'all's recent development. You seen her at all?"

David looked down the hallway at Hunter leaning against the wall, talking to someone Deborah didn't recognize.

"Thanks," she said with a hint of reluctance.

"Hey." He stopped her before she had a chance to walk away. "Do me a favor and let everyone do their thing before you start digging. We just brought him in."

Deborah had already failed once to get David on her side, and she didn't feel the need to push him any further. Besides, she was turning over a new leaf, her ambitions to the wind. The last time they had spoken, she was pressing him for a story that she felt obligated to pursue. A career being dangled in front of her like a piece of meat, dripping with the scent of a new title and more money. Of national recognition. New faces and better cases. But more than anything, once the days had passed, she realized that pursuing a position with *MurderoUS Weekly* was nothing more than a distraction. A numbing mechanism. A way of avoiding what she needed to do, at one point or another. It was nothing more than a device to protect herself from the uncertainty of her relationship. And from her past, more than anything. That wasn't Hunter's fault—or anyone else's, for that matter.

"Of course," she said before walking down the hall.

The stranger walked away as Hunter looked at Deborah like she was in the wrong place. At the wrong time.

"Hey, you," Deborah said, trying her best to keep things light.

Hunter's eyes didn't leave the floor. "Hi," she said.

Deborah leaned against the wall next to her ex.

"So they finally brought someone in, huh?"

Hunter only nodded, then looked down the hallway toward the rest of the department, scattering across the floor like an army of busy leafcutters, working frantically for the greater good of the colony.

"Yeah. It appears so."

Deborah was, in some ways, used to the discomfort that was a necessary evil of her job. Interviewing victims and their family members, ex-cons who had gotten caught up in something new, the anger and restlessness of the people she needed information from. She had always found a way to the story through the thick and thin of the drama. But standing there with Hunter was different. It was 49 percent work, 51 percent personal—a jarring split of the tension between them.

"So, that's it?" Deborah said. "We can't have a conversation like normal people anymore?"

It was a painful question, considering she'd been the one to break it off. But she needed to get it out. Somehow, some way, she needed to make an effort to right what she had done wrong.

"Like normal people?" Hunter said. She pushed herself off of the wall and folded her arms, standing point-blank in front of Deborah, pupil to pupil. Then she spoke in a private but taut voice. "I don't exactly see what's so normal about leaking information on a murder investigation. Maybe you can explain it to me."

And the split shifted.

Deborah didn't know what to say, much less how to say it. She stood in silence, hoping Hunter would move the conversation forward. Hoping she'd somehow settle the tension that, if not broken, could devour either one of them.

Hunter just waited.

"Yeah. I fucked up, okay?" Deborah said. "I had a chance at something better, and I took it. But that's not why I'm here."

"It's a little late to be changing your mind, isn't it? What's done is done, Deborah. Don't you think?"

"Yeah, I know. Look, I'm just—" She lowered her voice as one of the detectives walked by. "I'm just here to cover the case for *Crescent Crimes*. I'm done with everything else."

"Why the change of heart? *MurderoUS Weekly* isn't exactly a no-name journal. And by the looks of it, they got some good coverage from what you gave them. Or, should I say, what you and *Parker* gave them."

A tidal wave of shame washed over Deborah as she felt the heat move across her cheeks. The feeling that she had not only let Hunter down, but dragged Parker into it as well. The feeling that she had let the idea of a career consume her, personally and professionally. From head to toe. It felt dirty, gritty, like she had sold her soul for something that hadn't panned out. A gamble she had lost out in the open, for everyone to see.

"They wanted more," Deborah said. "I gave them two

stories, and it wasn't enough. And I realized that it never would be."

"So . . . what? After all that, you think everything's just gonna go on like nothing ever happened? You put the entire case and other people's careers in jeopardy. And for what?"

"It wasn't for nothing, Hunter." Deborah's voice jumped up an octave. She looked around once more, struggling to keep the conversation private. "I realized that it isn't worth it. It isn't worth giving up what I've worked so hard to build here. What I've built with you."

She had hoped to see more of a reaction. What she got was next to nothing, an unmoving expression of a mind that was seemingly decided.

"Yeah, well, not everyone can go back at the flip of a switch. Besides, if all you're doing is running back to what's familiar because you have a guilty conscience and things aren't going your way, then—"

"I'm not asking you to do anything of the sort. I just . . . I don't know, Hunter. I mean, I'm here. I'm trying. Isn't that enough?"

Hunter's eyes shifted, only a hair's width, past Deborah to the rest of the unit.

"A few weeks ago, I would've said that it was," Hunter said.

"A few weeks ago? What do you mean 'a few weeks ago'? Hunter, if having doubts about our relationship because of my past is the problem—which, granted, is 100 percent my fault—then that's something that I'm willing to work on. I'm trying to move past it. Really."

"It has nothing to do with what you said, Deborah. Or the fact that we split up the way we did. Yeah, I don't agree with it, but that's not it. But it does have something to do with the way things have played out. And what you've done."

Deborah shrugged. "What, then?"

"If things worked out with *MurderoUS Weekly*, and they'd begged you to come on board after one story, would you be working for them right now?"

No response.

"If Parker hadn't slipped up, and if I hadn't put two and two together as a result, would you be standing here right now, telling me that you did what you did?"

"Hunter, I—"

"You not only leaked information on a murder investigation, but you put my job at risk by going behind my back. With my boss, of all people. If that doesn't show your intentions, then I don't know what does."

"Hunter, I'm trying to apologize and own up to what I did. Doesn't that count for anything?"

Deborah was trying. She couldn't think of any other way to put herself out there. To apologize without making it feel overdone. Like she was begging.

"So, you think that apologizing and owning up to it means that it's only a one-time thing? That it won't happen again?"

"Really? You're just gonna assume that this is me now? That it's gonna happen again?" Deborah looked down the hallway, tugging on her emotional reins, doing her best to keep her image professional. "I don't think that's a fair assessment at all."

"Okay. And you have every right to feel that way. You do. But let me ask you just one more question."

She looked deep into Hunter's eyes. Her ex's normally soft lichen-colored irises were swelling, swirling into ominous whirls, cloudy funnels.

Then Hunter continued. "What about your last relationship, then? Did you go around handing out second chances after you caught your man tongue-deep in his—"

"Don't even," Deborah said. "That isn't even close to what's happened between us."

Hunter nodded, looking past her ex yet again. This time, Deborah followed her gaze, turning, looking back over her own shoulder.

Back to David.

"You're absolutely right. It isn't," Hunter said. "He only had one thing to apologize for."

The stranger from earlier returned and grabbed the door handle between the women. Then he spoke to Hunter, pointing to the sign next door: *VIEWING ROOM 2*. "If you're still up for a show, now's the time."

51

"CAN YOU AT LEAST take these off?" Mitch said to the detective. "Things are a bit tight." He held up his wrists, bound by the dull, ragged cuffs. The professor's hands were still stained with the dried blood of his wife. The silver of the restraints was accented by the small red flakes breaking free from his fingers.

The detective dropped a folder onto the steel table. "Well, that's one option," he said. He pulled out a chair and removed his leather jacket before hanging it over the back of the seat. Then he sat down and crossed his legs, leaning back, opening the folder in the process.

Mitch was still handcuffed on the other end of the table.

The man didn't look like a detective—more like a worn-out, retired memory of what a detective should have been. Perhaps someone who had once had it all and lost it to the wear and tear of living life in the fast lane. His aviators hung from the fork of his black V-neck shirt. His mossy granite eyes glinted under the tired lighting of the stark cinderblock room. His thin five-o'clock shadow exuded a rugged but clean exterior that harbored the tales of covert weekend shifts and bloody all-nighters.

"Before we get started, perhaps I should introduce myself. My name is Detective Asher Huxley, lead investigator of the New Orleans Homicide Unit."

"Who said anything about getting started?" Mitch said, leaning forward, his speech calm, hands folded on the table. "Like I told the cop at my house, I want my lawyer."

The detective played up a satirical agreement. "Of course, of course. I understand wholeheartedly. That's one way we could go about this. And you don't have to say a single word. As is your right." He put up his hands in surrender. His black pistol was clear as day, strapped to the side of his hip. "But you should know just exactly how fucked you really are."

Detective Huxley's eyes were a strange combination of piercing and hollow, with a mess-around-and-find-out type of glow.

Mitch inched himself back into his seat. Then he snapped back with his own type of one-liner, already weary of the detective's accusatory look. "Well, I'm not one to turn down some good entertainment."

"Excellent," said the man, slapping the table. He jumped up from his seat.

Mitch turned his attention to the wall of glass to his left. An unconvincing mirror, surely with two or more onlookers watching the back-and-forth between the cop and himself. Mitch knew how those scenarios played out. He'd seen the docuseries. The Netflix specials. Bad cop goes at it for hours on end, pressing, pushing. Relentless until the accused gives in and talks, cracking under the pressure, or insists that he has nothing to do with anything. Pleading with a dumbass look smeared across his face. Like the detective had been born the day prior. Then good cop arrives to save the day.

The small white camera on the ceiling caught Mitch's attention only briefly. A cherry light blinking from the darkened corner, a cobweb moving in the breeze of a nearby air vent.

Cop number two swoops in and asks for some time alone.

So cop one leaves the room, seemingly reluctant to be pushed aside. Then they go on to explain how all he needs to do is confess, because that's the only way to clear his conscience and give the families some sort of closure. And the last thing a murderer wants on their mind is distraught family members of the deceased.

Yeah, that made perfect sense. Kill someone and then worry about what the victim's family thought about it.

Mitch was insulted by how naïve the detective made him out to be. Like his only option was to talk when, in fact, there was nothing to confess. He was certain—they had nothing.

They couldn't possibly.

"So, you were promoted recently at your job. Is that right?" the detective asked.

Mitch chuckled, tossing the naïveté back across the table with no effort at all.

"What?" Detective Huxley continued. "I think that's a fairly simple question."

"Tenure," said Mitch.

"I'm sorry?"

"*With tenure,*" Mitch said in a firm amendment. "I was promoted . . . with tenure. You guys around the station might not understand exactly what that means. But in my world, it's a bit more than a pay raise."

The detective leaned against the wall, his arms intertwined. "Of course," he said. "How foolish of me. You were promoted . . . with a fancy title."

Mitch could feel the play between them, the delicate song and dance that was nothing more than an atrocious misunderstanding.

The detective stepped over to the folder and removed a photograph, sliding it across the way, the picture spinning until it hit Mitch's arm at the other end of the metal table.

"That's you, right?" he asked.

Mitch leaned forward, tilting his head to the side in a silent response. His hands remained folded between his legs.

Detective Huxley continued. "That's from a traffic cam at the nearest red light to Steve Daigle's camp the night he was murdered. Minutes after the estimated time of death."

"Of course," said Mitch. "That's no surprise to me at all. My brother lives right next door to the place. I was over there that evening before I drove to UNO for my party. My *tenure* celebration, that is. You can ask anyone in the department. They'll vouch for me."

"Oh, I'm sure they will. But there's only two problems with that."

Mitch lifted his bound hands, gesturing for the cop to continue.

"One—what time did you arrive to your party?"

"I have no idea. What are you implying, exactly?"

"Well, we've spoken to a few of your colleagues, and it turns out, everyone was on time. Except for you."

Mitch huffed, his chest moving but his voice absent.

"Congratulations. You have me leaving my brother's house, and I was late for a party."

"But my question is, why were you late? You knew that you had somewhere to be. And you weren't merely attending someone else's party. It was *your* party. So why the tardiness, Professor?"

No response. Mitch had no answer. After all, he was under no obligation to provide one.

"Maybe that's all a coincidence," the detective said. "But that's only part of my concern. You see, we don't charge people with something unless we're convinced."

"This is ridiculous. Ask my brother if I was over at his place."

"That's a great idea, Mitch. The only problem is that Paul was arrested on a DUI that very same night. That's mighty convenient, now isn't it?"

Mitch could sense the air between them snap tight like a rope thrown over the edge of a cliff, a body tied at the other end. Like the guilty jumping from a window, only to have their neck stop short of the rest of their corpse.

"But, somehow," the cop said, "I get the sense that you already knew that."

• • •

Hunter watched from the other side of the glass as the professor squirmed. Her focus moved over the detective inch by inch— his wavy pecan hair, the way his glasses tugged at the front of his shirt, hinting at his perfectly defined chest, the deep indentation of his forearm where muscle met elbow.

From the corner of her eye, she saw David turn toward her.

"He's one of the best we've got," he said. "If there's something to be found, Asher's on it."

"Looks like he's got something to prove," she said.

"Nah. Not him. That's just Asher being . . . Asher."

The detective removed another piece of paper from the folder, this time pushing it across the table, slowly and steadily.

"Maybe we can't prove where you were coming from that night," he said, "and that's fine. But what about this?" His finger tapped the printout.

"What am I looking at?" Mitch said.

"That's the specs on a certain brand of vial, sold by Electron Microscopy Sciences. You recognize it?"

The professor lifted his shoulders before lowering them what looked like one tense muscle at a time.

"Maybe I can jog your memory." The detective reached his hand into his jacket pocket, where it hung from the side of the chair, and pulled out a clear evidence bag with red tape across the top, two glass tubes inside. Matching vials with black caps.

He pushed the bag across the table without looking away from the professor, pausing, creating what Hunter took as pure dramatic effect. She thought it was beautiful, really.

"What about now?" the cop said.

Even from the other room, looking through a thick pane of one-way glass, Hunter could see the professor's demeanor change from Mach 1 to an airbag-deploying zero. The once-poised and objective man—on paper, at least—melted into nothing more than the panicked remnants of a fretting criminal.

"That's all you," David said, nudging Hunter with an elbow.

She glanced over, his touch adding even more pleasure to the already satisfying moment.

"Look, Detective. I don't know what you're getting at, here. But those vials"—Mitch picked up the bag and tossed it back in front of the cop—"are used by anyone and everyone in the research community. Besides, I'd love to know where you got that from, since I don't remember anyone showing up to my work with a warrant."

"This is the part I was worried about," Hunter said as she turned to David.

"Don't worry. Asher lives for this stuff," he said.

"What stuff?"

He pointed to the other side of the glass.

The detective opened the folder once more but this time turned it around, facing the professor. Then he pushed it forward.

"You're absolutely right. But not many labs have the same water profile. Being a scientist and all, I thought you would've been wise enough to use 100 percent ethanol and not dilute it when you left that sample behind at the Guidry murder. As it turns out, deionized water isn't as pure as you might think."

David raised his coffee to the glass. "Stuff like that," he said. Hunter's jaw was on the floor.

The man went on. "What we have on the Daigle murder might be circumstantial, but the vial and water chemistry link you to the fly left at the Guidry homicide, and the flies lead right back to Steve Daigle's body. It might not be the calling card you were looking for, but pretty soon, you'll have one call a week. Paid in full."

Mitch looked over to the one-way mirror—dead into Hunter's eyes, she felt. His focus was unmoving. Part shock, part anger.

"Moreover," Asher said, "this is all just lagniappe." He gestured to the evidence bag and paperwork. "When it comes to murdering your own wife, well . . ." He held out his hands as if to say, *Let's be real.*

That was when the door of the interrogation room flung open, Mitch's lawyer bursting onto the scene. "That's enough. We're done, here."

The professor continued to gaze into the mirror with a titanic, clownish grin.

52

THE LAB WAS EMPTY and dead silent. Eerily so.

Robert dropped the box of paperwork onto his desk, the cardboard pushing a dull thud across the room.

He longed for something more that he could do to help Meaux cope with the loss of her husband. The loss of his long-time friend and colleague. Something other than taking a box of Steve's work off her hands. He thought back to her home, in disarray from her hurried attempt to consolidate what shattered memories remained of her husband's life.

It had been a while since they collaborated. But at least Robert had a way of remembering Steve's impact on his career—the papers with their names side by side, collecting citations, adding to the growing catalogue of work that would surely lend itself to Robert's next grant application, and any accolades thereafter. Having his name next to Steve's gave Robert a sense of pride in what he had accomplished over the course of his career. In some ways, Steve would continue to be a collaborator, and that was what really mattered.

The science, above all else.

Robert removed the lid from the box and thumbed his way through the manila folders, their tabs protruding in a subtle left-to-right stagger. His friend had kept a busy hand in everyone's work throughout the department over at UNO. That was what was so great about Steve's research—there hadn't been a single collaboration that he had turned down for as long as Robert had known him. If it had led to a paper, Steve was all over it.

Like a tick on a reddish summer coat.

Robert and Steve had shared a common appreciation for how important the numbers were. Collaborations led to papers, papers led to citations, citations to grants, and grants to more collaborations. And so the pyramid was built.

But all Robert was interested in were the files on their own projects. As was the case with any tour de force, everyone had a role, and Steve's part had usually consisted of project design and overseeing the data curation and analyses for each study, which meant supervising any graduate students or postdocs who had worked on the projects. More often than not, Steve had been listed as the anchor author, his name printed last on the contributors list. But in the academy, the anchor author was viewed as being equally important as the first author—the investigator responsible for heading up the project and drafting the original paper. Typically, first authors were grad students or postdocs, and anchor authors their principal investigators or mentors. Academics fought over authorship like a fresh kill beneath the savannah heat, foaming at the mouth for that first-author spot—the name that would be listed in subsequent papers when the study was cited.

Robert could feel his sharp hyena grin come to light at the thought of how ridiculous it all was. Nonetheless, it was part of the game—a game that was just as absurd as it was brutal.

As he flipped through the dust-ridden files, he noticed several collaborations between himself and Steve, dating back more than two decades. The grimy powder fluttered into the air and formed a gray film across his desk. The files were mostly printouts of datasets and R code, which served as backups to the digital files that had been shared with the author list for each study. Nothing that Robert didn't have access to already. The box also contained similar files on projects that Robert was not privy to.

What stood out, though, were the red folders buried in the back of the box. Bound by a large, dried-out rubber band.

Robert grabbed them and attempted to remove the elastic strap. Then it snapped, falling to the floor like a dehydrated piece of flesh. The folders themselves were permanently bent and twisted from the pressure of the restraint.

The files were dated six to eight years prior, each containing much of the same information Robert had found in the files for their own work. But after flipping through the pages, he noticed something different about the other projects.

"Well that's . . . something." He sat down in his office chair, unable to look away from the ink-riddled pages.

He placed the folders onto his desk before flipping through the first one. *Chapter 1, Sex and Aging,* the tab at the edge of the file read. The first document was a published manuscript, followed by printouts of data files and modeling scripts. Robert spread everything across his desk and rested his glasses on the bridge of his nose, squinting, his chin up, eyes down.

The paper had been published seven years ago in *Ecology and Evolution*, a well-respected journal in the two fields, and the go-to publication for a fair shot at peer review, where editors actually took the time to look at reviewer comments objectively. Something was backward, though. Something jumped out as just . . . off, with the order of things. And then it hit him. Maybe Robert hadn't realized it at first because it was so peculiar. Strange to a T.

The published manuscript was marked up in a sea of red

ink. But it wasn't the writing, or the figures, or even minor suggestions from the editor during the production of the article.

The red ink was lathered across nothing but numbers in the final published version of record. Across the summary data itself.

He flipped to the other files in the folder, to the Excel data and R code. It was much the same. Ink on top of red ink. And much of it corresponded to what was in the paper. Errors, it seemed, that no one would have caught, outside of the authors and reviewers who should have taken the time to look at the data and code, included as auxiliary material—material that reviewers rarely paid attention to. One of the many pitfalls of blind review.

Why did Steve have the files to begin with?

Robert flipped back to the front page of the article, to the title page with the author list and corresponding institution listed below the names.

Kole B. LeBlanc, Mitchel R. Olivier, Steven D. Daigle, the author list read. And below it, the shared affiliation. *Department of Biological Sciences, University of New Orleans, New Orleans, LA, USA.*

53

As a PHD STUDENT, Mitch had been drawn to committee meetings like a buck to a food plot.

There was nothing more satisfying to Mitch than having his mentors sit before him, handing out compliments as if they were king-size Butterfingers on Halloween, gushing over his work like proud parents, pinning his report card to the fridge. They'd try to rattle him with off-the-wall questions from time to time, but such events were more an exception to the rule. They loved his work.

Almost as much as he loved hearing about it.

"So," Aura started in, "you said in your email that you have some updates for us on your dissertation chapters?"

During these meetings, the student was on one side of the table, his three committee members and outside reader at the other end. A parolee in front of the review board.

In addition to the three biology professors required to serve on a PhD student's committee, the department also mandated that an outside reader assess their work—someone not in the biology department. A professor with no skin in the game, so to speak, who could provide a more objective opinion of the student's research.

"Yeah," said Mitch, "I'm nearly done with the data analysis

on Chapter 3. I was hoping to get y'all's opinion on the project design for Chapter 4 today, so we can get started on it sometime soon. I'm also going through the data for a side project as well."

"So, you're three years in and starting your fourth chapter already?" Dr. Vincent Bailey spoke from the side of the group, separated from the three committee members. He twirled his pencil while avoiding the other professors. Vincent was the solitary variety of academic—a mountain of a man with long hair and signature polka-dot suspenders. He sported a new pair of the straps every other day, it seemed. His work as a professor in the Department of Earth and Environmental Sciences made him an appropriate external critic in Mitch's eyes. Someone whose work was close enough to the student's biology research to provide feedback but unfamiliar enough to ask the important questions that no one else would think of. Also, he was a softy when it came to committee meetings. At least, that was what Mitch had heard from other grad students.

"Pretty damn impressive, I think," said Steve. "If you ask me, you could defend early. Wrap up that fourth chapter and duck out as soon as possible. There ain't no point in sticking around longer than you have to."

Bailey nodded at the periphery of the table, bouncing the eraser of his pencil off of the oak desk.

"Well let's not get ahead of ourselves," said Bryan. "It isn't about the number of chapters but the quality of work. Besides, you still need to see how the fourth and possibly fifth chapter pan out. And then you can worry about scheduling your defense."

"Oh, calm down." Steve spoke to Bryan with a voice clearly meant to pull on the reins a bit. "You might be chair of the department, but you're not chair of his committee." He looked to Aura, then back to his ass of a colleague. "How much longer till we know if you're moving into the big house, anyways?"

"Dean positions take time to fill, Steve-O." Bryan spoke with his guard up. Sandbags on the front porch, windows boarded. "Why? You have your eye on something in particular?"

Mitch looked at his advisor.

"I think we're getting a bit off track," Aura said, rubbing her forehead. "So, you said that you're looking at the data on a side project. Is that the joint study between you and Kole?"

"Yeah. It's gonna be one of his dissertation chapters, but I told him that I'd help out with the modeling in exchange for a spot as middle author."

"Sounds good," Aura said. "Any idea where he's thinking about sending it?"

"I think he said either *Functional Ecology* or *Ecology and Evolution*. But that's really up to him and Steve." He gestured across the table. "It's their baby more than it is mine."

"Both of those are great journals," said Steve. "But *Functional Ecology* is a little more concerned with their impact factor. So they're picky about what they let in."

"I agree," Aura said, turning to Steve. "*Ecology and Evolution*, especially for that study, is probably y'all's best bet. Feel free to shoot it my way if y'all need another set of eyes to look it over before you send it out."

"Same," said Bailey, seemingly fascinated by how long the pink butt of his pencil could bounce on the tabletop.

"Well, I think it's great that y'all are pumping out papers like this." Aura spoke as she fidgeted in her chair. "Most grad students are lucky to put out one or two before they defend." Then she looked up and smiled at Mitch in the way he was learning to appreciate. The weird but cute way she drew her lips to a point. Her chin forming two petite dimples as her cheeks flashed a cotton-candy pink.

"So that modeling for Chapter 3," Bryan said, his nostrils flaring more palpably than the electric sheen radiating from the peak of his balding crown. "Anything significant?"

• • •

Mitch returned to the graduate student offices. A group of more than fifteen of them were packed into a single room with no windows, divided by a maze of claustrophobic, paper-thin cubicles, each one more run-down than the last.

The fact that he was corralled with the lesser minds of the department and forced to associate with other grad students was the bane of his existence during his time in the program. They weren't on his level. Not anywhere close.

Except for Kole. Maybe.

"So," Kole said, pushing his chair out into the walkway between their miniature wannabe offices. "How'd your meeting go?"

Mitch dropped his computer bag to the floor. "Good. Other than the fact that Guidry is a complete asshole."

"Ha. Well, that's nothing new, aye. They say anything about your chapters or when you should plan on defending?"

Kole spun in his chair, pulling his knees up to his chest, looking at the ceiling like a squirrel distracted by a shiny gum wrapper in the yard. His seat hardly missing the cubicle walls around him.

"Not a whole lot," Mitch said. "Other than it's good that I'm publishing as much as I am. Steve thinks I might be able to finish early, but Bryan—holy shit. Bryan wants everyone to suffer through a full five years."

"That's awesome, man. Well, other than Guidry. Hopefully you won't have much longer. If you've got too much on your plate, I can handle that modeling for my chapter if I need to. I'll put you on the paper either way, since that was the plan from the beginning."

Mitch shook his head while downing some water, trying to hydrate. His mouth was dry from the two-hour committee meeting.

"I don't mind at all," he said. "All I have left is to write up and submit Chapter 3, and then I need to get the ball rolling on Chapter 4, which shouldn't take long. I'll get some undergrads to handle the data collection. Hell, they'd probably let me defend whether I submit my last chapter or not, as long as it's done and included in my dissertation. Then it's just a matter of throwing everything together for the graduate school."

"You sure? That life history data is kinda messy. And technically, it is my chapter."

"Yeah, man. I gotchu." A fist bump signaled Mitch's appreciation for the guaranteed authorship. "I've run those generalized linear models a million times with count data. Besides, we're about to submit this grant that would allow me to stick around as a postdoc. I could use every pub I can get."

54

"So, what now?" Hunter asked the detective as they stood just outside the interrogation room, watching Mitch strut down the hallway with his pretty-boy lawyer, Floyd, by his side. Another officer was ushering the professor to a private room.

"Well, he isn't going anywhere anytime soon," Asher said. "We're gonna charge him, but it looks like we won't be getting him alone from here on out. I'll keep you posted."

He stepped away from her, then turned back and paused. His gaze tensed as if he were thinking about how to portray a thought, or perhaps whether he should say anything at all.

Something that resembled a grin worked its way to the surface of his rocky expression. But to Hunter, it seemed the result of saying something that he was forcing himself to admit, as well.

He nodded. "Good work, by the way." Then the detective walked off into the colony of frenzied investigators and rattling phones.

Parker turned the corner before Hunter could fully process the unexpected compliment. He looked back down the corridor as the man faded into a marching outpost of colleagues.

"I see you met Ash," Parker said.

In that moment, it was all starting to make sense—in a good

way. Her job wasn't at all separate from the responsibilities of the Homicide department. There was no sharp line where Pathology ended and the Homicide department began, only different players with their own positions, playing the same game. The departments were unique on paper, perhaps, and organized from dissimilar locations, but the two were meant to exist alongside one another, with a common ambition. And the goal was to find the truth.

Or, at least, the closest version to it.

"Yeah, we've met," Hunter said. "Although I can't say whether that's a positive thing or just—" She waved her hands in front of her, then rested her palm across her cheek, unsure what she was feeling after being thrust from the unfamiliarity of a new job straight into the nucleus of a homicide investigation. And now commended by a brand new and unfamiliar colleague for nothing more than following her gut.

"Asher has that effect on people," said Parker. "You're not really sure why, but you appreciate him. That about right?"

Hunter rested against the wall. "Yeah. Something like that."

"So, it looks like they're gonna hold him," Parker said.

"Do what?"

"Olivier. They're gonna hold him."

Hunter's focus had yet to be pried from the detective, though his back was lost to the crowd. "Oh. Yeah. Well, I sure hope so. Dude was caught playing patty-cake with his wife's blood while her body was slumped over his sofa a few feet away. I think holding him is underkill at this point, if you ask me."

She pulled a green, ragged pack of gum from her front pocket, jammed into her skin-tight jeans like a dollar bill wedged between the sofa cushions, flattened and indiscernible from trash.

Hunter was at a complete loss for how to bring up the

whole you-and-Deborah-sprung-the-leak thing to Parker. A new career wasn't exactly the sturdiest ground for questioning a colleague—or accusing her supervisor, at that. She needed to tread carefully, but she also couldn't bear letting it go.

She touched one of the green, aromatic sticks to her tongue, where it stuck just before she pulled it in. The mint cleared her sinuses, giving her the edge she needed to come out with it. Like ammonia hitting the weightlifter's nose before a record press. She couldn't hold it any longer. Not this, of all things. Not something that meant Deborah would get one over on her. And with her boss, of all people.

"Well, unless you need me, I think I'm gonna head on over to—"

"Actually," Hunter said with an awkward jolt in her voice. Almost a crack.

It was as if she were on autopilot, no off switch to power down, her mind not reviewing the words before they flew from her mouth. Only the end goal in mind—the innate need to do right by her own conscience.

Before she knew it, Hunter was stumbling over the words. "I hear Deborah's still around if y'all need to go over some more *material*," she said. She spoke as if it were a dare.

Parker shifted his head, turning one ear toward her. "Come again?"

Maybe he'd heard wrong? "You know . . . you and Deborah. I'm sure y'all have a lot to talk about, with the Olivier cases and all. Now that he's being formally charged."

Parker looked around the hallway. Forward, behind Hunter, then back over his own shoulder.

His mouth opened, but the words lagged.

"Work was probably the hardest thing for Deborah and I to deal with during the time that we were involved with one another," Hunter said. "Whether we liked it or not, at the end of the day, my job was her job. And keeping that from coming between us was pretty much impossible."

"Hunter, we don't need to make this—"

"But now, I realize that the cards were stacked against us the entire time. Were you ever gonna tell me? Or is this the normal back-and-forth between law enforcement and the media? Am I just that naïve, Parker?"

The man's high-and-mighty demeanor shifted to a sprawling plea bargain at the bat of an eye.

"Look, it was a one-time thing. Deborah and I go way back. It was nothing more than a friend helping out a friend. When you're in this type of career long enough, you realize that it's better for everyone involved if you just go along with it. Play the game."

"You ever hear the expression 'digging yourself into a hole'?"

"Hunter, please. We have a shared interest here. In more ways than one. Don't you think that it would benefit us both— or hell, all three of us—if we just—"

"No, Parker. I don't think so. There is no 'three of us.' You're not dragging me into whatever the two of you have going on. I've been burned enough at this point."

Parker's voice fell as he spoke. "Fine. That's fine." Then he crept his way closer. "But I'm gonna assume this stays between us. After all, that's probably in your best interest."

"And whose interest are we talking about?" David said.

How David had gotten so close to Parker without him knowing, she had no idea.

55

THE BETTER PART OF daylight had faded to a blood-moon tint, dripping from the lab windows. Robert caught a second's glimpse of the time, stamped at the bottom corner of one of the three computer screens.

Hours had vanished at a seemingly greater rate than that of coeds of the '70s before he realized exactly how lost in the weeds he really was. How he was turned around in a swamp of paperwork that all looked the same—published papers soaked in crimson errors, strewn across his desk. Data sets from journal websites open in Excel. One after another, steeped in subtle mistakes not obvious to the casual reader.

Or were they errors at all?

Robert placed his cup beneath the single-serve coffee maker before he dropped a pod into the chamber, the signature pop sounding as the canister was punctured. Then he pressed the flashing brew button without pulling his eyes from the scrolling pixels of open-access data.

The way Robert saw it, the problem was two-fold: Steve's folders contained more than one manuscript, and each of the papers had been published by the same three authors, one of whom was a postdoc in Robert's lab. So whether he liked it or not, Robert was invested by association.

Reputations were on the line. And if there was one thing that he was unwilling to handle objectively, it was his academic persona.

Kole popped his head in the door. "Hey. It's getting kind of late. You good?"

Robert sprung from his chair. "Actually, have a seat."

"Sure, what's up?"

He gathered the publications from his desk and turned them around for Kole to see, spreading them in an orderly fashion by publication date.

"These papers." Robert sat down, pulling his cup from beneath the coffee machine. "You have any idea why Steve would have kept these in his office? Or why they're all marked up after the fact?"

Robert adjusted his glasses on the tip of his straight-bridged nose, leaning his head back, looking through the two lenses. Kole leaned forward and adjusted the papers in a trivial way.

"Of course. My name's on them. Isn't it? These are some of the papers that Mitch Olivier and I published with Steve, back when I was in the PhD program."

Robert cream-and-sugared his coffee as he waited for his postdoc to elaborate.

"Where did you get these?" Kole continued.

"Like I said, they're from Steve's office. His wife gave me some of his work recently. She didn't know what else to do with it, and she didn't wanna throw it away."

Kole began skimming his way through the papers.

"Kole," Robert continued, "I've been looking through all of this for the last several hours. Please tell me you didn't have anything to do with this."

The postdoc pushed the papers back across the desk, his mouth an exaggerated gape.

"What is all of this?" Kole spoke while looking at the computer monitors. "I don't get it."

"I'm trying to figure that out myself. What it looks like is fabricated data, in some instances. In others, it looks like nothing more than lazy science. What I need from you is the why."

"Robert, I have no idea what—"

"Don't." Robert cut him off. His ego didn't have time for games, other than his day-to-day duties in the academy. "Your name is on these papers, Kole. Don't bullshit me with some excuse about how you didn't know. I mean, you're first author on several of them. And you want me to believe that you were just along for the ride?"

"How many papers were *you* on where you actually took the time to open up the data in R and run the code that a coauthor handled?" Kole flipped to several of the tables and figures in the papers. Then he tossed one of the publications in front of Robert. "Pull up the data for this one."

"It's already open." Robert pointed to the screen. "You don't have to look very far. It's like no one even tried to hide it." He ran the cursor across one of the cells in the spreadsheet, turning it from white to an evident, stark gray.

"And you think that all these are the same?" Kole asked.

"Not exactly, but they all have serious problems. Some of them are more obvious than others. How could you not know about this?" Robert ran his hand down his face, twisting the patch of hair below his bottom lip.

"I had help. I wasn't familiar with the modeling, so Mitch was thrown on several of our papers to help out with the R code. What should I do? This is almost every paper that he and I are on."

Robert stood again, wearing down the tile floor with his leather shoes, looking to the monitors, then back to the papers.

The difficult part was that he had had nothing to do with it, but his reputation would be affected in a big way if even a hint of misconduct got out, whether he knew about it or not. It didn't matter. Kole was part of his lab. What he was able to prove would be irrelevant.

What was done was done.

That was the funny thing about the academy: as long as it took to build a professorial image, it could be dismantled and forgotten in no time at all, given the right circumstances.

"Nothing," Robert said.

"What do you mean 'nothing'? If I don't get ahead of this, I'm fucked."

Robert didn't hesitate in his speech. "No. You're fucked either way."

"Rob, I need to email the journals. Tell them something. Hell, if I didn't know about it, maybe they'll just—"

"They'll what, Kole? Let it slide? Give you a hall pass? If you say something about it now, not only can you forget about a career in academia, but you're implicating me in whatever the hell happened, as well."

"Your name isn't associated with any of it."

"My name might not be on the papers, but you're part of my lab. And the only way you got here was as a favor to Steve Daigle. How do you think that's gonna look if this gets out? Whether you knew about it or not, you're not dragging me down with you. Besides, this goes way beyond your dissertation."

"What are you talking about?" Kole asked.

"Those papers have been published for years. They're cited in other studies. They've been used as the foundation for grants. Journal impact factors. Hiring and tenure applications. What's published in journals isn't written in pencil, Kole. It's etched in stone. So the papers aren't just gonna go away. *RETRACTED* will be next to your name, for good. I can tell you exactly how it ends if this gets released. And it doesn't take an ecologist to figure it out."

"Okay. So what do you propose I do, exactly?"

Robert sat down again, folding his hands beneath his chin. He looked at the data on the monitor, but it was more of a dazed look through the screen than anything else, into some infinite array of zeros and ones, weighing the possibilities one scenario at a time.

"Like you said, how often do coauthors—or anyone, really—check the data and R code that's handled by their colleagues? How many scientists actually download and go through the data and scripts that are published on journal websites?"

He collected the papers and removed each staple from the corners of the articles, flicking the metal prongs onto his desk with an exasperated jerk of the hand.

"Research is an imperfect enterprise, Kole. And there's no such thing as true, objective science. Remember?"

He pushed the top of the first article into the guard of the shredder, the machine pulling the paper between the rotating metal teeth, separating the red ink into thousands of indecipherable pieces of a past not meant to be found.

"So, as far as I'm concerned, the papers are nothing more than outliers that'll come out in the wash."

56

THE AUDITORIUM WAS STANDING room only as the newly cast dean, Bryan Guidry, presented the Dean's Research Awards for the College of Sciences. Mitch and Kole sat front and center of the herd of students and postdocs, professors and staff, with Aura and Steve at their side.

"We're here to acknowledge the outstanding achievements of the graduate students and postdoctoral fellows across the College of Sciences," said Bryan. His speech embodied a mind of its own as his words deepened through the podium microphone and reverberated from the naturally stained shiplap above.

Mitch had been waiting for that very moment for years, ever since he had applied to the graduate program. For nearly half a decade, he had exhausted himself, slaving day and night in front of a blinding screen. Writing, editing, submitting, revising. No other grad student in the department came close to touching his track record at publishing. That was what everyone on the outside never saw—the sacrifices he had made to be at the top of his field, at least as far as students were concerned.

But did anyone ever truly reach the top of the academic ladder? Or was every rung one step deeper into the clouds, obscuring whether there was a peak at all? The machine turning out one more cog to . . . feed the machine. An ever-expanding promise, like the edges of the universe itself.

At the end of the day, it didn't matter. Not to Mitch. He was being applauded for what he had done. And that alone was enough to keep the wheels turning.

"First up," said the dean, "are two students from the Department of Biological Sciences who, over the last four years, have excelled in not only their academics but their leadership across the college. Today, we're here to celebrate their research and, in particular, their peer-reviewed work."

Mitch tried not to, but he couldn't help it. He looked to the side, just to glimpse his peers' reactions. To see the faces as they changed, one thin turn of the lips at a time, in admiration of what he and Kole had achieved.

Their pictures flashed across the screen, projected over the stage in front of the flock. Mitch had been sure to provide the most recent portrait of himself, taken by a professional photographer from the graduate school the week prior.

"These students are Mr. Kole LeBlanc and Mr. Mitch Olivier," said Bryan.

The room broke out in applause. An acknowledgment that, to Mitch, was a few seconds too brief.

"In particular," the dean continued, "their list of peer-reviewed publications is considered an unprecedented level of achievement for any PhD program here at the university. But especially in our own department. Over the last four years, a total of nine manuscripts have been published between them, with many of those the result of coauthorship and their work together. As such, these awardees have demonstrated the embodiment of collaboration and perseverance that our college strives to both teach and display in our work, day in and day out."

Mitch felt Aura nudge his leg with a finger. A clandestine reminder, a smirk caught from the fringe of his vision, of how much he deserved his moment in the spotlight. He nudged his leg back against hers.

Then Bryan spoke the most beautiful of sentences. "Please join me in congratulating Kole LeBlanc and Mitch Olivier."

A round of applause followed that charged the hall and sent a wave of hair-raising cold down Mitch's arms. Kole extended his fist in a congratulatory thump as they rose from their seats.

• • •

Upon returning to their cubicle village, it was back to work as usual. But Mitch couldn't pull his focus from the plaque before him.

He ran his finger across the gold writing, etched into a reflective black background. *UNIVERSITY OF NEW ORLEANS, College of Sciences, Dean's Research Award, Graduate Student Mitch Olivier, Biological Sciences.*

"Congrats," Kole said from his chair, rolling back and forth in the walkway.

"Yeah. You too, man," Mitch responded.

"You got a minute?"

It was difficult to look away, so Mitch placed the award in his lap and rolled to the door of his thin, shadowy box.

"Sure. What's up?"

Kole had his computer open on his lap. He turned with his back to Mitch so he too could view the screen. On it was an Excel file, containing the data from their most recent publication.

"I'm a little confused about the dataset that we just published to Dryad," Kole said.

Mitch looked at the computer. The cursor flashed at the top of the second column, the input of a response variable. Kole pointed to the formula bar.

"Why are each of these modified in a different way?" he asked.

Then he pressed the down arrow on the keyboard. Each cell in the column showed a different formula than the last.

"I could understand if the whole variable was transformed, but it isn't," he continued. "Every cell is different. And then there's this." Kole clicked over to R, where two graphs were plotted in dark mode—one with the raw data, the other with the published results. One modified. One not. "What is this?"

Mitch set the plaque on his desk, then crossed his legs, folding his hands in his lap.

No one else ever checked data files once they were published.

Much less authors themselves.

57

THE CAMPUS WAS SULLENLY overcast, but in a narcotic way that made Hunter's senses grin.

She strode across the pay parking lot to the biology building as a faint mist loitered in the air, somewhere halfway between approaching thunderstorm and fading drizzle. A stratiform quilt of gray folded over the campus from above, sparsely lit by shards of blushing orange, cutting across the sky from the west.

The last time she'd been there, she had inadvertently stumbled into Mitch's lab after speaking with his wife. At the time, Hunter had been relying on her gut more than anything to guide her through her first murder investigation. But her intuition had ultimately led to the evidence, and the proof was more than enough to solidify her suspicions about the professor.

She walked through the automatic doors and into the darkened square hallway of the bottom floor. Unlike her experience as a student at Southeastern, and visiting other colleges during her stint as an academic and med student, there was something about UNO that set it apart from other universities. Something she had sensed during her previous visits to the college but hadn't fully clicked beyond her subconscious.

UNO was a professor's college—a modest, tight-knit community of diligent academics who kept to themselves and were satisfied with the state of the institution and their careers. Every building on campus conveyed the feeling. Empty halls, closed doors, and aesthetics from decades past. Perhaps that was the allure of the university for prospective students and faculty: its overall contentment and sense of calm. It drew you in with a feeling of Southern homeness, like your grandmother's one-bedroom cottage, tucked away at the end of a cul-de-sac.

Such characteristics weren't a bad thing, only unique. A melting pot of wandering professors, looking for a home. Like New Orleans itself. At least that was Hunter's impression.

Kole's office was in the corner of the building. No name plate or temporary tag—just a room number screwed to the door.

She leaned against the wall and knocked below the handle. "Doctor LeBlanc, it's Hunter Romero."

She could hear shuffling from inside, followed by the shrill of wooden legs dragging across the floor. Then soles, pacing to the door.

"Hey, come on in," Kole said. "I wasn't expecting you."

"Thanks. Hope I'm not interrupting."

Hunter promptly noticed how immaculate the office was—his desk organized better than her own, the walls adorned with two black-and-gray canvas prints of his microscopy work, and a tray of documents labeled more efficiently than a processed crime scene.

"No, of course not. Have a seat."

"I just wanted to stop by and see how you were holding up. It's not really my job or anything. I just . . ."

"I'm as good as I can be, I guess. Still processing everything while trying to get my work done at the same time. It's like living two lives, essentially."

The postdoc looked ruffled, as if he were treading water,

holding his head above the rising tide of the academy's expectations. The waves pushing against him as the brackish water dripped down the back of his throat, muddied with a tinge of salt.

"Well, I won't stay long. But if there's anything I can do, just let me know. I really appreciate your help with the case."

Kole pointed to himself with a curious, dancing brow. "Me? I don't really see what it is that I did for your case. Or, hell, how any of it can be considered good. I'm lucky there's still a department here for me to work in."

"Sorry. I didn't mean to make it out like it's a positive thing. I can only imagine how difficult it's been on everyone here at the university. Yourself included."

"No. I didn't think you did. I just wish someone would've done something sooner, aye. In hindsight, the whole thing with Mitch just seems a little—"

"Obvious?"

"I was going to say 'convenient,' but sure. Obvious fits."

"Yeah. I was getting that a lot, working on the case. Come to find out, I wasn't the only one who was looking at Mitch as a suspect."

"No?"

"Some colleagues of mine already had some evidence of their own. So it looks like, in the end, we were all headed down the same path. We just didn't know it."

Kole bowed his head, working a loose nail at his thumb's edge. "Well, I suppose that makes it go down a bit easier, knowing that the charges are solid, I'm guessing?"

"Oh, yeah. All too often, with cases like this, it ends up being someone close. Don't feel bad, though. I mean, the guy's wife didn't even have a clue about what he was up to."

"It makes you pause and take a step back, though, doesn't

it?" His attention floated off to the ceiling in a look of skepticism. "Did he even say what the motivation was? Or give any kind of explanation?"

Hunter stood up and snapped the scrunchie from her wrist, pulling her hair back into a tight ponytail as she shook her head in a silent *no*. "From one scientist to another—we have no choice but to follow the evidence, right?"

Kole remained seated. "The way I see it, that's the only way." Then he opened a small green pack of tightly wrapped silvery sticks and held one out. "Gum?"

58

KOLE LEFT, EASING THE lab door shut, and Robert was left alone with his thoughts, gaping at the now-hollow crimson folders. A shredder to the side, vomiting the remnants of mistakes he hoped would never again see the light of day—if he was lucky.

At least if they were brought to light by some overachiever of the future, Robert wasn't an author. Worst-case scenario, he'd have to run damage control, since Kole was working in his lab. Mild case, the errors would be found out once the postdoc was gone. He'd have some explaining to do, would have to convince his peers he had no knowledge of the misconduct. Best case? Kole moved on, and no one was the wiser.

But for the time being, Robert had done the best he could have. The problems that Steve had outlined in the papers were officially sitting at the bottom of the bin, in thousands of slivery pieces. An irreversible puzzle to be dumped at the bottom of some landfill. If they were to surface again, someone would have to figure it out for themself.

It was late in the day, but Robert couldn't leave just yet. His mind was too wired. What he needed was something positive to pull his attention from the calamity he'd been dealing with for the better part of a day.

And then he remembered—Meaux had returned his trail camera with the box of Steve's paperwork.

Hunting was a hobby that he and Steve had shared virtually year-round. Robert's winter months were spent hunting mostly at Steve's family camp; spring was devoted to maintaining the box stands and keeping the food plots in order; summer was spent scouting game trails and finding new hotspots to set up temporary ladder stands; and fall was a combination of clearing land, planting the fields, and scouting for bow season, which opened in October. It was a full-time gig, and as far as Robert was concerned, a healthy addiction.

If there was such a thing.

It was crucial for Robert to have something to hold on to, beyond the academy. Something to keep the mind sane. Such a drastic concept was foreign to most academics, and for the biologists he had known, research was more of a lifestyle. Weekends were nonexistent, a fairy tale for the less passionate, for the nine-to-fivers of the matrix. But for Robert, life beyond academics was critical to a successful career. Burnout was all too real, and he had no intention of foregoing retirement.

He opened the camera and pressed the SIM card, the thin drive clicking and popping out from the port. Then he inserted the card into the side of his laptop.

Scouting was a necessary part of deer hunting. Robert had loaned his cameras to Steve on a regular basis to help keep track of the deer population at the camp, as well as the hogs that had destroyed Steve's chicken coop on numerous occasions.

As he opened the file, hundreds of pictures littered the screen, dating back several months. As usual, the majority of them were nothing more than snapshots of nature in motion— branches sweeping the ground, leaves rustled by a firm breeze, rain pelting the mud like a battlefield of miniature bombs exploding under the indirect light of a bleeding moon.

Sifting through the images was comparable to doing the dishes or folding laundry. It put the mind on autopilot and gave him a chance to reboot.

After deleting what was useless, one of the pictures stood out among the lot. They were all black-and-gray stills, but one in particular was unusual. Difficult to read.

Robert had sifted through thousands of trail camera images, and videos, in the past—deer, hogs, turkey, coyotes. Anything that was part of the Louisiana woodlands, he had seen at one point or another, at this angle or that. But what he was seeing now was just confusing. A blur at the corner of the frame. Something in motion—hurried motion.

He recognized the contour. The color and shade. Only, he didn't. Like seeing the face of an acquaintance, accompanied by the feeling of a prior interaction, but blanking on the name.

Robert zoomed in on the image and opened the formatting tool, then upped the contrast and dragged down the brightness, normalizing the overexposed, blurry picture.

He had seen it before. Recently, even. Too recently.

Then it hit him, dead in the face.

The image wasn't a deer. No hog. No animal of the swamp, trotting to a nearby food plot, working a worn trail every morning and evening. But it was, nonetheless, a creature of habit.

The blur smeared across the figure was no branch or flash of moonlight in the night forest, either. The shape was an arm. And what he recognized was a scar.

59

WHY WAS KOLE DIGGING through published data to begin with? Once Mitch had clicked publish on the authors' behalf, he'd figured it would be lost to the online journal gods for good. It was done. Finished. Published meant official. *Of record.* The correct and final version.

Kole's question was ridiculous, like an interrogation following an innocent-on-all-accounts ruling.

"What does it look like?" said Mitch. His tone was meant to convey an air of certainty and annoyance with the question. A cut-and-dry instance of academic double jeopardy.

"Well, it looks like manipulated data, but I'm sure I need to give you the benefit of the doubt, aye? You're the one who uploaded the dataset and handled the modeling. So, I'm asking you."

Mitch looked at the computer screen, squinting as if he were trying to understand the contradictions in the data. It was hard to fake it, though. To act like what he had done was somehow out of the ordinary. He knew what each and every cell was meant to do.

"If I remember correctly—"

"Remember? Mitch, this was published a few weeks ago. What do you mean, *if* you remember?"

"I've been working on, like, five papers over the last year, Kole. And for most of them, I'm the only one handling all the stats. So, sorry if I don't remember every little detail about a dataset. Yeah, maybe it was published recently. But I haven't worked on that project in forever. It took us the better part of a year just to write up the paper."

Kole sat back in his chair, looking at the screen. Then he shook his head and glanced back at Mitch.

"This makes no sense."

"Stop worrying so much." Mitch leaned over to the screen, then pointed. "You know what, I think it's the transformation. Like you said before. Yeah, that's probably all it is. I think that response variable is transformed in the graph. Look." And he clicked Kole's computer, sending the screen back to the graphs in R.

Kole rubbed his eyes and let out a depleted, frustrated moan. "Mitch, you don't do that by hand with every single value in Excel. That's not what this is. I've looked at it every which way. It's not a transformation on the whole variable."

"What do you want from me?"

"Are you serious right now? I'm coming to you with concerns about our published work, and your response is what do I want?"

"You need to calm down, dude."

Kole spun his chair, stopping himself with his foot against the doorway, looking at the data but not really seeming to understand that it was meant to be forgotten. Published and tucked away for good. A line on the CV. Citations in the bank.

"No. I don't." He pushed his chair back out into the walkway. Then he slammed the laptop shut. "I can't just sit on this, Mitch. We need to bring this to Aura."

Aura was the last person Mitch needed digging through his

work, more than she already had been as his advisor. He was scheduled to defend a few months down the road. Kole's chapter or not, retracting a published manuscript would only blow up his entire timeline and set him back over a year—best-case scenario. If he wasn't kicked out of the department. His image would never recover.

Not to mention, he'd be single-handedly responsible for tanking Aura's reputation. It'd be bad enough if one of her students was accused of ethical misconduct, but a student she was dating? Forget it. It would end her career, whether she was let go or not. A cover story printed on the first page. One of those columns that spills over into the centerfold.

"Aura? You're gonna take your first-author paper that *you* published and bring it to *my* advisor because you don't understand what happened with *your* data? For your dissertation? Explain to me how that makes any sense whatsoever."

"What, you think just because I'm first author, and it's one of my chapters, that you don't have to deal with it? The modeling was your responsibility as a middle author. That's the only reason you're on it in the first place. And now you're telling me that you have no idea what you did?"

Mitch stood up and leaned against the doorway of his cubicle, arms folded. At the end of the day, what he had done should only have led back to Kole. Sure, he'd handled the data, done what he had to do to make the numbers fit. To get some results that journals actually wanted to publish. But that was what the game was all about—numbers. Number of publications, number of citations, journal impact factors. How many zeros were at the end of your grant. And none of that came from boring, insignificant results. Everyone knew it, but few had the nerve to decide their own fate.

It was Kole's dissertation. But whether Mitch had run the

data or not, he knew that it would lead back to the first author. It was the first and last authors who were responsible for finalizing a paper for publication, not the middle authors. So, if anything, Kole and Steve were responsible. In Mitch's mind, the path of accountability was clear.

"So, you're telling me that you're upset that you didn't check your own work before it was published?" Mitch said. "Whose fault is that?"

"I'm going to Aura."

"No. You're not." Mitch moved into the narrow entrance of Kole's space. His thirty-square-foot home, lit by the yellow light of a desk lamp and a small black candle—Salted Beechwood and Embers, by the fiery smell of it. The orange sparks floated upward as the wooden wick crackled and popped.

"Fine. Then I'll go to Steve. It's my dissertation anyway. If that's what you're concerned about, I'll go to him."

"Kole, I don't think you're hearing me."

Kole paused, looking to the floor as if the answer would scurry across the ground at any moment, barking, with a lost-and-found note pinned to its collar. Then his face twisted as he seemed to recognize the weight of his predicament.

Mitch continued. "One, there's nothing to show." He tried to fight it, but he felt the smirk tug at his bottom lip. "What are you gonna say? 'I don't understand my research that I just defended and published. Help me'?"

Kole's glance was nothing more than two white spheres harboring a trace of jet black.

"Two, Steve is chair of the department now. You really think he wants to deal with some case of misconduct by one of his own students? A study that he's anchor author on? Come on."

Kole dropped the laptop onto his desk, then rested his

elbows on the table's edge, pushing his hands back through his wavy, feathery locks. His fingers rested at the back of his neck, interlocked, his head hanging between his arms.

"And three?"

"Oh, three is the most important one of all. Three you already know."

Kole looked over. Mitch spoke in a monotone grit, in a way that required no emphasis to get the point across. "Three, the paper is a chapter of your dissertation."

For Mitch, the great thing about being a middle author was the safety net of accountability. Sure, his misconduct, the data manipulation, sloppy research, fabrication—whatever they wanted to chalk it up to be—might be found out. But no one would tarnish his reputation without sinking their own. Authorship was an all-or-nothing affair. Either coauthors admitted to the wrongdoing, or they claimed that they had no idea of the misconduct, which was just as bad. Either they had a hand in it, or their science was lazy enough to miss it. There was no median.

And that was where Mitch had Kole—with his back against the beauty of middle authorship.

"It's a chapter of the dissertation you just defended. Doctor."

60

STEVE HAD ENOUGH ON his plate as it was.

Since he had moved up and into his role as the department chair, his lab had shrunken down to a smoldering three grad students and one postdoc. Between the department politics and keeping his research above ground, he was spread thinner than he cared to admit. But administrative duties aside, his lab came first. It always had. Without the science, there was no chair position for him to serve. The lab was his baby. And when the grandkids called, he answered.

Over his decades of service in the academy, Kole was without a doubt the most independent PhD student whom Steve had advised—and mentored. Steve's approach with his students was off the beaten path and down the trailside, but purposeful. Most professors never discerned between advising and mentoring, and assumed that because a student worked in their lab, they were, by default, both advisor and mentor. But few were. Few had the wherewithal to pull it off.

To Steve, the difference was simple: advisors provided advice and guidance on coursework, research, and all matters collegiate. What courses to avoid, where to submit papers for publication, how to write a paper. Or simply how to write—the basics, essentially. But mentors did the same and more, providing advice on a student's career trajectory, outreach, personal guidance, and other matters. His students were not only his employees but his colleagues. They were in training, but collaborators all the same.

Kole had sent Steve an email, requesting to speak in person—something Kole had never done during his four-plus years in the lab. But Kole was on his way out. He had defended, and all that was left was the menial task of getting him out the door. Graduate school paperwork and dragging himself across the stage, if he cared to do so.

Steve's role, as it pertained to Kole completing the program, was simple. But he had a hunch that their meeting would be about more than the tedious duties of an advisor. Based on Kole's panicky tone in the message, Steve was expecting to play mentor. And his predictions were rarely off center.

Two taps on the metal doorway signaled Kole's arrival.

"Hey, Kole. Have a seat," said Steve.

The kid was known for having his shit together. Well-dressed, well-spoken, polite, smart, a clean set of manners. But from the moment he walked into the office, Steve could sense one thing or another was out of place. Something was off-kilter. One side of Kole's shirt had found its way out of his pants, his face was sheet white, and his usually modelish hair was morphing into some sort of Einsteinian sculpture.

Steve had no clue why, but he found himself on the edge of his seat, clicking his pen, half nervous habit and half anticipatory death grip.

"Yeah, thanks for meeting with me. I know it's short notice."

Kole sat down and placed his laptop on the desk, facing Steve. No computer bag, no papers, nothing. Just the student and his already-opened computer. A strange enough start to the meeting.

"So what's up?" Steve asked.

Kole adjusted his collar and leaned forward. He rolled his shoulders in what looked like an attempt to calm his nerves.

"Well . . . I, uh, wanted you to take a look at something."

"Okay."

The student slid his finger across the mouse pad, awakening his computer. An Excel file was already pulled up on the screen.

Kole pointed.

"Some data from one of your chapters?" Steve asked.

Then Kole clicked a column heading, highlighting the values in gray.

"The chapter we just published. I think there's a problem with one of the response variables."

"Okay." Steve's attention was officially aroused.

"I just met with Mitch. And, apparently, he has no idea how this was calculated. Or at least, that's what he says."

"What do you mean he has no idea? Isn't this your chapter?"

"Well, yeah. That's the problem."

Steve was partly confused, and partly shocked by the lack of accountability. But he needed something more before he passed judgment. His lack of response said all he cared to say in the moment.

"It's my chapter, but Mitch was the last one to work with the data. He did all the modeling and deposited the dataset online."

"I'm not sure what you're getting at, Kole."

"I was going back through the data for another project, and I noticed that the entire column for age is modified. Cell by cell."

"What do you mean?"

"Every cell has a custom formula that modifies the value.

Nothing complicated, just a plus two here, a minus three there."

"Did he transform the entire column somehow?"

"That's what I originally thought, but that doesn't make any sense. If that was the case, the entire variable would have the same formula. Every cell would be adjusted the same way. But they aren't. Each one is different."

"And you asked Mitch about it? And he has no idea what happened?"

Kole pulled his fingers across his cheeks, squeezing his mouth in a tiresome cinch of the lips.

"That's what he claims."

"Well that's nice," said Steve.

He let it linger for a second. Would Kole add anything on his end to hold himself accountable? To point out the fact that it didn't matter what Mitch had done? It was irrelevant. The paper was Kole's work. A chapter of his own dissertation that he was responsible for.

"I guess my question is, what do we do?" Kole said.

Steve shoved his finger into his own chest.

"What do *we* do? This is your chapter, is it not?"

Kole said nothing.

"A better question is why did something like this happen in the first place? You're telling me that the data was uploaded, and the paper was published, without you looking at all of the code?"

"I did look at the code."

"Just not the data."

"I did look at the data."

"But not after you gave it to Mitch for him to analyze."

No response.

"Kole, that project was your responsibility. All of this could've been avoided if you would've checked everything. It's your chapter and your name as first author on the paper. What about the other ones that he's on?"

"I haven't gotten that far yet. How was I supposed to know that the dataset was modified after I gave it to Mitch?"

"Easy. You should've looked at the data after he ran the models and before he put it up on Dryad."

Again, Steve waited. Any ounce of liability would have been appreciated, anything at all. But instead, the conversation turned sour in a bad way.

"And at what point did *you* look at the data?" Kole said.

"Excuse me?"

Steve was anchor author. Anchors were different from first authors. Anchors were a position to be coveted, not questioned. Anchor authors were immune to the responsibilities of the less privileged. Last authors went nowhere near the raw data.

"Your name is on the paper just like mine, aye?" Kole spoke with accusation. "At what point did you check the data and look at the code? Mitch screws up, and it's all on me?"

"Yes. It is on you."

"Well that's convenient."

"No, what's convenient is that y'all messed up, and now I'm expected to clean up the mess."

"Just tell me what to do. Do I need to email the journal?"

Steve was sure to tread carefully from that point forward. His name, whether he liked it or not, was on the paper.

"I'll take care of it."

"I think I need to email them and explain what happened. Maybe they'll let us submit a revision once we figure it out."

"I said I'll handle it."

Steve didn't need help. All Kole would do, all any student would do, was dig the hole even deeper. He would hit ground water and drown the entire author list. And fixing the problem didn't mean begging the journal for a second chance. That was a last resort.

"I'll email them and copy you on it. I'm sure they'll understand and—"

"No. You won't."

"I don't get it. Aren't we supposed to be upfront about—"

"You want a career, right? You're wanting to stay in academia?"

"Of course I do, but—"

"Then you'll listen and let me handle it."

Steve assumed he had gotten through. That he had made some sort of impression. That he would be appreciated for taking on the problem himself.

But the kid had other plans.

"Why should I?" Kole said.

Steve stood up and leaned forward, placing his hands on the other side of the desk, nearer to the foolish side of the table.

"You just defended, right?"

"Yeah."

"You have a postdoc lined up?"

Steve knew the answer before he had asked the question. Kole huffed in a pissy sort of way.

"That's what I thought." He eased the laptop closed, then pushed it in front of Kole. "Now you do."

61

HUNTER LOOKED OUT OVER the Mississippi as she waited for the detective to arrive. A ripped blanket of ragged fog lay scattered across the adjacent bank like a thin layer of paint on a canvas, hinting at the river's surface below. The choppy brown-green water shimmered against a passing barge as the clamor of fading hooves knocked the pavement in the background—the city coming to life, lost under an early-morning haze.

She'd been pleasantly surprised to get a call from the Homicide department two days after they had arrested Olivier. The call was to follow up on her work, more than anything else. But the conversation ended on a cliff-hanger, with Asher asking to meet at the riverwalk the following morning—at a picturesque stretch of dock adjacent to the French Quarter. Unsure what the meeting would entail, she'd waited on a positive note and was happy just to be included in something more than her day-to-day lab work.

She found a bench on the inland side of the walkway, tucked between two live oak trees on a grassy pad. Hunter sat and rested her arm over the back of the seat, breathing in the salty mist that hovered nearer to her side of the water.

In her mind, Asher's request to meet away from the distractions of an office was peculiar. But from what she had heard, that was his way of operating—beneath the radar of everyone else. Against the grain.

No sooner had she crossed her legs and settled in to the temperateness of the Louisiana morning than she saw the detective approaching, drinks in hand.

"Good morning," he said, holding out a coffee.

"And good morning to you."

Hunter lifted her sunglasses to the top of her head before grabbing the drink, the warmth pulsing in her hand as a steady cloud of vapor meandered from the opening in the lid.

Asher looked out to the river and sipped his drink. Then he spoke. "It's a beautiful morning, huh."

"Yes, it is. And quite the spot for a business meeting."

The detective gestured to the waterfront. "Why don't we walk. It's too good to get only one perspective."

"Okay, then."

They ambled down the walkway of weathered timber planks.

"Just for the record," he said, "I wouldn't consider this a business meeting. I like to keep things a bit more casual than that."

"Yeah. That's what I've heard."

"Ha. So they do talk."

She noticed a way about him that put her at ease. It wasn't a politeness or even a reserved type of demeanor. Truthfully, she didn't know what it was.

"I hope you don't mind," he said, "but the coffee's black."

"Mind? I'd be judging you a little more harshly if it wasn't." She tested the brew, opening the lid, then sipping with caution from the rim of the paper cup. "Wow. That's, uh . . . that's straight-up rocket fuel."

"Well, the whole point is to wake up. Is it not?"

She replaced the lid, pushing the edges of the top in a circular pattern. "You'll have to let me in on who your dealer is."

He lifted his cup in agreement. "Last name Beignet."

Hunter raised her own before taking another sip. "So, what can I do for you, Detective? I've only worked one case with Pathology, so I'm a little confused about why we're here. Especially out *here*, in particular." She looked out to the river.

"We're here because of what you did on the Olivier case—talking to potential suspects and looking into leads that were, really, nothing more than hunches based on some lab work. That's the kind of stuff that's usually left to Homicide."

Of course, she had overstepped. It was her first case. What was she thinking? She couldn't afford to lose this. She had worked toward a pathology position for years. All of the academic work, the technician jobs, the part-time gigs. Med school. What was she thinking?

"I'm sorry. I . . . I wasn't sure . . . I didn't mean to—"

"You having an aneurysm or something?"

"What?"

"Calm down. I'm not here to complain. Hell, I'm not in any position to push back on your work even if I wanted to. Sure, our departments work together, but I'm not the one to tell you how to do your job, Hunter."

Then what was it? He'd dragged her all the way out there for what, then?

"I'm confused," she said. "What's the problem with my work on the Olivier case?"

"Who said anything about a problem?"

Maybe she was getting ahead of herself.

"Sorry, I just assumed that—"

"And stop apologizing."

"Sorry, I just—"

He gave her a look.

"I'm just a bit touchy after being questioned so much about what I did on the case. Parker wasn't all that supportive of my approach."

"Parker? You're worried about Parker? Oh, please. The rest of us have been waiting for him to leave that position for months now. You can ask anyone who's even remotely involved with Pathology. He's on his way out. I'm not here to question your work, Hunter. I'm here to give credit where credit is due."

She had no idea what that implied. "Give me credit? I'm not sure what that means, exactly. You just said you're in no position to comment on my job."

"No. I said that I'm in no position to tell you how to do your job. But what if I was?"

How could she respond to that? Her mind was lost somewhere between being judged and being congratulated.

"I don't follow."

"As it turns out, a spot recently opened up in our department. In particular, on my team."

"Okay."

"How would you like to work as a detective?"

Surely, she had heard wrong. "Do what?"

"Aw, man. You're gonna make me repeat it, aren't you?"

"Sorry, I just . . . I thought that maybe I overstepped with my first case, is all."

Asher leaned against the railing, looking out to the river as his hair was ruffled in a whirl of warm breeze. "Yeah, in my world, that's called 'doing it right.'"

"But I'm one case in with my current position. I'm sure you can find someone more experienced than me. Besides, I have an academic background. What in the world is that gonna do for your team?"

"Working with me isn't about experience," he said. "I wanna work with people who follow their gut." His unshaved, sharpened jawline was cut by the rising sun. "Sure, there's some stuff you'll have to pick up along the way. But that's the least of my concerns."

"Yeah?" She let it linger. The feeling of being wanted for her intuitions. For the raw inclinations of her conscience and not some resume in a pool of applicants.

He turned toward her. "So . . . what do you think?"

She was still trying to process the question. It was a simple one, really, but it caught her off guard. In a good way.

"What all will the job entail, exactly?"

"You know, the usual stuff—calculated risks, dealing with stubborn people like myself, a willingness to be wrong more times than not. Impossible puzzles."

"Well, when you put it like that, sign me up."

Asher lifted his cup, and they clanked lids.

"My boss and I, we have somewhat of a longstanding relationship. I'm pretty sure I can get him on board with bringing you on, but you'd probably start off small. There's an ongoing case that we've been at for a while. Something I think you'd be perfect for."

"So, what? Your boss doesn't trust you or something?"

His expression slightly faded, in a way that she might not have noticed if it weren't for the morning light.

"It's a little more complicated than that. Let's just say it might take some convincing on my end to get him on board with the idea."

Hunter turned around and put her back to the air, her hair crawling over her freckles. "What if I said that I might be able to help with that?"

"Oh yeah? You think you know my boss better than I do?"

"No. But I think you and your boss would rather not have your hard-earned puzzle pieces leaked to the public."

62

COMPARED TO THE HOT and rainy air beyond the window that stood cracked open behind his desk, Robert's lab was set to a chilling morgue temperature—the glass fogging as the two worlds collided at the room's edge.

The professor watched Kole as the postdoc completed his normal morning routine at the other end of the space. Brew first, email second. Then the usual round of checkpoints before the day could begin. An assessment of new citations on Google Scholar, then ResearchGate. He opened his website and stared at his publication list for a good twenty minutes, adding a PDF to his most recent paper—one that was likely still embargoed. Then it was on to Manuscript Central for two journals, where he looked to see whether "in review" had changed to "pending recommendation" for the papers he had submitted with Robert, one of them a nauseating eight months prior. Social media was last. Then it was back to Manuscript Central, just in case the status had magically updated in the last ten minutes. A second cup of coffee, one more glance at Google Scholar, and then he opened R and imported some data to play with. That would probably do until lunch.

"You got an update on that dataset?" Robert spoke from his desk.

Kole swiveled in his chair. "Give me one sec." The printer began to chatter in its jittery, mechanical tone, spitting out pages one line at a time as it shook and beeped, jarring in place.

The postdoc pulled the papers from the tray, tapping them on the desktop until they formed an annoyingly perfect square. Then he punched a staple in the top corner. He walked to Robert's desk.

"This includes everything except the plots on that last model."

Robert didn't care about the plots. He wanted to see it up close. To get another look at it and ensure he wasn't caught up in some sort of crossover between dream and reality. To confirm he wasn't putting the face to the picture after the fact.

Kole held out the papers, the white sleeve of his button-down rolled to the top half of his arm. The brown leather band of his mechanical watch covered the majority of his wrist—and the wound that ran from the base of his forearm to the center of his palm.

The healed remains of flesh, once opened by the glass shards of a shattered vial.

Robert recalled the incident as it had once played out in that very room. Kole had processed the samples, capping the glass tubes between solution changes. The pressure shattered the vial as blood leaked from Kole's palm and formed a purplish-blue pool at the center of the lab floor, each drop splashing against the tile and onto the legs of a nearby stool.

It was an unfortunate incident that had come full circle, back to Robert himself. An incident that, more likely than not, would remain beneath the radar of NOPD. And Meaux.

"Why don't you have a seat," said Robert. "It's been a while since we've caught up."

"Yeah, sure."

Robert tossed the printout onto his desk.

Kole began, "So I think I can have the plots graphed by the end of the—"

"I'm not interested in the plots," Robert said.

Kole pointed to the unmoving papers sitting between them. "Okay, then." And their eyes met. "What's up?"

"How are things going over at UNO with your teaching and all?" The professor was anticipating his own words, looking ahead to a sentence formed but not yet spoken.

"Same as before, really. You know, lecturing and doing what I can to stay ahead. To play the game—just like you taught me, aye."

"Is that right?" Robert swiveled his chair, looking to the water dripping from the edge of the window. "And what did I teach you, exactly, when it comes to 'the game'?"

"More than anyone else has."

"Oh, I find that hard to believe, Kole."

"It's true."

Robert interlaced his hands behind his head, turning back to the postdoc. "More than Steve?"

Kole's gaze moved to the side, just enough to avoid his boss's look. Then back again.

"Steve is the only reason I'm here." He spoke with intent. "And if there's anyone with a mentoring style like you, it's Steve."

"*Was* Steve." Robert could see that his correction was unwelcome.

"Sure."

"What about Bryan?"

"Bryan Guidry? I never really had any—"

"And Aura Theriot? The two of you worked together. No?"

"Of course. But none of them were honest about their role

in the academy. Not like you. They were merely players. Second string at best."

"Ah. I see." Robert turned his monitor to the postdoc, the black-and-gray photograph from the trail camera plastered across the screen. Then he pointed. "And this? What advice would I give, here?"

Kole leaned forward, narrowing his eyes, looking at the date and timestamp at the bottom corner of the image. "Will you look at that. Now that's what I call a close-up. You know, that's probably worth more with an autograph. I don't mind." He pulled a pen from his jacket pocket.

"So what's the next move? I taught you well, no? What's next?"

The postdoc's maniacal laugh would have given Bundy a run for his money. "Move? What move? What you taught me, *Rob*, is that the academy is all about numbers. Results. What you taught me is that the game, that the image of every player in it, is worth far more than that picture ever will be."

"And what makes you think I'm just gonna sit back and watch you go after Bailey?"

"Bailey?"

"Well, I'm no expert on the matter, but Bailey is the only one left. No?"

"Oh, you think you have it figured?"

Robert paused before continuing. "You couldn't care less about the committee members. It was Mitch."

And Kole's laugh returned.

"You knew about the data," Robert said, his mouth all but touching the floor.

Kole lifted his hands in a you-got-me fashion, palms up. "Like you said"—the postdoc's face turned disdainfully genuine—"it's all about the numbers. Mitch was the problem.

But so were the professed collaborators who put tenure before the science."

"Right—three committee members and an outside reader. That's the requirement. What about the outside reader, Kole? What about number four?"

"When's the last time you saw an outside reader with any skin in the game? Come on, Rob. There are many things that I am. But unjust is not one of them."

Kole stood up and slid his arms into his olive plaid coat, bouncing his shoulders until the fit was just right.

"And how would it look if the one opportunity I had left was wasted on another white guy, and Aura—the only female—wasn't included? That doesn't sound very diverse to me. Or inclusive." He stopped and looked out the window. "HR would have a field day."

He buttoned his tweed jacket.

"Besides, you should cheer up. Our paper is pending decision." Kole leaned down, across the table, and spoke under his breath. "Don't forget to check the data."

About the Author

KB Fisher is an independent author of mystery thrillers. He lives with his family in the Southeast United States and is a native of Greater New Orleans.

One of the most valuable things a reader can do for an author is to provide an honest review of their work. Please visit the book's review page on Amazon or Goodreads to do so.

Email: authorKBFisher@gmail.com
Website: authorKBFisher.com
X: @authorKBFisher
Facebook: KB Fisher

www.ingramcontent.com/pod-product-compliance
Lightning Source LLC
Chambersburg PA
CBHW021217310726
48971CB00006B/1598